NEVER

CW00556693

‐

JENNA KIRBY

Giving with love.
Jenna
X

Copyright © Jenna Kirby

Registration No: 284749715

Books by Jenna Kirby

Love's a Bitch

A Dangerous Mistake

My Name is Angel Love

Dark Dangerous Love

Love Hate Revenge

A Dangerous Love Triangle

Passion & Betrayal

Never Look Back

Never Let Me Go

PROLOGUE

LOS ANGELES

Gerry Swane had his booted feet propped up on his desk, and his butt comfortable in his soft leather chair. He was lazily studying the latest financial report of the Santi Corporation. A corporation he ran with four other directors.

Suddenly his office door swung open with a bang. He didn't even bother to look up, because it was late and the office was closed, and had been for five years. "Sorry, I'm not a private dick anymore, and Ben our lawyer left an hour ago." He still didn't bother looking up, as he took a drag of his cheroot, and gave out a cough that sounded like losing a lung. "Would you mind closing the door behind you, it's fuckin' freezing in here."

He was already cranky and short tempered, because Los Angeles was suffering a cold snap, which was unusual even for January. The residents of L.A. were used to 70°, and being cold was making them extremely antsy and unpredictable, and especially Gerry Swane. He hated the cold, that's why he lived in California, but should probably relocate to the Caribbean. But over the past five years he had become close to Marcus and Mia Medina, and their four amazing kids. He had never had a family of his own, so they

3

had become his surrogate family. He couldn't leave them behind, although he was a solitary human being, they would always be there for him.

The door closed, but Gerry knew his privacy had been invaded. His insides dropped away, because he knew who it was, her perfume gave her away. He would know that perfume anywhere, it haunted his nightmares, and his past mistakes, and he had plenty of them to lose sleep over. If he was being honest, she was the last woman he wanted to be acquainted with again.

Slowly he looked up, and couldn't believe his eyes. It was Leanne Zeema, but not the Leanne Zeema he remembered. She would always be extremely beautiful, with long, curly dark hair, but it was hidden under a colourful silk scarf, wrapped around her head like a turban. Her amazing café au lait skin was still her trademark, and she was tall for a woman, but had lost a cartload of weight. Her usual immaculate clothes hung on her like a bag lady, and those exotic slanting multi-coloured eyes of green, blue, and hazel, were sunken with dark circles under them. This woman was a pathetic, physical wreck, not the Leanne he had walked away from without looking back over five years ago.

Something he had always regretted.

She looked as if she was going to pass out at any moment, and then he noticed under her warm coat she had a small child snuggled against her body, and it was fast asleep. At least he was certain it wasn't his, because it definitely wasn't five years old, probably about two years young.

"I'm s-so sorry Gerry, but I don't know who else to turn to. I need somewhere to rest. Somewhere to organise myself, and look after my little boy." She tried to stop the tears from filling her eyes, but they just spilled over, and down her cheeks.

He wanted to take her in his arms, and help her, but controlled the urge. If he touched her, he wouldn't be able to stop. "Sweetheart, I am not the right person to help you. You know I'm a selfish, self-centred bastard, and a solitary S.O.B." But he couldn't help himself from asking what had happened to her. He would put her in a hotel, or motel, tonight, but that was as far as he would go. "What's happened? Where have you come from? You look dead on your feet."

She sniffed the tears back, and stiffened her spine, she was at the end of her capability to look after her toddler son. Staying upright was a problem right now. "I've been driving for four solid days. Have slept with my baby in Walmart car parks, and eaten at McDonald's drive through." She took a deep breath and blew his safe world apart. "I killed my husband while he slept early on Sunday morning. I think it was Sunday?" She closed her eyes, and rubbed her forehead with one hand, because she had to hold on to her sleeping son. "It must have been Sunday, because we don't have any staff working on a Sunday, and I-I needed to make sure nobody would see me do it, or hear the shot."

Gerry couldn't breathe! Couldn't speak! Which must have been a first for him. He wasn't known for keeping his council, or opinions to himself.

Fuck! Shit! Fuck! Dear God, why him? Why did she have to drive four days to get to him?

He soon found out, when she gave him the tattered remnants of the card he had left next to her in bed when she was asleep, and he had left without saying goodbye, five years ago. It was his personal card with his cell number on, and he had written it for his sins. 'If ever you need me, don't hesitate to get in touch.'

Now, he had to honour that pledge, and step up to the plate. Immediately he came round his desk and helped her to sit down in one of the armchairs. He knelt down in front of her, and took her hand. She was so bedraggled, and needed a shower badly, and most definitely a good nourishing meal inside her.

"You need to tell me exactly what happened, meanwhile I'll order in dinner for us, and whatever your little boy wants. We both need a large, strong drink, which I can provide, but it will have to be a scotch, straight up." Slowly he got up and went into the next room where a convenient bar was set up, and poured two hefty slugs of really good vintage scotch. When he came back she was fast asleep exactly as he had left her, and her son cuddled up even closer to her. Gerry had to wake her up, because he needed to know what had happened, and were the police looking for her. But first he put an order in for them from his favourite Mexican restaurant, who would deliver within thirty minutes. Hopefully she would have food for her toddler, he didn't know what small kids actually ate.

She drank down the scotch in one hit, even though it made her throat hurt and her eyes water. They had eaten the wonderful meal in silence, and he had his answer about small kids, because he tucked into his mother's food. They were both ravenous. Gerry cleared away the empty cartons, and poured a glass of water for Leanne, and another scotch for himself. She had refused another drink because she was so exhausted, and wanted to go back to sleep. But Gerry needed to know exactly what had made her commit murder.

"Take your time, sweetheart, but tell me the whole truth as it happened. I need to be able to work out what we are going to do. Not tonight, as you need to rest and so does your son. In the next room there is a shower, and a Put You Up. You can sleep there tonight. I'll stay here with you, so don't worry about anyone knowing where you are. You are safe from prying eyes. I need the keys to your car, so that I can put it around the back, nobody can see it there."

She went and put her son to bed in the next room. He hadn't made a sound the whole time they had had their meal. Gerry began to wonder if he was traumatised with all the travelling, and being on the road for four days. It wasn't normal for a child of that age to be so quiet, and docile.

But Leanne had told him that her husband was overly strict with him, and sent him to his room if he made any noise. For that piece of information Gerry already hated her husband, and was sure after she explained why she had cold bloodedly murdered him, he would hate him even more. For all his faults Gerry loved women, spoilt them, would never hurt them, and stupidly put them on a pedestal. But definitely could not commit to a relationship of any kind.

Marriage and kids were totally out of the question, with anyone, ever.

Leanne walked silently back into the room in her bare feet. Gerry had taken her case from the car, and left it in the next room for her. After a shower, and wearing a silk kimono, he couldn't stop himself from picturing what she was wearing underneath. She looked like the beautiful woman that he remembered, and for a brief couple of days had fallen in love with. That was why he had sneaked out in the night, because he did not want to love anyone, that was a path he didn't want to wander down, and suffer a broken heart.

He had been a tough Private Dick, with no morals, and a different woman in his bed every night, until Leanne.

Instead he had almost drunk himself to an early grave, and took every dangerous assignment the F.B.I., D.E.A., and L.A. police, could throw at him. But he had survived to tell the story, and live for another fuckin' boring day.

Now, he slowly drank his third scotch, as she slowly sat down with those fabulously long legs tucked under her. His brilliant blue eyes gazed greedily at her, as he waited hopefully for the truth of what had happened to cause such a dire confession.

Her voice was still as sultry, warm and soft as she began to speak, and she never took her eyes from his face, which was watching her like a hawk, because he believed she wasn't going to tell him the truth. Perhaps her truth, but not anyone else's truth.

She began by admonishing him, which he knew he deserved. "Five years ago you were my first, and I couldn't believe it when I woke up and found you had left me in that informal hotel room, with just a small card telling me to get in touch if I ever needed you. We didn't acknowledge that I was totally inexperienced. You were kind, patient, unselfish, and so loving. I thought, as naive as I was, that we had connected. Ridiculous of me, but I believed we had fallen in love over those two nights and a day, we never left that hotel bed, only for room service."

Gerry looked extremely uncomfortable at her words of truth, because unusually for the hard bitten male that he was, he had fallen in love. He had never been anyone's first, and it had totally side-swiped him. It had made him run, hard and fast, away from a situation that had scared the crap out of him.

"I left for Atlanta that morning as I had been offered work there. Quite a lot of important work, and I needed the money, I was almost on the bread line. New York had become my home, and it wasn't cheap living there. My Agent had managed to set me up with some modelling, and a big magazine photo shoot. So I didn't have time to wonder what I had done wrong in that hotel room for two nights, giving everything I held sacred to a man I believed would hold it dear." She sadly shook her head at Gerry, who had the grace to look guilty as hell, and had actually blushed with embarrassment.

"Unfortunately, at a party I met a charismatic, extremely handsome man, who seemed to be completely bowled over by me. He was the assistant District Attorney of Atlanta, and his family old money Atlanteans, who seemed to take me in their fold, and circle of close friends and associates. Believe me that was a figment of my imagination. They were all bigots, and cruel. I was black and of no consequence whatsoever to their circle of old money and genteel manners. I was slave material."

She took a long drink of water, and a long breath of air before continuing. "Edward Connor had married me as arm candy, and for my womb to carry his two children. To show the large majority of voters when he needed them, that his family were not bigots, and embraced blacks, ethnic minorities, and migrants, because one day in the future he would need all their votes. Everything was a lie, but they all probably believed his glib tongue. But definitely not me. On our wedding night he called me a disgusting black bitch, that was when I found out he was gay, because he didn't even share a bed with me." Her voice wobbled when she carried on valiantly. Gerry didn't dare console her, as he knew she would break down completely.

"When he wanted to get me pregnant, he beat me up when I refused, because he disgusted me. Edward was addicted to sex, but not with me. I threatened to leave him, but he just laughed and said I would be dead. He would put out a contract on me. Teddy, our boy, was conceived after he raped me, and *he* has been my love and joy, and well worth

11

the agony of being thoroughly beaten up until I had to give in to save my life.

"This Sunday morning he came home reeking of sex and booze, and I knew I was in big trouble. I locked myself in my bedroom, but he crashed the door down and dragged me to his bedroom. He had previously got rid of my contraception pills, so he was trying to get me pregnant again, because he needed the perfect family. An obedient wife and two children. Perfect parents with old money, and high ranking associates, and his own family also supposedly perfect. We never had staff working on a Sunday in our extremely large, vacuous mansion. A family home that didn't have a heart and soul, especially not mine."

The part of this story that she was leaving out worried Gerry to death. She hadn't explained how she had managed to leave without anyone seeing her, and had been on the road for four days, and no one seemed to be following her, especially with her young son who would have been missed. So her departure must have been organised to the last letter. When she went to bed he would track what the police were doing about her high profile husband, and herself missing.

"Tell me exactly what you did after your husband raped you, and he obviously went to sleep, or had a shower?"

"Since Teddy was born almost two years ago, Edward has never come to my bedroom, unless he thought or

12

believed I had embarrassed him in some way when we had to be together at a function. Either my dress was too low, or too short, or I was too beautiful and taking the attention away from the golden boy of Atlanta. By then he had become the D.A. of Atlanta. His elderly boss had retired and put him up for election by endorsing him. Whatever I did when we went out was always wrong, even breathing had become a hazard for me. He constantly hit me, knocked me unconscious, and often broke my bones, all treated at a private clinic, so the media wouldn't find out. He was a complete nightmare. I think he is a psychotic narcissist, and believes he is above the law and cannot be judged whatever he does."

Leanne got up wearily and began to pace around the room, touching everything around her. Gerry didn't stop her because he realised the past two years must have been hell on earth for her to cope with. And those years would be crucial for her defence.

"I began to realise that the only way I could get out of his cruelty was to plan to kill him. I had to be at least one step ahead of him. I needed to get my son away from his father before he could turn my baby against me, and he would throw me out. I have a dear friend who now lives in San Francisco. He was a black escort to many high profile men in very high places. Now, he has retired to San Fran from New York, but we shared a small apartment when I was working in New

York. He never brought anyone to our apartment, and I never questioned who they were. But a lot of seemingly straight men, who were closet gays, owe him a lot of favours. Bazil de Frey is my best friend and confidante. He wanted to expose Edward, but I knew that my husband would somehow get his own back. And I didn't want Edward knowing about Bazil, he was my friend exclusively. Knowing Edward, if he had found out about my friendship with a black gay, Bazil would have gone missing without a doubt. And I am even more worried now. Once the immoral men around Edward realise what I have done, and not been kidnapped as I have planned, I am sure Bazil will be a target. Through his help I have been able to disappear."

Gerry had to interrupt her, he needed to know exactly what had happened four days ago if he was going to help her now. "What did this Bazil actually do to help you? And what did you do to your husband? Try to keep it short sweetheart, you are almost asleep standing up." He was getting seriously worried about her, she looked beyond exhausted, and so frail.

"Bazil somehow managed to obtain a completely new identity for me and my son. I have a new passport, driving licence, and social security number. My name is now Anna Weist, and Teddy is now Jayden Weist. He managed to get all the relevant documentation to a post box in the next town to me, and I managed to get away from my security long

14

enough to hide it all in my new car, that was hidden in a lock-up unknown to my husband and his security. It took me two long, frightening years to be able to set all this up, and execute it."

She wiped away the tears that were now tracking down her pale, stricken face. "And, all the time I knew the only way I would be able to get free of Edward and his complicit goons would be to kill him, and get my son away from his dark, evil world.

"Sexually he left me alone, so that was a bonus, but of course the joy of hurting me continued. I was his punch bag, and he sure loved to humiliate and de-humanise me, until early last Sunday morning. Honestly Gerry, I fought him until I lost the will to live. He raped me in the worst possible scenario. It seemed to last for hours, I was degraded, sodomised, used for his own sexual deviations. Throughout the whole time I kept silent, I was not going to beg, or ask for mercy, because I knew what I had to do, as soon as he went to sleep. That day was the last time he was ever going to hurt me, abuse me physically and sexually, and of course mentally.

"I had gone into that marriage a naive, loving, excited young woman. After four years I was a mental and physical wreck, and would never, ever, trust another living soul."

She looked straight into Gerry's eyes, obviously including him in that comment. And, Gerry couldn't agree with her more. He didn't usually blame himself for other people's bad luck, or bad choices. But, it was pretty obvious that Leanne had married that obnoxious pervert in part because he had walked away from her without knowing he had broken her innocent, trusting heart. He had always been a selfish, self-centred, singular bastard. Had used up a lot of years just fucking, boozing, and using gorgeous women as a warm body, and inventive mouth, as long as they didn't use that mouth for talking too much.

At the time he had loved Leanne, but soon got over that stupid melancholy of lost love. Then he had stupidly fallen for Mia Maxwell, with two brothers who absolutely adored her. He had stood back and waited to see who would win her, and in the end they both had, within months of each other. Luckily he had been far too old for her, he had been forty then, and Mia just twenty-two. Yes, she had loved him, but like an elder brother, not what he had in mind of course.

Leanne was talking again, so Gerry brought back his roving mind to concentrate on what had happened four days ago. He sincerely hoped that she had really covered her tracks over the time she had left Atlanta, otherwise he was going to be in shit street with her. Not his favourite part of town.

16

"I got up and went into the bathroom, and got into the shower to wash his stink off me. I scrubbed until my skin bled in places. I was bleeding underneath anyway, so more blood didn't seem to matter." She was talking as if she was reading the newspaper to him, in a melodic sing-song voice.

"I quietly walked back into his bedroom, he was fast asleep, and snoring, as if he hadn't done those awful things to me, his wife. That alone made me mad enough to kill him, in cold blood. I walked around to the side of the bed where I knew he kept his loaded gun. I had already put on a pair of thin plastic gloves from a drawer in the bathroom, pointed the gun behind his ear, and pulled the trigger." She smiled eerily, and whispered, "job done! He was truly fucked by the wife he hated, as I hated him.

Still smiling she carried on, so calmly. "I kept the gloves on, and opened his safe in the wall, and took out all the cash, not moving anything else. I dropped the gun by the bed, as if in a hurry to leave. Then went back to my room, got dressed in warm clothes, because like here, Atlanta was cold, even colder. I put just a few items of clothing in my small travel case, that nobody would notice I had taken, and just a few toiletries and make-up that I had bought earlier to take with me, so anyone would think I had left everything behind. As if I had been forcibly kidnapped. Only then did I go into Teddy's room and packed his little holdall that again I had

17

bought earlier. He would want his special blanket and stuffed animal, and his bottle for milk to go to sleep of a night. I believed a kidnapper would make sure a tiny child would need, and a few necessary clothes.

"My poor little boy never murmured while I got him ready to leave, because he was so used to Edward shouting at him if he made any noise, at any time. I went straight to Edward's study and blocked out all the cameras that were outside. He never allowed cameras inside as he had many clandestine dodgy business meetings in his study. Nobody wanted their photos on a camera, least of all Edward."

Leanne was running out of steam, but was determined to finish. "I carried Teddy, and pulled my travel case for about a half mile, going around the back streets so we didn't meet anyone, even though I had a large warm coat on, with a hood covering my hair. I could not have anyone being able to identify me once we left Atlanta. I had already put cushions and blankets, and bottles of water in my new car, ready for when we managed to leave.

"I planned this for two years, knowing I couldn't leave a trail anyone could follow. Honestly Gerry, I made it look as if we were being robbed and Edward was shot trying to defend me, and had to give them the keys to the safe. The thieves then kidnapped me, and Teddy. That gives me at least a week before anyone thinks that I killed him, and left." She put up both hands at his look of disbelief at people believing she was missing, possibly dead. "I know that everyone believes he is a wonderful husband, and father. And, he admires blacks and ethnic minorities, but all of that is utterly untrue. Edward was a bigot, and a bully, and had his fingers in anything that was unlawful, and earned a great deal of money. He was a pig, disgusting and psychotic, and – and I killed Teddy's father. May God and Teddy forgive me, but I really had no choice. If I had walked out on him earlier, he most definitely would have had me killed, and brought up Teddy himself." She began to cry in earnest. "I-I couldn't let that happen, Gerry. I just couldn't. My baby is too precious to me, and always will be. I would die for him."

Gerry couldn't sit still any longer, he pulled her up from the armchair, and held her close to comfort her. She was shaking with exhaustion, and misery. Had driven thousands of miles with a baby to look after, and had bared her soul to him, and had killed another human being, however bad that human being had been. In his book that was never easy, and it never got easier, Gerry could vouch for that, it marked your soul, forever.

"Sweetheart, that's enough for tonight. You go to bed with your baby, and try, I know how difficult that will be, to get a good night's sleep. We will sort all this out in the morning, and see what the best way is to approach this. I'm going to get into the Atlanta Police Department system, and find out what they are making of your situation. I would give them at the most a week to realise that all is not as it seems. That's if they've got one detective with a working brain cell. That gives us a couple of day's leeway to get you hidden somewhere safe with your son. At some level this has to be sorted out, because you can't be on the run forever. Believe me, I know how stressful that can be." He kissed her forehead, and turned her towards the other room. Of course he would have loved to go to bed with her, but that not only would muddy the waters, but she had a two year old keeping her company.

Gerry didn't have much of a moral compass, but kids were an absolute turn off for him, and he didn't think that situation would ever change.

Tiredly she tried to snuggle closer to him, but he wasn't going to allow her to change his mind. Far too much was at stake here, her freedom, and his libido. Both were too important to fuck with.

"Come to bed with me Gerry? Please! I don't want to be on my own tonight. We don't have to have sex, just holding me will be enough."

"Sweetheart, you are kidding me. I have never slept with a woman just to sleep. My dick would never forgive me if I ever did that, probably would go on strike, never to rise again." He gently pushed her towards the rest room. "I've got a great deal of work to do before I can sleep, so please leave me to do it. Go look after your baby, he needs you more than I do." Gerry knew that was a lie, because his dick was already twitching in response. But, it could stand to attention and sing Dixie for all he cared. Nothing was going to happen between himself and Leanne now, or in the future. By killing her husband she had become trouble with a capital T, and especially with anyone stupid enough to help her.

When she left he went straight to work. He had been right when he said that all police weren't stupid, they were still reporting that she had been abducted with her small son, but also indicating her husband's death appeared to be very suspicious. Gerry knew it wouldn't take the detectives working in that police force long to dot the i's, and cross the t's, And Leanne would be the main suspect. He had to get her hidden away ASAP, so they could work out what to do next.

He reclined in his comfortable soft black leather chair, with another large vintage scotch, and his usual cheroot clamped between his teeth, and let his mind wander back five years ago. For thirty six hours Leanne and himself had been as close as two bugs in a rug, and so sexually compatible, as if they had known each other for years and years.

He had asked her why she didn't have any family, and was living in America, and obviously was of mixed race. It was pretty obvious to him, because Gerry was very astute

21

and very observant, that she hadn't always lived in the USA. And, she intrigued him, because she appeared to be well read, well educated, and originally from money.

When she told him about her life before America, he totally wished he hadn't asked. Leanne had certainly been through the mill, but had in time accepted that shit happened, and you had to stay strong and get through whatever life threw at you. And, now it had happened again. It really wasn't fair, because that sick psycho Edward had dealt her another crap hand to deal with. Gerry prayed that she managed to get through this without spending the rest of her goddamn life in prison. That diabolical thought had his meal congealing in his stomach.

He had found her to be overly kind, very loving, too fragile, and he was sure she would give her last dollar to anyone in need. He would probably fight to the death for this beautiful woman. Possibly take a bullet for her, but truly hoped that would never happen, because he had never welcomed pain, never had, never would.

Five years ago when they had almost fucked themselves senseless, Leanne had opened up to him and told him her life story before she had met him.

He leant back in his recliner, completely relaxed, and let her story wash over him, as he closed his eyes and drifted off into a shallow sleep.

CHAPTER ONE

KENYA
SOMALIA

Leanne Zeema was born thirty years ago to Ana and Lee Zeema in Washington D.C. Lee was assigned to the Somalian Embassy, and had married Ana Adams, who worked as a secretary at the Embassy. It was a love match, that would last until their demise. Leanne was their first child, and was absolutely loved, and incredibly beautiful as a baby, and as an adult.

When she was five years old the family moved back to Somalia, and bought an impressive house on the outskirts of the main city, Mogadishu. Lee was now a high ranking politician in the government. There were many different militia groups always trying to overtake any particular group administrating the welfare and stability of the country. Lee was a steady hand at the centre of government.

Leanne had a wonderful childhood with parents who adored her, and she was a bright, loving child, who did extremely well at school, and then college.

Every two years her mother Ana produced another child, always a son to swell their family unit, four sons in total. Every one as bright, and mischievous as their elder sister.

23

Leanne adored her parents, and most of the time her brothers, who constantly played jokes on her. So she was pretty good at sticking up for herself, and getting her own back on four troublemakers.

Her father encouraged her with her education, often helping her with homework, she could read and write by the time she was four years old. Her mother Ana was the ultimate homemaker, always there for her husband and children. They were a tight, close, loving unit. Happy and content to stay at home, and when their father had to socialise, their mother often stayed at home with her family. Their home was totally organised, but also full of love, laughter, and hugs from their doting parents.

Leanne was cocooned in this wonderful family life, and didn't see any danger lurking in her young life, and future. By anyone's standards it was too perfect.

When she finished her education with top honours of course, she decided, because of her height, and being naturally slim, she would try her hand at modelling. Her father knew a lot of influential people, and she soon became famous on the designer circuit of modelling, and the catwalk.

Then offers trickled in from the USA for her to join an Agency, who could get her plenty of work in magazines, and designer houses. She didn't really want to leave her family in Somalia, but her parents encouraged her to leave, and get out into the world of glamour, and prestige. But Leanne still wasn't sure if she really wanted to leave everyone behind. Her mother said she would visit as much as possible, and Leanne would always be welcome back home if it didn't work out.

There was a lot of unrest in Somalia at that time, with breakaway fractions of terrorists causing a great deal of aggravation and hardship to the official government. In truth, Lee, her father, was extremely worried for his family's safety. He encouraged his wife to accompany their daughter for a few weeks to settle her in the USA. He breathed a huge sigh of relief when she agreed.

Ana loved her wonderful husband, and didn't want to be away from him for any length of time. But also knew he was worried for all his family, even though he hadn't said a word to her. It wouldn't be too long before a couple of his older sons would be called up into the army, and that worried Lee intensely.

He was a man of peace, and his wonderful sons deserved a better future than being in the army.

"Papa! Mama and I are going shopping today in town as soon as we finish at the American Embassy. I need decent clothes if I'm to get work in America, and you love it when I am all dolled up, 'cos you are proud that I am your daughter."

Uh-oh, thought her father, this sounded as if it was going to be a very expensive day for him, and his wallet. He put down the newspaper he was studying before he left for work, and looked at his beautiful daughter, who had that beguiling expression on her perfect face. That expression meant he was expected to give her the extra money for shopping. It was an old routine he'd had to get used to. Leanne had been earning money now for two years, but was hopeless at saving any. Whatever she earned she spent with great enthusiasm, and without a doubt enjoyed doing so.

He should really start lecturing her on her finances, but he loved and spoilt her far too much, and he couldn't see that changing anytime soon. "Okay darling, I will give you my credit card, but don't go too mad with it. Your mother will need it as well." He never minded his darling wife spending money, because she rarely did so. She always spent money on her family, making sure they were presentable with his stature in the Government. In Somalia presentation was highly regarded.

Unfortunately his oldest child didn't adhere to that regard, but he loved her too much to ever say 'no' to her. She looked like her mother, who was very American, tall, blonde, and beautiful, but the only difference was Leanne had glossy, black curly hair, like him. And her skin was more Western than dark like his culture. Her four brothers were like their father, tall, dark, and very handsome, and they all knew how handsome they were, attracting females like bees to honey. They were now eighteen, sixteen, and fourteen year old twins, and every one of them becoming a handful.

"Would you like me to come with you today, sweetheart? I don't mind waiting while you are at the Embassy, and then go shopping. I really prefer that you don't go alone with your Mama." In truth Lee would rather stick pins in his eyes than watch women get excited over clothes that looked similar to what they already had in their wardrobes. But Mogadishu wasn't settled at the moment, and there was a militant group of Shahaab using hit and run tactics, trying to destabilise the rebuilding of Mogadishu.

"No Papa, we don't need you pacing up and down, and sighing heavily while we are trying to enjoy ourselves. Mama will be happy if you pick up the boys as usual when they leave their schools and college. Otherwise she will be worrying herself sick that they aren't safe." There was no way that Leanne was putting up with her father breathing down their necks while her mother and herself were on a spending spree, and having a mother and daughter bonding day.

"Yes my darling, I most certainly can do that, but please be careful where you shop. Keep to the main mall, and then drive straight to the Embassy."

27

"OK Papa. We completely understand. Please don't worry about us. Mama is like a tiger with her cubs, where her children's safety is concerned. We will see you later, Papa." She kissed him as she left the kitchen to find her mother. She couldn't wait to start using her father's credit card, which she was holding tightly in her hand.

Not knowing that in a few hours her safe, comfortable life would change forever, and not for the better. She would have clung to her beloved Papa, and would never have left her home for a fun day out, with the Mama she also adored, and who also was her best friend.

CHAPTER TWO

The two striking women decided to shop first, have a leisurely lunch, and then go to the American Embassy to renew Leanne's American passport and VISA to allow her to work in the USA. She hadn't visited America for fifteen years, so needed new documentation that she was still a citizen of that country. Her original passport had expired, so she had to produce her birth certificate, and anything else pertaining evidence that she was still an American citizen.

Arm in arm and laughing about the ridiculous antics of her four brothers, they entered the silent hallowed mansion on the dot of four, and expected to wait however long it took to get an appointment with someone in authority.

But when they gave their names at the reception desk, they were quickly ushered into the nearest office, and very gravely asked to make themselves comfortable until someone could see them.

Leanne sat next to her mother on the couch, and gave her a puzzled frown. "That was weird Mama, she looked very grave when we gave our names." Under her breath she said 'shit'. "Oh for Godsake do you think they are going to turn me down for a new passport and VISA?" She blew out a disappointed breath. "So big deal! I don't need to work in their bloody country. There is plenty of work here." She grinned at

29

her mother, "and I'd much rather stay with my family, instead of earning a fortune in the States."

Just as she was about to get angry the door opened, and the actual Ambassador strode purposefully into the room with two assistants following him. He asked them to stay seated as he pulled up a chair next to them. Again he looked very serious and sad. Leanne's stomach lurched, knowing they were not going to like what he had to say.

"Look, it's obvious that you are not going to give me a new passport, and a VISA to work in your country." And, she was royally pissed as to why she was being turned down. "But, I would really like to know why?"

"Mrs Zeema, and Leanne, I am so terribly sorry, but I have some truly dreadful news for you both." He looked really uncomfortable, and looked at his assistants for help, but they stayed silent. "There is no way to sugar coat this. About an hour ago your husband and your four sons were gunned down in cold blood. We believe by one of the militia groups that are ravishing Somalia."

Ana and Leanne just looked at the Ambassador as if he was spouting a load of rubbish, and they were sitting in an alternative universe, and what he was saying didn't affect their safe, loving world.

Leanne was the first to find her voice. "What *are* you talking about, sir? My father is a respected government official, and my brothers are innocent of any crime to anyone." She took a deep calming breath, believing he was talking about someone else, definitely not her beloved family. She put her arm around her mother who was visibly shaking, and beginning to cry.

"I am so very sorry, Leanne. But this *is* official. Your father and brothers were all pronounced dead at the scene, and have been moved to the local mortuary. The ME knew your father, and confirmed their identity. I am so sorry, but there hasn't been mistaken identity. Your neighbours have also confirmed what has happened." He quickly turned to talk quietly to one of his assistants. "Ask the Embassy doctor to come immediately." Mrs Zeema was looking as if she was going to collapse at any moment, and he couldn't blame her. The thought of losing his beloved family would be too much to bear.

Leanne took her weeping mother into her arms, but knew she would never be able to console her. Her mama lived and breathed for her husband and children. Leanne wanted to scream out her denial of what was happening. Wanted to get a gun and shoot every fucking terrorist in the world, especially the ones who had done this.

Instead she went freezing cold. Couldn't cry! Couldn't let out all the pent up misery that was overwhelming her! Tomorrow or another day, she would scream and cry until she couldn't manage either emotion. Her world had just gone dark and without compass. Her beloved papa was her world. She absolutely adored him, and couldn't believe she would never see him ever again. Bur now her distraught mother needed her strength and all encompassing love.

But then her bleak misery compounded itself. Her mama clutched her chest, gave out a blood curdling scream, and fell out of Leanne's arms onto the carpet. Immediately the assistant still in the room went down on his knees next to Ana, and began CPR. But only Leanne knew that her mother had a serious heart complaint, and that he wouldn't be able to save her, however hard he tried.

He worked on her for what seemed a long time, and then he looked up at Leanne with despair written all over his young face, asking for permission to stop. With tears now streaking down her beautiful face, she gave her permission by nodding her acquiescence. That was when the doctor rushed in, and immediately confirmed her loving, kind mother was also dead, and beyond anyone's help.

Leanne knelt down next to her mother, and took her in her arms to feel the warmth and energy that was still her beloved mama's life force, but that was all too readily leaving her. "Sleep tight Mama. Papa and your boys are waiting for you. Now you can be together into eternity, and never be parted again. I will always love you forever and a day. I know I was truly blessed to belong to a family so full of love, hugs, and kisses. Wish me well and pray for me, as I try to carry on without you and Papa, and the boys." She kissed her mother's cold lips, and gently laid her back down, knowing she would never feel her mama's loving arms around her ever again.

Leanne Zeema was an orphan at the tender age of twenty. The kind and concerned Ambassador waited until her mother had been taken to the small hospital within the Embassy, to tell her that the murderers had also burnt their house to the ground. Leanne was now homeless, without funds, without family, and too distraught to really care what happened to her now. She wished she could go to sleep and never wake up to reality again.

But the Ambassador had children of his own, and would not let this courageous, gutsy young woman leave the safety and security of his home. "Leanne, you can make the Embassy your home for as long as you want to. I cannot allow you to leave until the police investigate what actually happened today. You could be at risk. We don't know why your father was singled out. We have many empty suites in this Embassy, and you are most welcome to occupy one for as long as it takes you to get back on your feet."

Leanne realised she didn't have the strength, energy, or moxy to find somewhere to live. Plus money was going to be a huge problem, she didn't have any. "Thank you sir, I am sure you are right. You are so kind to offer me sanctuary until I can work out what I am going to do." All she wanted to do was get to a room that was private, where she could let go, and grieve for her parents and brothers. She really didn't believe or understand what had happened.

This morning she had hugged and kissed her handsome Papa. Had said goodbye to her brothers as they left for school or college. Had spent a fantastic day with her amazing Mama. Now they were all gone. How could that be? Never to laugh, argue, and cry with them again. And, how was she going to cope with her heart shattered into a million pieces? Why? Why was she still living and breathing when her beloved family were all cold and dead? Her Papa had been revered and loved.

What had gone so terribly wrong?

"Please call me John, Leanne. If you are going to be living here for a while, Ambassador sounds a trifle stiff, don't you think? Andrew, my assistant will take you to your suite, as I am sure you need time alone right now. And, please ask my secretary if you need anything, anything at all. I can see that you have a lot of bags with you, so hopefully will be OK." He took her hand and looked at her with such sadness, and empathy. "Everyone at the Embassy is horrified at what has happened today. I know we can't take away the awful pain you must be feeling, but please remember we are all here for you. Your father was a truly great man, and a grievous loss to the government. I promise that you will want for nothing while you still live in Mogadishu. And, if you still want to go to America I will expedite that whenever you want to leave."

Andrew got hold of her shopping, and she followed him out of the room. For the first time in her young life she was totally alone, scared, and heartbroken.

Really scared! Really on her own! Totally heartbroken!

The next day an official from the government, and the Police Commissioner came to visit Leanne at the Embassy. Andrew stayed with Leanne to help her with any questions she had for the two officials. He didn't want her to be overwhelmed with what the two men were going to tell her. She wasn't to know that she was *so* going to need his strength and empathy when they explained what had actually happened to her family.

She asked the commissioner to tell her exactly what had happened to her father and brothers, as she needed to understand why her family had been targeted. Her family had believed that their father was an honest, caring politician in a country that was riddled with greed and corruption.

"I am truly sorry this awful situation has happened. Your father was well loved and revered. Do you really want to know what occurred yesterday?" She nodded her head grimly and waited. She had to know how her family had died, bravely or begging for their lives. But already knew, because her father would have tried to save his sons, he had loved his children far more than his own life.

"We have already questioned your neighbours, who all gave exactly the same story. That around three p.m. six armed men with masks pulled your father and your four brothers from the house. Made them kneel down on the front lawn, then proceeded to shoot each one in the head, leaving your father to last, having to watch his children one by one be executed. Not one of your family begged for their lives, after your father quietly asked them to be brave, and that he would see them in heaven, and never leave them on their own. Your neighbours are heartbroken, because they couldn't help them, four of the assassins continually held their Kalashnikov assault rifles towards the neighbouring houses."

Leanne hadn't moved, hadn't blinked, hadn't shown any emotion, which intensely worried everyone in the room. They had never seen anyone in such control when being told their family had been murdered so coldly, so well planned, and executed so easily in front of an audience.

All Leanne asked was why? The commissioner looked across at the official from the government who answered her question, she certainly needed a truthful answer. "Our good friend Lee was determined to rid our country of the terrorist groups that are trying to take us back to the bad years of Somalia being held to ransom by those controlling, blood thirsty murderers.

"The government wishes to give your father a state funeral, which he absolutely deserves. But with your permission of course, dear Leanne."

That morning Leanne had had a discussion on her family's funeral and burial, with John Anderson, the Ambassador. He had told her that there was a small discreet church annexed to the Embassy. There was a large empty plot in the corner of the garden behind the church. An ancient Acacia tree spread its branches over that large plot, which was empty. The Embassy would be overjoyed to lay her family to rest there, if she thought that would be what her father would have wanted for them.

She had told John that her father had always said that if anything untoward happened to him, he did not want pomp and ceremony. But just a simple Christian burial somewhere quiet and peaceful. She had accepted John's offer without a second thought. And it was scheduled for early tomorrow morning, with only the staff at the Embassy there.

Her father, and Levi, Luca, Lari, and Leni, with their beloved mother Ana, would all be buried together in a beautiful place. Only the staff of the Embassy knew they were there, and their grieving daughter and sibling of course.

A close, loving family, were even closer in death.

For Leanne it was a truly difficult time to cope with. She cried constantly for a whole month, but nobody knew. She cried in the shower, and out walking in the gardens, and by her family's graves. Hardly slept an hour at a time, because her mind kept seeing her family gunned down, and slaughtered.

At the end of that month she decided to leave for America. To start a new life as an adult on her own. She had to live, and make something of herself in her family's memory.

Be someone of consequence and stature, especially for her parents. They had brought up their children to stand on their own feet, always to be kind and considerate to others, and to never hate anyone because of their colour or creed.

And, especially to be true to themselves, always.

CHAPTER THREE

Leanne entered the USA, excited but with a heavy heart. She had hated leaving her family, but Andrew had promised to tend the graves, and make sure there were always fresh flowers available. Of course she realised that Andrew had wanted her to be more than a friend, but she wasn't capable of being anyone's friend or more in the foreseeable future.

She was empty and hollow inside, and incapable of love. Incapable of worrying about anyone else. Putting one foot in front of the other was all she was capable of, right now. Work and somewhere to live was the top priority in her lonely life. She knew she had to pull herself together, and get on with living.

Her first stroke of luck in a month came out of the blue, and would last for the next five years. The most beautiful young black male came over to her while she was waiting patiently to start her day's work modelling for Vogue magazine. To say a guy could be perfect in face and body was really unbelievable, but this guy was, and Leanne had worked with a few gorgeous specimens of manhood, but he beat them all hands down.

He had a natural, nonchalant body movement, and a killer smile, which unfortunately didn't make Leanne's heart rate accelerate. Taking her by the shoulders he gently kissed

39

her on both cheeks. "Well! Leanne Zeema, our Agent, Mandy Ellis, told me that you were stunningly beautiful, and she wasn't overstating, my darling. If we ever get pregnant together our kids will be absolutely gorgeous. But, I am about as gay as a gay can be, and evidently you are as straight as straight can be, so that ain't ever going to happen."

He raised his eyes to the ceiling as if in prayer. "Thank God for small mercies, my darling girl. Look, Mandy also told me that you are desperate for some decent digs that you can afford. I rent a large open space at the top of a warehouse, and really need someone to share the outrageous rent with. I've had a couple of disasters with men of the same persuasion as myself." He blew out a breath of utter disbelief. "Didn't work out, darling. It was misery personified. Please, pretty please, would you consider taking my sincere offer? It's spacious, has wonderful views, two large bedrooms, modern kitchen, and bathroom, and a warm, comfortable lounge. Honestly, I love living there, but the rent is killing me." He could see that she was considering saying yes, but wasn't a hundred per cent convinced.

"It's in the meat packing district, west Chelsea, in fact near Chelsea Market. An old district of New York, with gay clubs, department stores, and elite fashion houses. On the ground floor of my loft is a delicatessen, a coffee shop, and a fantastic beauty salon, and an organic revitalising therapy shop." He raised his elegant hands in the air. "What's not to like, Leanne Zeema?"

But Leanne didn't know this gorgeous man from Adam, and for the past month her life had been shit street, and she didn't want to make any mistakes for her future. "I'm sorry, but I don't want to cause you anymore problems. Perhaps you should stick with a male renter. I'm new in America, and don't know anyone to talk over such a big commitment. It wouldn't be fair on you. I don't even know your name yet, and you are inviting me to move in with you. You can't blame me for not taking up your offer, even though it sounds too good to be true." She stepped back a pace as he was intruding on her personal space a tad. Something Leanne never felt comfortable with.

But he could see she was hesitating, so went in for the kill. "I promise faithfully that I will never intrude on your personal space or time. I will never, ever, bring anyone into our shared home, male or female. And I will expect the same courtesy from you. Our home will be a haven of peace and tranquillity that we can share after the crap work we endure every day. Any problems that arise we have to share and talk over, and agree on. I am an amazing cook, and love to clean, so you don't have to worry about either, if you don't want to of course." But he took in another deep breath before his next exposé. "Just between you and me, I am a VIP escort, and will never reveal who my client at the time is. These men are high powered individuals, mostly happily married with families. Often CEO's of big companies, or politicians, etc. You will never know where I am going, or who with." He grinned, a dimple appeared in his cheek, and even Leanne couldn't help but think what a waste for the females who must fancy this gorgeous package.

"Sorry, I forgot to tell you that my name is Bazil de Frey, and yes, I am totally gay, and will never be a problem sexually to you. Please share my home. Be my friend, and I promise to try and keep you safe in the cesspit that is New York."

Leanne jumped in feet first and took a big gamble. She was staying in a cheap, tacky motel, and hated it. It really was a no-brainer to move in with Bazil. She would of course check with Mandy Ellis, their Agent, but her gut told her that this smart, elegant man was everything he said he was. If not, she would be in deep trouble, and that was nothing new to her lately.

For the next five years Leanne led a comfortable, relaxed but busy life. Bazil became her surrogate brother, and beloved family. They got on like a house on fire, and loved living together. He took her to all his favourite gay bars and coffee shops, and helped her become outrageously fashion conscious. He cooked and cleaned everything but her bedroom and bathroom, because he complained she was too fucking untidy, and a slob. So he continually shut off her part of the apartment so he couldn't keep complaining about how she lived in perpetual untidiness.

They were both earning very good money, so often ate in the best restaurants locally. She never queried Bazil as to where he went or who with, when he disappeared of a weekend, or a couple of nights in the week. But she knew it would be someone of importance, because he was often quite nervous, but did tell her that his work was becoming dangerous, because he knew too much about too many high profile men in New York and Washington D.C.

Leanne did worry about him, and begged him to stop that part of his life. And with great sadness he admitted he was going to leave New York and relocate to San Francisco. She had to promise faithfully to *never, ever,* tell anyone where he was, as he was going to change his name, and just disappear to live a quiet life in the countryside, not too far from his favourite city. But also close to the thriving gay community, when he needed some lively company.

Leanne was really sad that he was leaving, but knew she would leave as well to start another part of her destiny, another new beginning. And Bazil had taught her so much. How to eat at the best restaurants, how to dress in her own style. How to negotiate the true rate of her worth as a beautiful woman in the meat market of snakes and pimps that were the advertising and photographic world of high end fashion.

As Bazil left for San Francisco, she left for an assignment in Los Angeles, and for her eternal sins met and fell in love for the first time with a charismatic heartbreaker called Gerry Swane.

A S.O.B. personified!

Leanne was sitting in the lounge of The Excelsior Hotel in Los Angeles, nursing an excellent cup of coffee, and missing Bazil, and feeling morosely lonely. But the young woman playing the piano was utterly amazing, as if she had been born to play for the Gods. She was also beautiful and reminded Leanne of someone, but she just couldn't bring her to mind. It was on the tip of her tongue, and would annoy her all evening now.

"She is the image of Madeline Maxwell, don't you think, and plays that instrument like an angel?" Leanne looked up into the deep blue eyes of a man who wasn't actually the best looking man in the room, but not far off. For a change he must be taller than her, as she was almost six feet tall. His blond hair was a trifle shaggy and long, with strands of silver at the sides, so she believed he wasn't quite so young

44

anymore. As he spoke he had twin dimples that deepened when he smiled, and a permanent tan that made her think he spent time on the beach. But his perfectly aligned face wasn't so perfect, as his nose must have been broken at some time, because it was slightly crooked.

He was immaculately dressed in obviously designer casual clothes, all matching in colour, but anything would look good on this man, because he was slim but well built. She realised she was staring at him when he spoke again. "I don't bite, beautiful lady, unless of course you ask me to. Can I buy you a decent drink, or another coffee? And I'm not chatting you up, unless you want me to."

"I'm so sorry, I am feeling a bit low and fed up. I've just come in from New York, and don't start work for a couple of days, and was wondering what I was going to do with myself. Plus I don't accept any drinks from strange men. My Papa was very strict on that subject, and I always took notice of what my Papa told me." She turned to watch the angel at the piano, and completely tuned out the egotistical jerk trying to pick her up. Where was her friend Bazil when she needed him?

"I can't blame you for being overly cautious, because GHB, and Rohypnol are endemic in L.A. right now. I will call John, the barkeep over to take your order and serve you personally. And, I've never had to drug a woman yet to be able to talk to her." He sat down at her table next to her, because now he was determined to get to know her better. In her bed of course. He actually didn't have a date this weekend, which was totally out of order. So he had popped into The Excelsior to hear Mia Maxwell play her magic on the piano. Instead, he had seen this stunningly beautiful woman sitting alone looking sad and lonely.

"OK, I give in. Ask John to bring me another coffee and a sandwich if possible. Anything but meat, please. I am really trying to be a vegetarian, but honestly, failing miserably."

For the next two hours the two strangers didn't stop talking to each other. Leanne began to realise that Gerry Swane, her new friend, was actually one of the good guys, and she really liked and fancied him. But she also realised that he was in love with Mia Maxwell, the tiny, gorgeous, very talented piano player.

"You're in love with her, aren't you?" Leanne couldn't help but make the comment, because if she was being truthful, she was unusually jealous.

Gerry grinned, but couldn't deny the truth. "Yeah, I am. And being absolutely stupid. The owner of this hotel has made it pretty obvious that he is smitten, and what Anton Santi wants, he always gets. Unfortunately I am twenty years older than Mia, and wouldn't stand a chance with her. And, unfortunately I think she has fallen for Santi, who for his sins is amazingly good looking, and can sweet talk the birds out of the trees. But! He is the head of all the dark, nasty, underworld in L.A., and I am truly worried for her safety. Believe me Leanne, every red-bloodied male who comes in contact with Mia falls in love with her. She is her mother's daughter. Difficult, obstinate, bad tempered, but also utterly gorgeous, and loving, but often sweet, and always giving to others."

"Wow! That's a young woman who is hard to compete with. After what my beautiful family went through, I pray that this Santi takes good care of her, and keeps her safe." Leanne could tell that Mia was as innocent as she was, and truly hoped that she would find happiness with this Santi guy, because it would be a terrible tragedy if she was hurt in any way. After listening to her amazing talent on the piano, the young woman needed to be looked after and encouraged to go further with her career, and future.

Thinking about Mia made Leanne make a decision about her own future, and Gerry Swane. Bazil was her best friend and confidante, but never her lover. She had a gut feeling that this charismatic man sitting next to her would always be in her future, and would always try and keep her safe, and extremely happy in bed and out.

"Will you sleep with me tonight, Gerry? I have a lovely suite here, and I don't want to be on my own this long weekend."

Gerry had never been stupid, or slow on the uptake. And, had been sitting there very uncomfortably, with an acute hard on, wondering how he was going to sweet talk this stunning woman into bed. He couldn't believe his luck, it wasn't usually so easy.

Without a word spoken, he stood up and took her hand and gently walked her out of the lounge, giving Mia a nod and a wink as they passed her playing the piano. She mouthed 'good luck' and gave him a wicked grin in return. She knew that Gerry always had a beautiful woman on his arm when he left the hotel. But this woman was exceptionally beautiful, tall and slim, and knew how to wear clothes to her advantage. She *had* to be a model, or a movie star.

Mia Maxwell was colour-blind, and hopeless with choosing the correct style. She was short, a trifle chubby, and only ever bought clothes etc in charity shops.

But she loved everyone she came in contact with, and everyone loved her. At the moment she loved two brothers, and wasn't sure who she wanted to be with. But knew that her indecision was short lived. Anton, the youngest brother, who was the boss of every shady deal in L.A. fancied her, but was gentle, kind, and loving towards her. Only her. She knew he

48

controlled his empire with a heavy hand, and if anyone tried to cheat him, they just disappeared. He was dangerous, edgy, and lethal, but that excited her, and he was the perfect storm for her innocent, naive persona. She might be an innocent, but never stupid. She had him by the balls, and she would never let him go.

He was also a billionaire! So problem solved!

CHAPTER FOUR

She watched him walk over to the bar and settle his bill. Then she couldn't believe it when he put a hundred dollar bill into Mia's tip glass. And was a trifle jealous when Mia kissed him with a brilliant smile on her beautiful face, and he gave her a loving hug in return.

He came back and took hold of Leanne's hand and led her to the lifts to get to her suite. The Excelsior wasn't a mediocre hotel, and didn't have standard rooms, only suites, which were all extremely luxurious. They held each other's gaze as the lift ascended. Gerry never took his deep blue eyes from her gorgeous face, as if he was worried she would change her mind after all. She in turn gripped his hand tightly, because this was a momentous decision for her to allow a man to use her body for pleasure for the very first time. And, she had no intention of letting Gerry know that she was a twenty five year old virgin.

Best keep her mouth shut and act nonchalant, as if she did this every freakin' weekend, because for sure he most certainly did.

"Do you always tip the hired help so extravagantly? I know she is fantastic. But, a hundred dollars is a trifle extreme."

Gerry laughed at the absurdity of that statement. "You're kidding me! My finances, however good, would not allow me to be so reckless. No! Marcus Medina asked me to keep an eye on her, because she is new to L.A., and is naive and innocent. Every night he gives me that note to give her, but I have to keep to myself where it comes from. Personally, I think he is bonkers, but he loves her and just wants to keep her safe. And that ain't going to happen, 'cos his brother Anton has set his sights on her, so believe me, he will stake his claim, and good ol' Marcus will lose out. Anton is edgy, dangerous, and the most beautiful male I have ever had the pleasure of not knowing personally. He is a complete shit, but evidently can charm the birds from the trees. So I fear that we are going to lose our gorgeous girl, as shits usually win the end game, unfortunately.

"Anton Santi has been my involvement with the FBI, DEA, and LAPD for the past two years. I have been deep undercover trying to get enough evidence on him to bring him to justice." It exasperated him that he hadn't been able to get anything reliable on Santi, everyone was too scared to speak up against him. He shrugged his shoulders as the lift came to a stop, and then he grinned. "Of course I will have to kill you if you dare breathe a word of what I said, because Santi would kill me in a heartbeat if he knew I was the undercover guy shadowing him everywhere."

She put her finger to her very kissable lips. "I will never tell on you, even if I am tortured to death. Gerry Swane, you have my sacred word on that." She grinned back at him. "Anyway, I don't believe a word you tell me, because you are a pussycat behind that hard veneer you show the world."

Thank Christ for small mercies, thought Gerry, as he gave her a kiss that promised a spectacular night. He never, ever, told a living soul what work he actually did. This stunning woman was scary, and he had to be exceptionally careful around her.

She was definitely a keeper. Would not take a one night stand lightly. If they had another date would expect a ring on her finger, and one through his nose.

Oh shit! What had he got himself mixed up in for a piece of fine ass, and a sleepover?

He did *not* do responsibility!

Did *not* do marriage under any circumstances!

Did *not* want kids, or an interfering mother in law!

Only wanted to fuck his brains out, and have some fun over a boring weekend!

So what was he doing in this lift with the most beautiful woman he had ever been with?

Fuck me! He didn't have a clue!

*   *   *   *

He closed the door behind them and locked it securely, not wanting anyone unexpected to invade their privacy. He knew what work Leanne did, so knew she wouldn't worry about being naked. In modelling, and advertising, the girls were used to taking their clothes off in front of anyone they were working closely with, male or female. And, he sure as hell wasn't expecting to wear any clothes over this weekend, which was an extra bonus.

He crowded her against the nearest wall, putting both his hands either side of her head, and went in for a deep, full of sexual interest, kiss. His erection already hard and expanding as it pushed against her soft, womanly lower body. His dick evidently very keen to get where it most wanted to be. Deep and deeper still inside that womanly warmth and solace, to begin the journey of extreme pleasure and satisfaction for both of them. Gerry was determined to make this the best performance he had ever given, because he was pretty sure she would be very experienced in sexual intimacy with a lot of very good looking and highly sexed men in her profession.

And Gerry Swane never shied away from any problem, especially sexual. He was definitely up for it, and that wasn't a pun. He hadn't been first in the queue when equipment was given out, neither was he the last. Pretty normal was his take on his penis, but he certainly knew what to do with it, and give his partner the best time ever. His ever-ready dick was always primed like a homing pigeon, racing to get home, and do the deed satisfactorily.

He broke the kiss and looking straight into those multi-coloured eyes, he undid the four tiny buttons holding her long loose top together. And almost came when he saw she wasn't wearing a bra, and her breasts were perfectly formed, small, but with large brown mouth watering nipples.

She smiled endearingly and just said "Do they meet with your approval?"

He could only stutter. "Er, absolutely. My imagination came up short, believe me." My God, he couldn't believe it when she undid the clasp holding up the long matching skirt, which pooled around her sandaled feet. He thought his beating heart actually stopped for a moment, because she was wearing a miniscule thong that just covered her, and was see through, and he couldn't help but notice that every part of her amazing body was hairless. Probably because of her work that would be normal to her, but not him. Never him!

His heart started to beat again, and his erection now was about to erupt without any help from him. Taking her face in his hands he took her mouth in a kiss that was full of sexual intent. Then with one hand undid his trouser zip, pulled her legs around his hips and tried to enter her with one strong push, but she was too tight, and he came against resistance.

He stopped, not believing what was happening, and with a worried frown looked straight into her smile.

"Don't you dare stop Gerry. Whatever is building inside of me needs more, a lot more. I've never done this before, so you make it fantastic for me, or I will kill you personally, without Santi's help. Do you get my drift, Swane?"

"Yes maam, I will do my best work, especially for you, I have to admit, this is a first for me." He grinned like a much younger man on his first fuck. "I'm going to start over, and go much slower, 'cos my ever-ready dick ain't so ever-ready at this moment. But, don't worry, it's like a homing pigeon, it will always find its way home."

He picked her up and made his way to the bedroom, because if there was going to be a delay, he wanted to get comfortable. Gerry wasn't a teenager anymore, and his back wasn't his strength, but he was still up for it, especially with this gorgeous, untouched woman. He had never had the privilege before, and was determined to make it special for her.

But also realised he was in big trouble with this woman. Big Trouble.

He was a very experienced tutor. She was an exceptionally sensual student.

That night they didn't sleep at all, but made slow, erotic love, only stopping to give Gerry time to recuperate, and that's when Leanne came into her own, and made love to him with her mouth and sinuous body. He had never made love to a woman before who actually took him in her mouth, and wouldn't stop until she had tasted his essence. God forbid, if this exceptional woman was out there taking on lovers, she would have a queue a mile long for the privilege. And God help him, that made Gerry angry and nauseous with worry.

He couldn't get enough of her. Sucked and lightly bit her nipples until she actually had an orgasm without him entering her. Leanne was a high octane sexual being, and had never known it. When he did manage to get his overworked penis to work its magic, she screamed for him to go deeper, and higher, until he didn't know who or where he was. They became one on a higher plane of existence, and love.

They showered together and he held her against the tiled wall and fucked her until they were both boneless. Then told her to hold onto the vanity and as he looked into her stunning face in the mirror, he took her from behind, and she screamed out her violent organism, and his.

They both ordered a huge breakfast through the service menu, and ate quickly to get back to bed to be able to continue. Now they were both addicted to each other, and couldn't stop kissing, touching, and loving without a break.

That day Gerry told her stuff about himself that he had never told another living soul, because he had never thought anyone would be interested. But Leanne was greedy to understand what had made this loving, giving, gorgeous man, the exceptional person he had become.

Quietly and patiently he had told her, while they lay in bed, their arms around each other, just resting.

He was a teenager when his whore of a mother died of cancer in his arms. For all her faults, he did love her, and mourned her deeply, because he was alone and penniless. As soon as possible he joined the Marines, and wasn't really happy, because he didn't take to rules and regulations. When he got his first furlough, he went with three of his newly found friends and travelled to Las Vegas. They decided to get absolutely blotto with drink, and he woke up the next morning to find he had married the pole dancer from the last club they had visited. Both parties woke up the worse for wear and screamed the motel almost out of business.

Luckily the owner of the wedding venue wasn't legally allowed to marry anyone. It was a bad joke organised by his so called friends, and the marriage was annulled before it had begun. Gerry had almost shit himself with fright, and never spoke again to those three idiots. And, that was why Gerry had vowed never to say the marriage word ever again. He had never been so frightened in his life.

Because of an aggravated back problem, he was discharged from the Marines. Then joined the L.A.P.D. to become a high ranking detective in just a few years. But, could not cope with the police force that was riddled with back-handers, evidence being lost, prisoners going AWOL, and gangsters like Anton Santi becoming multi-millionaires. So he left all that behind, and was now a Private Investigator, and was trusted in the community, and often worked for the Agencies to find who was making a great deal of illegal money out of drugs, guns, and gambling to the detriment of hard working people.

The next night was even better than the previous one, as they had learnt what each other really liked sexually. A couple of times after they had enjoyed cataclysmic orgasms, Leanne had quietly cried because she was so happy and content after her previous years of trauma. That was when Gerry started to worry what was going to happen when he had to leave for work the next morning. He was going deep undercover for the FBI, and needed to be free and unencumbered for that serious work, because if it went wrong he would be in deep shit, possibly dead.

Leanne was fast asleep, laying across his chest, all arms and long slim legs entangled with his. For the past two hours he had watched the digital clock slowly moving forward, knowing he had to make a diabolical decision to leave before she woke up. If he waited too long he would never be able to do it. Out of the blue he had fallen in love, deeply. Something that had never happened to him before, and he had always hoped it would never happen. Life became too complicated when you attached yourself to another human being. Gerry was a solitary S.O.B., and enjoyed his own company when he felt the need. But Leanne could change that in a heartbeat, because he knew she had fallen in love with him. The sex had been incomparable to any other. Sex without a condom was beyond comparison, and so much more close and loving. She was on the pill, and had shown him her prescription, but he had believed her anyway. In her line of work she travelled extensively in America, and further afield, so rape was an ongoing danger for her.

Taking one last, long look, at the amazing woman he had spent the last two nights making love to, and it had been love, even on his side. Gently, he untangled himself from her loving arms, and quickly got dressed, and taking a card from his wallet, he wrote those ridiculous words to get in touch with him if she ever needed help.

What a joke! Why should she ever trust him? He was skulking out of her room without saying goodbye. He was the worst kind of shit imaginable, with a soul that was damaged through the life he had led previously. While Leanne was the most beautiful, giving, loving woman he had ever been with, and most probably, never be with another half as good.

Silently, he opened the door, but then stopped with tears forming in his eyes, and that was unthinkable, because he never, ever cried. Not even when his mother had died, and was laid to rest. He knew what he was doing now he would regret for the rest of his goddamn life.

How had he been so lucky to have been her first lover? That had truly been a privilege he would never forget.

He could have had an amazing future with a woman who would have loved him, as he would love her.

Was he a fucking idiot? You bet your sweet life on it!

Gerry laid back in his soft leather recliner and let those memories of five years ago still rattle around in his brain. He didn't get much sleep that night, because he had an ongoing nightmare tomorrow. What to do with Leanne Connor, now Anna Weist, and her silent young son, Jayden? He had to have a plan, a very good, water-tight plan. She had murdered her violent husband, calmly and premeditatedly. It certainly didn't look good for her. He would have to be a fucking magician to keep her out of prison.

But he was pretty certain he was up to the challenge. Hopefully her husband's family didn't have a lot of clout with the legal system in Atlanta. Again, that was a long shot, with money everything was possible, and so far his Anna wasn't being very lucky in love, or murder. So Gerry had to think on his feet and be ahead of the cops, and possibly the FBI, because her husband had been the D.A. of Atlanta. A top job in the justice system. Once they all realised that Anna and her son hadn't been kidnapped, or killed, they would be on the hunt for her whereabouts. In the morning he had to get her hidden away safely where no one could find her.

He already had a plan, which was the easy part, but would his friends help them? Gerry was pretty certain they would. But a woman who had murdered her husband, and planned it for two years, was a huge commitment, especially for an upstanding lawyer in his local community.

Well! Time would tell? Gerry could only do his very best for her and her son. If he didn't, she would spend the rest of her life in prison without her baby.

Gerry was not going to allow that to happen. He would bust his gut to keep her safe, and to spend the rest of her life *not* looking over her shoulder.

He had let her down once, and now he was paying the price.

And, it was about fucking time!

CHAPTER FIVE

Gerry didn't really sleep all night, just catnapped, which wasn't unusual for him. Worried that he wouldn't be able to come up with a feasible plan for Anna's safety, at three a.m. he gave up and got ready for the day ahead.

Ten minutes later he quietly went into the room where Anna and her son were sleeping. Very gently, he shook her shoulder and put his finger over his mouth to stop her from waking her baby, and indicated for her to follow him back into the office. Gerry didn't know how this woman managed it, but she was still so beautiful without a scrap of make-up on, her hair a mass of tight curls, and heavy eyed from a deep sleep.

And shit! He fancied her like no other female, and his morning erection was making itself uncomfortable again. But he didn't have the spare time to take her back to bed and fuck her until they were both brainless, and exhausted.

He knew he sounded hard and impatient, but he had to get her out of these premises, because it was always busy here. Ben, their lawyer, always had a line waiting for him to give out free advice to the migrants, ethnic minorities, and poor blacks. "Anna, we have to move quickly while it is still dark out. I am going to take you to my apartment on the beach for a couple of days, but no one, and I mean no one, can identify you there. Then hopefully my friends living outside Fort Worth will let us stay with them.

"Now be a good girl, and get ready quickly, and then wake up your boy. We need to leave here ASAP. I don't live too far, and we can pick up breakfast in the deli close by my home. But first I'm going to hide your car under a cover where no one will find it. Best we take my Range Rover from now on in case a nosy detective manages to find out that you have purchased a vehicle in the past year. Believe me, it can happen by sheer luck that they stumble on what you have managed to do." He gave her an encouraging grin, because she was looking fragile and worried, and he didn't need her falling apart on him. He had enough on his plate right now, and didn't need any further mishaps.

She whispered "I can't thank you enough Gerry, I honestly didn't know who to trust. But somehow I knew that I could rely on you." Anna knew that Gerry would bust his gut trying to help her and Jayden. He was that type of man who would go the whole nine yards, and more. Without hesitating, she went back to where her son was sleeping, from now on she would do whatever Gerry told her. He was in charge of her destiny now, because she was in dire trouble with no one else to turn to.

Thirty minutes later they both came back dressed and ready to go. In fact Jayden was back in his mother's arms fast asleep again. Gerry had never seen such a quiet, placid child. Marcus and Mia's four children were noisy, bright, and articulate to a fault. But then Mia was enthusiastic, full of life, completely bonkers, but so loveable.

Swiftly Gerry put them into his British Range Rover. It was his new acquisition now he was earning exceptionally good money with Marcus. He could afford a little luxury to go with his Triumph TR6 Roadster, which was his pride and joy. Gerry only took the Roadster out of its lock-up when he wanted to coerce a certain female into sleeping with him.

In truth that vehicle rarely came out into the sunshine. Gerry was over confident that his skill in the bedroom was in the top league, because he practised that skill to the extreme.

Gerry owned an apartment on Hermosa Beach in a Motel called Gloria. A two storey with one large bedroom, lounge, small kitchen, and bathroom. But the bonus was two verandas overlooking the busy but immaculate beach. On the veranda off the bedroom upstairs he could sunbathe naked and no one could see him. That was why he was a beautiful colour of bronze all over. Something that Leanne had commented on when they had spent the weekend together. She was lucky that she had been born a café au lait colour all over, because of her parents.

Somalian women were well known for their beauty, and Leanne had it in spades. She was tall, slim, and gorgeous. A package not many red blooded men could resist. And Gerry had fallen for that package, and had often regretted walking away from it, because he was the ultimate coward where commitment was the order of the day. Once bitten, twice shy.

As soon as his visitors had eaten the breakfast he had bought at the deli next door, they both went back to bed, which suited Gerry. He realised they were exhausted after the four day journey from Atlanta, and sleeping in his comfortable king size bed was the only answer.

Straight away he video called Marcus, knowing that his boss and friend always got up at four a.m. His household was noisy, busy, and frantic once Mia and the kids woke up for the day, ahead of them.

Apart from running his late brother's legal acquisitions, which were many, Marcus actually had earned his millions on gambling on the International Stock Market, and futures. Also he owned a small ranch where he bred thoroughbred horses, longhorn cattle Herefords, and a mixture of other smaller animals. His four children lived an idyllic lifestyle, and Marcus was a seriously hardworking, busy man, but always had time for his kids, who adored him, and their step-mother Mia.

His two boys, Milo and Micah, were nine and eleven and the result of his first marriage to Bianca who had died nine years ago. The twin girls, Maddie and Mel, were four years old, absolutely as gorgeous as their mother Mia, but were not Marcus's children. They were his brother, Anton's children, but he had been murdered before they were born. Marcus had immediately stepped in and married Anton's widow, because he had truly loved her.

Mia had loved both brothers. Even though Anton had captured her heart, Marcus had stayed in the background waiting for his chance. But hadn't wanted his brother to die for that chance. A chance that didn't rely on Anton being murdered. Even though his brother worked and survived in the underbelly of Los Angeles, Marcus still loved his bright, loving, younger sibling. Anton had fallen in love with Mia and married her within weeks, and then died a week after.

They had all been devastated, but now the children of the two brothers lived, laughed, and loved together. It was a sight to warm Gerry's disillusioned and dysfunctional heart. This amazing family were his only family, and he loved every solitary one. He would do anything for Marcus and Mia, they were the best friends anyone could possibly have, especially for a solitary, selfish being as he most definitely was.

"Morning Boss. I know it's not too early to talk to you as you've probably been awake hours already. If I waited too long, your household would be manic, so hopefully I've caught you at a reasonable time?"

Marcus grinned, Gerry knew his family, and the trauma that always followed Mia. "Yeah, you're so right. I'm in my office getting a head start on Anton's affairs, there is always a pile of problems coming from Sonny, even though we have great management in all the key areas." He rubbed his forehead as if he had a headache. With his excitable family, and his exhausting business affairs, Gerry assumed he must always have a headache on the go. He didn't know how Marcus stayed so patient, and understanding, with everything he had to cope with.

"Something wrong with the Company that you need to get in touch on a Saturday? Honestly, give me a break, and sort it out yourself. That's why I pay you big bucks to take the heat off me."

Gerry took a deep breath, hoping Marcus was going to help Anna and her son. "Personally, I have a huge problem that's come out of the blue. A problem from five years ago, when I was looking out for Mia at The Excelsior. I can't say anymore over the phone. It's nothing to do with Mia, or Anton, I promise you. And that's all I can say over the phone. Could I possibly visit you ASAP and bring a friend, who is in dire need of help? I'm sorry that I can't say who it is, but will explain when we get to you."

When Marcus went to butt in to say of course that was OK, he was a man always ready to help anyone in need, Gerry stopped him before he could say it. "I will understand when you hear what has happened, that you could change your mind. To be honest, after hearing the story I was blown away, but realised I had to help, because of what happened five years ago. But this is my problem, and not yours. Again, to be honest I don't know what to do, I just need some breathing space to work out the best way to jump on this, and where to go."

"Look!" Marcus didn't hesitate, "I have an eight a.m. meeting with Sonny our accountant on Monday at his office down town. It will be over by ten a.m. at the latest. I can leave here around four a.m., it's flying time of about four hours. I can pick you up at the small private landing strip where I usually go in and out of L.A. Does ten a.m. suit you? I don't like staying in L.A. longer than necessary, and Mia hates me being away from home for any length of time. She's not great at keeping the kids occupied, and on good behaviour. Also my mom Sophia likes to leave early as she does have a husband who needs to eat occasionally."

"Thanks Marcus, I expected to have to drive to Fort Worth, which takes at least twenty hours from here. You are a fucking God-send. My friend drove solidly for four days to get to me, so wasn't looking forward to being in the car for that length of time, again."

"My pleasure, Gerry. Whatever has happened we can work it out together. That's what friends are for, to help each other when in trouble. I've gotta go, I can hear the family on the move. And if Mia finds out you are on video, she will never let you off, and I'm starving, and need a large, strong coffee. See you Monday around ten-ish, and don't worry, everything is solvable in life, everything!"

Gerry shut down his phone, and could only pray that Marcus was right. But his gut told him otherwise. What Anna had done was understandable, but totally stupid. She couldn't run for the rest of her life with her young son, because someone would find her, however long that took.

Days – weeks – months – or even years. But it was inevitable it would happen. All Gerry could do was work out how to get round the legalities of murder. And make sure she was the victim, not the perpetrator of the crime.

But for now the hardest part of this ongoing problem was keeping his dick under his zip, and under control. Not an easy thing for Gerry to do, because he had never gone without sex for any length of time, like a week. And he really fancied Anna, and remembered what sex had been like between them five years ago.

Hot! Very hot! They had been two people merging as one. So compatible they had fucked like there was no tomorrow, but would die happy. He had fallen in love totally. And knew she had also fallen in love with him.

Jesus Christ, he was *so* screwed, and going over the waterfall without a paddle, or even a fuckin' canoe.

CHAPTER SIX

Mia Madeline Medina hurtled down the steps of the house, and threw herself into the open arms of Gerry Swane. He caught her and swung her around, laughing at her enthusiastic antics. He had quickly got out of Marcus's vehicle knowing this was how Mia always welcomed him.

He loved this exciting woman, as a younger sister, a constant friend, and a lover that was never going to happen in this lifetime.

Marcus would end Gerry's life, very painfully.

Mia was loving, giving, adored by everyone, but had a fearsome temper, which she often vocalised. Five years ago Gerry, with others close to her, had saved her life, but unfortunately couldn't save the life of her beloved husband, Anton, Marcus's younger brother, who had been murdered in front of her, and she had been left for dead by two of his security guards. Marcus had stepped in to look after her and Anton's unborn twins. Mia had decided to marry Marcus, and the whole family were now a tight, happy, loving unit.

Marcus absolutely adored her, and the twins, who were now four years old, and the image of their mother. And she was the image of her movie star mother, Madeline Maxwell, who had also been murdered more than twenty years ago.

Gerry had turned to Marcus to help him with Anna's huge problem, because he was a man Gerry trusted implicitly. Marcus had a legal mind, and limitless money to help anyone in need, and Anna and Jayden were in desperate need.

"Sweetheart, will you please let Gerry go, as we have other guests to welcome." Marcus was always a little jealous of his chaotic wife's over-enthusiastic greeting to his friend.

Gerry had sat next to him in the plane, but hadn't spoken about Anna and her baby. They had been asleep behind them, but Gerry had told Marcus he would let him have the entire story when they got to Fort Worth. Marcus had respected that request because, by the worry on Gerry's face he realised that he was going to ask a huge favour of him. Usually Gerry sorted out other people's problems, so this must be really serious. Of course Marcus would try and give him legal, and personal help, but would never do anything to put his family in peril, or danger.

Anton's lifestyle had managed to do that in spades, even his death had caused huge problems for Marcus, and Gerry. They had to bury him in secret at night, so that his enemies couldn't get hold of his body. Marcus had always lived a corporate life, and was a family man with a loving family, and wouldn't do anything to change that life for anyone.

"Mia darling, will you show Anna and her baby where their suite is, as I'm sure she will want to freshen up. And, ask Ria and Elena to rustle up some food for us all." He smiled at his wife who was looking mutinous, her bottom lip stuck out, which didn't bode well for himself, or anyone else in the vicinity. Mia was her mother's daughter, absolutely gorgeous, and loved sex beyond any man's wildest dreams. But, would not follow any rules or regulations, did in fact fight them with all her fury, and absolute determination. Luckily Marcus was her complete opposite. Yeah, he adored her, but wouldn't allow her to walk all over him.

When Anton had been murdered in front of her, she had fallen apart, and just about survived. Marcus had picked her up, and put the pieces back together, like a puzzle. For the rest of his life he vowed to keep her safe and secure, and wasn't about to relinquish that trust, not even for Gerry.

Mia knew that the two men would disappear into Marcus's office, and leave her out of any interesting conversation. But Marcus knew that she would want to help her new found friend, and that would end up in an overload of emotion for either man to cope with.

Marcus breathed a sigh of relief when Mia took hold of Jayden's small hand, and then grinned at his mother. "Come on baby boy, the kids are all playing in the stables, as it's too cold outside. After we have all eaten we can go look for them."

Jayden looked worriedly at his mother, he had never been allowed to play with other children, or talk to strange grown-ups. All he said, in a plaintive little voice, was "Mama?"

Anna took hold of his other hand. "It's alright darling. Mia is taking us to our bedroom, where you can play with your toys while Mama changes her clothes. Then we are going to meet all the children, who are going to show you all their animals."

Anna could see that her little boy looked really worried at meeting anyone he didn't know. "It's OK Jayden, Mama will stay with you, there is nothing to be frightened of." She tried to explain to Mia who was frowning at the thought that a child was scared of meeting other children. "His father didn't allow him to mix with other children, nor have friends." Her beautiful eyes filled with tears. "Edward was an extremely strict, out of touch father, and would shut Jayden in his room if he disobeyed him in any way." Then she whispered to Mia, "And I got much worse, unfortunately."

Mia looked absolutely horrified, and couldn't imagine anyone treating her children like that. Marcus was the most loving, patient, extraordinary father to their combined children. If he hadn't been, she would, without any doubt, have left him, and taken all the children from him.

"Shit Anna! I am truly sorry. You are safe here with your baby boy. You did the right thing by leaving your husband, and asking Gerry to help you, and now my darlin' Marcus."

The two women, who had become immediate friends, walked into the house together. Mia desperate to help Anna stay safe away from her bully of a husband. Anna fearful that Mia would understand that she had murdered her husband in cold blood. Also sick with fear that Marcus would ask them to leave the safety of his home when he found out what she had done six days ago.

It seemed a lifetime away! She still lived in terrible fear from the consequences of that Sunday morning. Edward had a younger brother, Charles, who was unbelievably more hard bitten and cruel than Edward, more immoral, if possible. Charles would never give up looking for her, and her baby. He was a serious crime investigator working for an Agency affiliated with the Atlanta Police Department.

If Charles did manage to locate her, he would without any doubt in her mind, kill her, and get away with it. His job gave him the kudos to commit murder and not be judged. Anna would kill herself, and her gorgeous son, because Charles would make her demise extremely slow and painful.

He would never believe that the brother he idolised was a wife beater, and had sexually brutalised Anna. Of course he knew that Edward was gay, but she was his wife, and must somehow have deserved everything that Edward had put her through.

Anna had feared Charles more than Edward, and now that she had murdered her husband, would have to pay the penalty. Charles would show no mercy, and Anna didn't expect him to. The space that Edward had left in his diabolical family would never be filled again. And, she had caused that family unmitigated pain, and agony.

The two men stood back and waited for the women and boy to go inside. Mia was talking animatedly to her now latest friend. Everyone that Mia came in contact with became her best friend, and the little boy walked between them holding their hands, feeling safe at last from his overbearing father.

Marcus watched his wife put the much taller, much more sophisticated woman at ease. His woman was a one-off. She was an eclectic dresser, and couldn't care less that she wore colours that never matched, in fact were eye wateringly mismatched. Never wore anything on her small feet, unless playing with the kids outside. Sometimes he wondered who were the kids, and who were the grown-ups, because it was really hard to tell the difference.

He still couldn't believe that she had married him, after losing Anton. But he would take every moment she was his wife as a bonus, a gift he thanked God for every day. And, she told him every day that he was loved absolutely, especially in their bed. No man had ever had such an amazing lover as Mia, who needed sex like an alcoholic needed their next drink.

Marcus Medina was the luckiest bastard living, and intended to be that bastard for many more years to come.

Gerry couldn't take his eyes from Anna, she didn't walk, but swayed her body in a fluid movement. Christ, he found that so incredibly sexy. She was at least a foot taller than Mia, and had to bend her head to hear what she was saying. Jayden never took his eyes from his mother, a worried frown on his sweet little face, everything seemed to worry him. Gerry presumed that all the travelling, and meeting new people, were a huge worry at his age. Also, Gerry noticed that any man in the vicinity had him clinging to his mother, which was to be expected with his cold, cruel father.

Anna wore clothes like a professional, and was always dressed in soft flowing tunics, with matching silk trousers or skirts in beautiful pastel colours. She was of course a Somalian woman, exotically beautiful with perfect features, and almond shaped eyes, but her eyes were not dark, but mixed colouring, which she must have got from her American mother.

77

Gerry was amazed as he watched the two women walk into the house, because they were poles apart in stature and culture, but were both laughing at something Mia had said, already becoming good friends. That was Mia, always loving and giving.

Fucking hell! He had to put his dick into cold storage, or he was going to get himself into a shitload of trouble. Fucking that gorgeous woman had to be the end game, but he couldn't do commitment, marriage, love forever. Anna deserved much more than Gerry Swane, and he didn't blame her, because he was a selfish, self-centred bastard. A one night stand Lothario.

Always had been! Always would be!

Marcus shut the door of his office behind him, and turned the key, because his sweet, nosy little wife was very good at eavesdropping, so he wasn't taking any chances. "Well Gerry, what's going on? And who is Anna? Are you involved with her? I can tell that she means a great deal to you, and lastly, who is Jayden's father, and where is he?"

Marcus had sat down behind his desk, and had a fixed, stern expression on his face, which wasn't his usual demeanour. But he had to have the truth, all of it, because this was his home and family, and he kept them safe and secure in a world that most certainly wasn't.

Gerry settled down in a comfortable armchair as it was probably going to be a couple of hours explaining to his friend. He wasn't going to sugar coat anything, Marcus deserved the truth.

"I'll try to keep it tight and as short as possible, because Anna's life hasn't been easy, especially the last five years, which is why I am asking for your help. You know if I could have worked this out by myself, I most certainly would have." Marcus nodded his head, it was unusual for Gerry to ask for anyone's help. That was why he was intrigued.

"Anna was born in America to an American mother and a Somalian father. When she was two or three the family moved to Mogadishu, Somalia. Her parents had four more children, all boys, and her father worked his way up into politics. He spoke out against the Government, and said that they were lining their pockets with the people's money, and that a lot of the people were suffering in poverty." Gerry pulled out a packet of cheroots and asked Marcus if it was OK to smoke. Marcus of course said it was fine, but not to let Mia know, because she hated those small cigars, and always said he would get cancer sooner rather than later.

"Just over five years ago when Anna was twenty, she decided to renew her American passport. She was finding plenty of work with modelling and advertising in Mogadishu, but realised she could be much busier in the States. Her mother went with her to the American Embassy, but while they were there, her beloved father and four younger brothers were assassinated at their home in front of their neighbours. To worsen the tragedy, if that's possible, her mother died of a heart attack when they were told."

Marcus couldn't believe what he was hearing, and literally was speechless. The poor woman must have been overwhelmed with grief and despair.

"I know, it must have been far too much for a young woman to cope with, but it doesn't get any better. Anna managed to get to America with the help of the Embassy, and did really well in her chosen profession. Well! She is exceedingly beautiful, and elegant. She also had someone looking out for her, another male model, who was extremely good looking, and very astute. He was also gay, and black, and she lived with him as best friends for around four years, and was very safe and happy with the arrangement. Everyone thought they were a couple so they were left alone.

Marcus raised his eyebrows, as if to say, I believe you, but thousands wouldn't.

"Then I come into the situation, and fucked it all up, as per usual. We met at The Excelsior, and for two nights never left her suite. She was in L.A. for a magazine shoot, and I was looking for my usual one night stand. Marcus, if I'm telling the truth, we both fell in love. But, you know me, can't deal with love, commitment, and marriage. And, I knew Anna would expect all three. I left without a goodbye in the night, and just left my card. What a fuckin' idiot I was, because I never forgot her, and have regretted that decision over and over again."

"Gerry Swane, sometimes you astound me just how fucking stupid you can be. You had the chance there for a stable life, a loving wife, and a family. What is it with you, that you are so scared of commitment? Look what I have with Mia. I wouldn't change a second of my time with the love of my life, not for anyone or anything."

"I know! I know! I am a fuckin' idiot, but that fake marriage in Las Vegas scared the crap out of me for anything down the line. Anyway, Anna's next work was in Atlanta, and she met and married the assistant D.A., who turned out to be her worst nightmare. He was a closet gay, and a very mean one. Also, he was a bigot and a right wing prejudice, with a hatred for blacks and ethnic minorities. He married her to silence his critics, because she is of colour, very beautiful, but also Somalian. He raped her to get her pregnant after beating her to a pulp, and threatened to kill her, and their son, if she attempted to leave him."

By now Marcus was shaking his head with tears in his eyes, that any man could treat a helpless woman in such an appalling, disgusting manner. Marcus treasured women and would never lay a hand in anger on them.

"Early last Sunday morning she knew he had drunk too much, and he wanted another child, and she waited until he fell asleep for her chance to get her own back. For two years she had plotted her revenge, after Jayden was born. Edward was a cruel, cold father to his son, and that is why Jayden is overly quiet, and scared. Anna managed to build up a new persona, with the help of Bazil, her black friend, who was now living in San Francisco.

"So with everything in place, she waited for Edward to fall asleep after he had raped her, as usual with horrible consequences of a beating and a painful rape. Their home didn't have any staff working on a Sunday, so she knew she could get away with murdering him. She shot him with his own gun, cleared out the safe to make it look like a kidnapping, and burglary gone wrong, and left with Jayden."

"Jesus Christ, Gerry! It was premeditated murder! She will never get away with it, especially as he probably is the D.A. by now. What were you thinking, helping her and bringing her here?" He blew out a held breath, and shook his head again. "And, what the fuck can I do to help? She has to hand herself in and take the consequences of her actions. It's the only sensible thing to do." He blew out a breath again.

"Honestly Gerry, what were you thinking?"

"Her husband *was* the D.A. in Atlanta. She will be crucified if she has to go to Court. Everyone thinks he *was* an upright, hardworking Justice official, without a stain on his character. Instead he was into everything corrupt. He is from old money, and even older lineage of Atlanta. She won't stand a chance, and her family will take Jayden from her, and make him as corrupt as they all are. She threatens to kill herself and her boy rather than give herself up."

Gerry was heartbroken at that threat, because he believed her. Anna was that strong and determined, and would never let her son be taken away. He was her only family and she would rather die before Edward's family got hold of him.

Marcus got out of his chair, and came round to comfort Gerry. It was pretty obvious he was extremely upset for Anna and her boy, as was Marcus. But trying to be sensible in this dire situation didn't work for anyone.

"Gerry, let's not get ahead of ourselves, and get someone who knows the legal system for murder, it's not my forté. I'll get in touch with one of my partners, Lenny Hayes in Houston, he is shit hot on defending someone like Anna. We can only ask him for his opinion and experience on her situation."

Gerry was so relieved at his friend's honesty and help, because he realised that Anna was in a no-win situation, and he felt helpless for a change. "Oh fuck! I forgot to mention that Edward has a younger brother who is in a Serious Crime Investigating Agency in Atlanta. And, Anna says he is worse than Edward, if that is possible. And, he will kill her if he finds her, and will get away with it."

Marcus's terse reply was, "Oh shit! Anything else you've forgotten to tell me, because this gets worse every moment. And, I am begging you *not* to tell my wife *anything* that you have told me. You know when she gets a bug up her ass, she will try to sort everything out on her own. We have to get this right from the very beginning, because one misstep and Anna will lose her freedom and her son. This has to be like a tactical legal manoeuvre. If we go down the wrong pathway we will lose, and I am not a person who likes to lose. Keep the faith Gerry, because there has to be an answer, there always is. Now, we have to go find our women, and pretend we have been discussing our Company's finances. And, you know Mia, she won't believe a word of it. Also, don't dare smoke in front of her, because she will be checking you out for signs of ill health, and you won't like that, believe me, she is very thorough."

The two men left the office and found all the family in the huge solarium. Mia's eyes narrowing to check them both out, and she knew that they were not going to tell her the truth. They both looked as guilty as hell. But she knew that she would get the truth out of her husband in bed tonight.

Oh yeah! She would know everything they had discussed in that office, or she was losing her touch. Sexually speaking and satisfying of course. That was her forté in life, and she loved every minute of it, especially now she was married to Marcus Medina.

He was gorgeous and sexy. Thankfully he loved her just as much as she loved him. So it was a no-brainer. She would fuck him senseless tonight, and he would spill the beans as per usual. He was a man, and men were defenceless against the wiles and ways of their women, and sex.

Mia would bet her last dollar on that, and so far had never lost a bet, and never intended to.

CHAPTER SEVEN

Gerry and Anna spent a couple of days with Marcus and his exuberant family, but now Gerry had decided they had to leave. He hadn't informed Anna of what was going to happen. They had to leave Jayden behind. It was impossible to evade anyone who was looking for Anna, because her son would give her away. And Gerry, Marcus, and Mia had all come to the same conclusion that it wasn't fair, or right, that he should be traumatised any further. He was a shy, quiet little boy, who needed the love and support of a regular home, and family. He needed lots of love and hugs.

Marcus's family hit all those buttons. Jayden was already conversing more, and happy to play with all the other children, something he had never done before.

Last evening Anna had gone to bed early to be with Jayden, as he wouldn't go to bed on his own. The twins had begged their papa to let Jayden sleep in their room, as he was like a fascinating new pet to them, but Anna had refused as her little boy wasn't ready for all those hugs and overly exuberant loving.

Anna wanted to visit Bazil in San Francisco, but Marcus and Gerry agreed that she couldn't go on her own. Gerry had offered to drive her, even though Marcus had said he would fly her there. But Gerry had refused, as he didn't want Marcus to be any more involved than he already was. The three adults were left to discuss what was going to happen to Jayden. Mia, Marcus, and Gerry decided that he should stay with the Medina's, as it would be safer than with his mother. But convincing Anna was going to be a huge problem, as she had never left him alone since he was born.

Mia had argued that Jayden was already talking more with the rest of the children, and was playing with all the small animals in the stables. Also Sophia, Marcus's mother, who had been a teacher locally, was tutoring the twins for a couple of hours every morning, and Jayden was a bright child and could sit in at the lessons.

Everyone agreed that it was the only feasible solution for Anna to be able to visit Bazil safely. Convincing Anna of this was going to cost Gerry's patience, and logical mind, because kids were a no-go area in his bachelor persona. They should be seen, but not have an opinion on anything seriously affecting him.

As he slowly made his way up to her suite the next morning, he took deep calming breaths. It was a battle he had to win, otherwise she couldn't go to see her beloved friend Bazil.

Anna might seem to be a sweet, loving, caring female, but Gerry knew she had a backbone of steel, especially where her baby was concerned. She had come through some diabolical situations in her thirty years, and somehow survived. She was never going to be a pushover, especially where he was concerned – Mr Playboy of the year, who couldn't hold down any relationship longer than a one night stand.

But Anna wasn't to know that Gerry loved her, something that was alien in his life up until now. Yes, he had sort of loved his whore of a mother, but she had died in his arms when he was a hard-bitten fifteen year old, and older than his years, even then.

So this love he felt for Anna was a complete anomaly to the ex-marine, ex-detective, ex-private investigator, and FBI deep undercover expert. He never did emotion. Never had given his attention or heart to another human being in case they trampled all over it.

Gerry Swane was a one-off selfish bastard, who had fallen in love, and didn't know what the fuck to do about it. But was he proud of what he had become? Of course not. But on the other side of the coin he was proud of what he had done with his life.

He had been born into a poverty struck single family. His poor uneducated mother had prostituted herself to put food on their table. She had died in his arms when he was fifteen, and he lived on the streets until he was eighteen, when he enlisted in the Marines. From then on his solitary life changed completely, and he became the man he was today. Never without food! Never without money!

So fuck everyone who thought he was a hard bitten S.O.B. because staying alive had always been his top priority. Hunger clawing at his gut a constant pain when he was young. As he grew up he vowed to always enjoy himself, and screw every woman he could without exception, unless they wore a wedding ring.

And, for years that had worked for him, but Leanne Zeema had walked into his life five years ago, and changed the compass of his single existence, and mindset.

Now, she was back! Gerry knew that his single, selfish, wonderful life was in jeopardy. What could he do to stop the wheels of change?

Absolutely nothing! Because love had hit him hard and wouldn't go away. He looked at Marcus and Mia, and wanted what they had. Laughter, love, family, and trust. And, he knew he could have all that and more, with Anna, and her sweet little boy.

Now, it was up to him to be worthy of her and her son. If she would have him? But would she? She had a huge problem to contend with. Keeping her out of prison was as big as it got. But Marcus was an amazing lawyer, and had extremely good friends in the justice system. The one fearsome worry was Charles, her brother-in-law. If he got hold of her, would she survive? Gerry feared the worst from that piece of shit. From now on he would be looking over his shoulder, not wanting a knife in his back.

Best keep on the move so she couldn't be found was his best answer. But in truth he couldn't see a good ending to this fiasco, and he was up to his ears in her problem now. His gut was telling him to turn her in for her own safety, but that was the last thing he could do.

Loving someone was the pits. He had always known that, but she had got under his defences and into his heart. Now, he might have to take a bullet for her, and he really hated pain. But knew to save her life, he wouldn't hesitate.

Oh shit! He was definitely in love!

CHAPTER EIGHT

Gerry pulled over into a safe area, and stopped the truck he had been driving for a couple of hours. Once again Marcus had come up trumps and produced the nondescript black truck that morning for Gerry to drive on the four day trip to San Francisco. It was registered to a non-existing company with California plates, so if Gerry was stopped for any reason, it would pass the ownership criteria.

He walked around the vehicle and opened the passenger door, really angry. His patience with his passenger at breaking point, and he couldn't drive another mile until he shut her up. In fact felt like strangling her, because she had been sobbing for the whole two hours. Anna had left her baby behind with Mia and the kids. Jayden had walked away with the twins without a backward glance. Anna had been man-handled into the truck, and locked in while Gerry said his goodbyes to Marcus and Mia. Mia already crying for a distraught Anna, and Marcus giving Gerry a man hug in total sympathy for having to drive to San Francisco with an emotional mother in complete meltdown.

"Get out of the truck Anna!" She didn't move, and kept staring out of the windscreen. "Out Anna, or I will pull you out. I am seriously pissed off, and don't want to hurt you." She turned towards him and glared at him, giving a melodramatic double sob. She was an absolute soggy mess, her usually beautiful eyes swollen and red rimmed. For the first time in over two hours she spoke, her voice wobbly, and strained with all the emotion she had bottled up inside her. "I – I c-can't do this, Gerry. I want to go back. I need to be with my little boy. He needs me, Gerry. I have never left h-him b-before. Please, I am begging you. Please take me back."

But Gerry was made of sterner stuff, and never having had a family of his own, couldn't really understand what was going on between a mother and child. He took her by the shoulders and shook her, that was the least he could do when he was *so* angry. He had never hurt a woman, and wasn't going to start now, however fucked off he was.

Anna kept her head down looking at her feet, still crying quietly, because she couldn't seem to stop, however angry Gerry was with her. She just wanted to go back to her son, and hold his chubby soft body close to her, just love him, and keep him safe.

Gently he put his hands around her face, and made her look at him. She was a complete mess, a soggy mess, but still unbelievably beautiful. He pulled her closer to his body, and met her lips with his, putting all the love he felt for her in that single moment. Anna put her arms around him, and gave back everything she felt for him. It had been a long, unhappy five years for her. She had been in a wilderness of pain and trauma in those five years, but at last was finding peace and love with Gerry.

Gerry didn't prolong the kiss, because his lower body was already primed to get even friendlier. For crissake, he hadn't had sex for a couple of weeks, and his ever-ready dick was going into an overload of sexual withdrawal.

He spoke quietly but with authority. "Enough now, Anna! No more crying, or sobbing. I cannot drive safely with that female racket in my ear. We have another three hours before we reach Amarillo, and can stop for the night. We cannot go through the main area, but have to go around the outskirts. We can pick up our dinner at a drive through, and then find an unobtrusive motel for the night. Then you can get in touch with Mia to make sure Jayden is OK. I am one hundred per cent sure that he is happy and probably sleeping in the twins' room." He most certainly wasn't going to sugar-coat the rest of the night, because he wasn't a gentleman, and couldn't sleep in the same room as Anna, and not fuck her, probably all night.

"I'm warning you now that I am going to fuck you until I can't fuck you anymore. Because once we start I am not going to hold back. I have never forgotten how it was between us five years ago, and I'm certain that hasn't changed. I'm not asking for your permission, because I am going to erase those five years from your memory."

Anna nodded her head, and tried to give him a watery smile, because Gerry was always in control of every situation, and right now she was relieved at his no-nonsense way of speaking. She was too tired, too exhausted at what her life had become, through no fault of her own, just a stupid, stupid mistake in trusting that monster, Edward Connor.

"I'm sorry sweetheart, but we have to go find Bazil in San Francisco. He understands your situation, and hopefully will have a different perspective from Marcus and myself. Believe me, we certainly need Bazil's help in this ongoing serious situation." He pulled out a handkerchief from his jeans, and wiped her soggy, beautiful face dry. Swiftly kissed those luscious lips, and turned her towards the passenger side of the truck. "Now, let's get started on those three hours to Amarillo. I'm starving. I need a shower. A comfortable bed with you in it. And you can have a nap while I drive with the country music station on, which will definitely keep me awake, as I fuckin' hate country and western music."

Gerry pulled up at the seediest motel he could find, because his gut was already telling him that her cover had been blown. Her brother-in-law evidently wasn't stupid, but must be very, very angry that his older brother was dead, and all the pertaining evidence pointed to Edward's wife. He would be sure that she had fled the scene of the crime with Edward's son. Charles had lusted after Edward's wife, but she had always cut him off cold, and made her distrust of him very evident. Now, surely he must be intent on getting the boy back for Edward's parents, as they must be distraught at the loss of their kind, loving son?

Gerry sat in the truck for a quiet moment, just looking at Anna. She had been fast asleep for over three hours, even through the Mexican fast food restaurant. She looked so young and peaceful while she slept, that he was loath to wake her. But he was in need of a shower, food, and a bed with Anna next to him, preferably under him all night.

He gently shook her, but she didn't wake up. "Come on sleepy head, I need to put this truck away from prying eyes, and get my butt off this seat, and back into the land of the living."

Anna moaned, but sat up immediately when she realised they had stopped, and she had slept throughout the rest of their journey. But then grimaced when she saw where they had stopped, it most certainly wasn't the Ritz.

"I'm sorry sweetheart, but we can't be seen anywhere that the police will be looking for you, or by anyone trying to track you. This ain't home from home, but it hopefully has a bed, and a shower that actually works. So that is good enough for me, right now. Get your sweet ass out of the truck with our luggage, and I will drive around the back out of the way."

When he walked back to her she was sitting on her luggage waiting patiently for him. He had already paid cash for the night at the so-called reception. If it had been a decent lodgings, they would have wanted his credit card as a reference to who he was, and as a deposit. Gerry always had an alias lined up with cards to match, but tried to keep everything kosher if it was possible. Tomorrow night in Albuquerque he would probably have to be someone else. His gut was acutely letting him know that they had an experienced tracker on them already. But Gerry was an extremely accomplished tracker himself, so had a head start on anything he felt was suspect around them.

Gerry had known when he had taken on Anna's diabolical problem that the outcome would be a bad one. But he never walked away from danger, because danger seemed to follow him, and so far he had been extremely lucky. Often close to death, but always coming back smelling of roses.

But this time he couldn't see a way out for Anna. She had committed pre-meditated murder on the top man of the justice system in Atlanta. A man who had been revered as a man of the people; all be it as long as they were white from moneyed upper class parents, who were complete snobs, and anarchists.

He came out of the shower still drying his over long dark blonde hair, and couldn't believe how patient he had been. To be truthful, he had wanted to tumble her onto the bed, and be deep inside her the moment they had closed the door behind them. But for once he had been a thorough gentleman, and had taken care of his woman. They had eaten, quite quickly though, and Anna had claimed the shower first. Luckily she had put a couple of soft, luxurious towels in her luggage, at Mia's request. Thank God for Mia, because the towels in the bathroom were pitiful, as was the entire contents of the motel room.

But then Gerry would have had sex standing up. Sex was sex, however you managed to get it, and with whom. Sex with Anna was a privilege, and the best fuck ever, and he wasn't going to waste a moment of it worrying about the cleanliness of the furnishings. He had slept in much worse surroundings, and was by now immune to any creatures lurking in places they shouldn't lurk.

Oh Jesus Christ! He had just pulled back the blanket covering Anna, and she was naked as a Jay-bird. Still utterly and amazingly perfect, as perfect as she was a female of colour. He took a really long, deep breath to slow his libido down, and to stop him from coming.

This was going to be a long, long night, and he didn't want to wear himself out before the main event started. Gerry

97

knew what he was capable of, and knew he had to pace himself. He wasn't twenty, or thirty, anymore. He had moved onto early forties with experience, and control on his side. But Anna brought out the male animal in him, and he prayed that his dick was in control of the situation, because *he* could never be where Anna was concerned.

The moment she had entered the room she had got in touch with Mia. She was desperate to find out if Jayden had settled down. Anna had never left him before, and had assumed he would go back into silence, and probably cry for his mama. But couldn't have been more wrong, as Mia pointed out. "He is fast asleep in the twins' bedroom. Marcus put up a small bed for him, and after a bath he went straight to sleep with Maddie's spare soft toy, and of course he had his own toy dinosaur clutched to his tiny chest. It was hilarious when he got out of the bath and the girls saw him naked, and couldn't understand why he had a penis and they didn't. So Marcus explained the reason for the difference, and that Jayden pee'd out of it. The girls couldn't stop laughing and called it his winkie. Now, they both want one, and he is quite proud that he has got something they haven't." Mia took a breath at last, and added, "Oh, by the way, Jayden hasn't stopped talking, and can we adopt him, as we all love him? He is so sweet and loving, he puts my naughty girls to shame."

Then the phone went dead, evidently Marcus and Mia were in bed, and he was getting extremely impatient with his wife talking too much, as per usual, especially at an important moment.

Now she knew that Jayden was asleep and content in his new environment, Anna was determined to get past the last excruciating three years, and enjoy her special time with the gorgeous man she loved. She wasn't naive or stupid and knew that Gerry was incapable of really loving anyone else but his selfish self. He would never marry. Never commit himself to a partner. She would never hear him say the words she longed to hear – I love you, heart and soul. But she loved him enough for the both of them, and always would. But, when he found out her secret, he would probably run as fast as he could out of her life.

But now he was standing by the bed just staring at her with a really weird look on that extremely good looking face. She put her arms out to him in blatant invitation. How embarrassing if he turned her down after five years of being with other people. She had only been with Edward, and what a god-awful disaster that had been. While Gerry had bedded the most glamorous women available, and had probably never been without a willing bed partner every week.

"My God, Anna, you are *so so* beautiful, and after what that piece of shit put you through, I am terrified of hurting you. I'm going to apologise before I get in that bed if I'm not up to my usual standard of sexual expertise. In other words, this fuck isn't going to last more than a minute if we are lucky, and I can keep control of my dick, that seems to be starting without me." He glanced woefully at the offending appendage.

Anna laughed at his usual outspoken foreplay. Gerry never held back in bed, and always made sure his partner was with him when he came. But this time she had a feeling he was so close to losing it, she would have to wait for a replay.

He dropped the towel he was wearing, and knelt on the bed. One hand went around her neck and brought her mouth to his for a wet, hungry kiss, that was full of sexual intent. The other hand went under her hips and brought her body up to his penis, that was already iron hard, throbbing, and dripping with his essence. He shifted her legs open wider, and entered her with a grunt of impatience and obvious need. But he didn't hurt her, because Anna was ready for him, and took him deep inside her until he touched her womb, and her heart again.

They both climaxed immediately, as if they had been waiting for five years for this joining of two souls in perfect harmony, and dare she say love. The world seemed a million miles away. As if darkness covered the earth, and they were the only two humans left alive, and alone in a seedy motel in Amarillo.

They lay together in the aftermath of a truly amazing sexual encounter. Gerry still embedded deep within Anna, because her body was still holding him tight, and he could feel his penis starting to revive itself, ready to start the process all over again. Anna rubbing her soft, gentle hands over his muscled back, and tight buttocks, pulling him closer, if that were possible. Encouraging her lover to take it slower this time, and eventually would put her mouth to him to encourage him even further. Gerry's intake of breath and the groan he always gave when he was about to come, always made her come in unison with him.

Gerry was an expert in the art of making a woman feel as if she meant the world to him when he slept with them. But he rarely stayed the night, because that would be too much of a commitment, and some women would expect a ring on their finger, or through his nose. But this time he had nowhere to go, and was extremely happy to be inside Anna, as they both fell asleep. But as usual he had to have the last word, which made Anna laugh as usual.

Gerry carefully manoeuvred Anna to lay on top of him, as he was far too heavy to be on top of her. He moaned an expletive as he almost came out of her, but somehow they

101

managed to be locked together by him rocking his body closer to her. That stimulation was enough to get his erection up to speed, but not enough to go into action. He put his mouth to hers and began kissing her erotically. She had the softest, fullest pair of lips he had ever had the pleasure of kissing, and couldn't seem to stop tasting, licking that luscious mouth. He sighed with happiness and total pleasure. "I never want to leave this lumpy, hard bed, awful room, and disgusting motel. Well! That is until we are all fucked out, and too exhausted to walk." He grinned at her, his dimples appearing by his sinful mouth. "The way we are going, and we do have to leave early tomorrow, we could be fucked senseless by morning. I'm going to take a little nap, so that John Thomas can get some steam up, and hit the revival button."

He kissed her again, using his tongue to remind her of what was in store for her. Ran his strong, calloused hands all over her soft, silky body, touching and marking out his territory, especially between her legs.

Gerry let out a big satisfied sigh, and gave a slow, sexy wink, and the lights went out for Gerry immediately. He was fast asleep, and he was surely going to need it.

Anna snuggled closer, and also gave a huge satisfied sigh. She had never felt so safe, so secure, and so – so happy. She knew that Gerry would look after her, and her darling boy, whatever happened in the future. And if things went badly for her, she realised that Marcus and Mia would take care of her son, as if he were their own. They were really good people.

That was the most precious thing that anyone could do for Jayden and for her. She went to sleep smiling for the first time in three long years, and counting.

CHAPTER NINE

Gerry had stated that at his age he was slowing down, but that hadn't happened. They had made hot, sweaty, sensual love all night.

At dawn Anna had woken up with her feet over Gerry's shoulders and his mouth sucking and teasing her clitoris, while two long fingers were impersonating his already hard and swollen erection. He was a man on a mission, and already winning the war. She almost left the bed as she climaxed, bucking and screaming to an orgasm that seemed to go on forever.

Anna had to admit that Gerry Swane was a past master at giving amazing orgasms. But early morning was her worst time of day, and she wrenched herself away from Gerry and ran to the bathroom, her legs as weak as noodles from her orgasm. Slamming the door shut from his prying eyes, she bent over the toilet and was violently sick, again and again.

Swilling her mouth with her mouthwash, she washed her face, and brushed her luxurious long hair, calming down the tangled mess. She needed to be calm and assertive at Gerry's anger when she confronted him. She couldn't blame him for his anger and disappointment in what she had done to him. What they had done last night, all night, would make him even angrier, because he would believe she had been using him all along.

He was leaning against the small dresser opposite the bathroom. His face was thunderous, and hard as nails. He was wearing a pair of black boxers and nothing else. Whatever he was going to say to her, she would accept, because she loved him with every fibre of her being, and always would. She could only hope he would forgive her when she explained her situation.

For Anna he was the perfect specimen of male physical embodiment. At least six foot two, slim, but with a strong muscular form. Long dark blonde, shaggy hair that often flopped over his face. A face that could have been called beautiful, but for a crooked nose that had been broken in a fight he obviously hadn't won. Eyes the deepest blue that always had a twinkle in them, except when he made love, and they changed to almost navy blue, and very sleepy. His clothes were always immaculate, but designer casual, and looked as if they were made especially for him. However old he got, he would always be an extremely gorgeous package, as he was now.

And Anna Weist had loved him for five years. But knew this could be the end for them both, because he was a solitary unit, and did not want anyone getting too close to him, and taking away his independence, and singular way of life.

"Well! When were you going to tell me that you were pregnant? Remember me sweetheart? I'm the stupid fucker who is desperately trying to get you out of a shitload of trouble." His voice was sharp, hard, and totally without any sympathy for her having been so violently unwell. The twinkling blue eyes were now cold and devoid of love and understanding. A baby in the mix was definitely far too much complication for his problem solving, and patience.

She still felt decidedly unwell, so went and sat down on the unmade bed, where the evidence of their hectic love-making all night was pretty obvious. She was just going to explain when he put his hand up in front of him. "And p-lease don't make up a fanciful explanation. I might not know much about pregnancy, and foetuses, but I do know that being raped a week ago does not cause a woman to be that sick so early." He almost bit out the words. "And sweetheart, I have never given my bed partner a screaming orgasm where she has had to run to the bathroom and throw up. Believe me, if it had happened before, I would have locked myself in a monastery and become a suicidal monk." He shook his blond head in despair. "Honestly Anna, I don't know how we can come back from this, because I'm pretty sure I have never made love to a pregnant woman before. I find the thought pretty irresponsible, and might I say, pretty disgusting."

She really tried to stop the tears from falling down her face, but she was two months pregnant, and her hormones were causing havoc with her emotions. She hadn't told him because this was the outcome she had dreaded, hopefully he would understand when she explained what had happened to her; or probably not. She didn't have a choice. She had to tell him the absolute horror of the past three months, and why she had murdered Edward in self-defence. Her children could not be subjected to his violent, cruel anger that could erupt at any given moment, especially against their mother. She had killed her psychotic husband for them, and not for her own sake. She would die for her children, and in the end might have to.

Prison was not an option for Anna, because Edward's family would fight to get his children, and win against her.

She sniffed back the tears, and wiped her runny nose on the edge of the towel that covered up her naked body. She had an awful tale to tell, and needed to be in control of her runaway emotions. Gerry would not listen to her if she kept on crying. He hated female hysteria, and wouldn't have the patience to stay around her, let alone listen to what she had really gone through, and she was embarrassed to tell him.

"When Jayden became two years old, three months ago, Edward evidently decided he would get me pregnant again. In truth he had left me alone after our son was born, because he had no interest in me sexually, physically, or emotionally." She stopped for a moment, and gathered herself together, blew her nose on a tissue, then continued. "At that time he had a young, gorgeous gay athlete as his preferred bed partner, so to have to fuck me he had to get extremely drunk. I saw the signs, so I made sure that our son was in his own bedroom, fast asleep, when I knew that night he would come rampaging into my bedroom. I locked the door as I was terrified of what he was going to do to me, because his rage against me had been building for weeks. But he was a really strong, big man, and just booted the door crashing open. I had decided that whatever he did, I would not make a sound, wouldn't beg, wouldn't cry, just let him do what he wanted, and perhaps he would then leave me alone. Previously that evening, he had asked me when my period was due, so he knew there was a good chance I would get pregnant."

Anna was getting more pale and disturbed by the minute, but Gerry let her carry on, because he really needed to understand how a kind, giving, loving woman like Anna could murder her husband in such a cold, calculated manner.

"H-he lurched into the room, and backhanded me across the face so hard I fell onto the floor in a daze. Then he shouted 'you disgusting black bitch, get up and lay on the bed, so I can fuck you in so many different painful ways, until I can't fuck you anymore.' I scrambled onto the bed, and he ripped my nightgown off me, and threw me onto my stomach, and sodomised me. The pain was unbelievably bad, but I only screamed in my head, because I was terrified he would cause me irreparable damage, he was so violent. But that was only the beginning, because he had removed his belt, which had a metal buckle, and gave me the beating of my life, while he shouted the most obscene language regarding black mother-fucker bitches like me. That was when I lost consciousness with the excruciating pain. But I know that he must have raped me again, and again, because when I came to I was bleeding from my vagina. He had left me a broken woman without pride, and a hatred that burnt deep into my soul, and psyche."

Gerry hadn't moved, but stood against the wall, white faced, fists clenched, and beyond normal anger. If she hadn't killed the fucked up psychopath a week ago, he would have done it for her. But she hadn't finished. He didn't know if he could listen to anymore, even though it surely couldn't be as bad.

By now her beautifully modulated voice had become scratchy and sore, because of throwing up earlier. "Two months ago it happened all over again, because I knew he hadn't impregnated me last time. That night he used his fists instead of his belt, and again he raped me until I bled, and the pain was truly dreadful. But I knew he had impregnated me. A mother always knows when she is fertile, and receptive. But this time I began to plot his downfall, if he ever touched me again, and he did, a week ago. He didn't know I was pregnant, because I wouldn't give him a reason to celebrate with his murderous, bitter, white supremacy family."

She raised her tear drenched eyes to the man she loved, and actually smiled at his obvious distress for her. "So, for two long years I had waited patiently after my darling baby was born, and engineered a new, clean, persona for both of us. And with the help of my bestest friend in the world, became Anna Weist, and buried, with hate in my heart, Leanne Connor.

Gerry was shell-shocked and still hadn't moved. He was a man of the world, and had seen some shit, a lot of shit. But this had happened to his Anna, and he wanted to kill someone very slowly, very painfully, to ease his heart-ache and despair that sick psychos like Edward often got away with brutalising their women constantly. Gerry loved women, and would never intentionally hurt one, and especially the brave, beautiful woman who had opened her heart and soul to him.

"I'm so, so sorry Gerry, that I couldn't tell you what really happened with my husband, and that I was pregnant. I have to live with all that knowledge for the rest of my life, but I can truly understand if you want to go back without me, and I will go and find Bazil on my own. He has done so much for me, and I have to say thank you to him for literally saving my life and Jayden's, when I was at my lowest, and wanted to end my life, and my baby's."

Gerry didn't hesitate for a nano-second, and sat down next to her on the bed and took her in his arms, and held her as tightly as possible, without hurting her. She'd had enough hurt to last a lifetime, and he would defend her with his last breath, and couldn't love her more if he tried, and Jayden, and her pregnancy.

Would he take a bullet for her? You bet he would! He would probably scream like a girl, but who cared when you were bleeding out, and probably dying.

CHAPTER TEN

That morning they headed out for the eleven hour drive to Albuquerque in complete silence. Gerry still trying to get his thick head around the dire circumstances of Anna's huge problem. He was definitely going to use everything in his power to stop her from going to prison. She had suffered enough at the hands of that bastard, and deserved a lot better in the future. A loving home and security for her and her two kids, but Gerry wasn't sure he could be that person. In fact was pretty certain he wasn't up to having that noose around his neck for the rest of his life.

Anna silent because she was so worried that she had cut the ties between them by telling him all the lurid, and disgusting things her husband had put her through. Surely a man like Gerry wouldn't want a woman like her in his life. Whatever way you looked at what she had done, she was damaged goods. A murdering wife, who was pregnant by that psychotic madman. None of it had been her fault, but that didn't matter. It had happened, and she had fled to Gerry for his help, putting him in danger by helping her.

She believed in her heart that he loved her, but Gerry was an enigma. A one-man-band, who listened to his own drum beat, which no one else heard. Anna realised he would never admit to loving her, but he showed her every time they made love. It was never just sex between them, it was an act of love, always.

That morning after the trauma about her pregnancy, he had helped her into the shower, and soaped her all over, washing her personally everywhere. Which of course led to making love under the relentless spray, but he had so sweetly asked her permission if it was OK to make love as normal, because he didn't want to cause her anymore pain, now or in the future. He had entered her slowly and carefully, while he had kissed her carnally and deeply, showing her that he needed her closeness and welcoming womanly body, as much as he needed his next breath. She had grabbed both of his tight buttocks, and pulled him even closer, he couldn't stop himself pumping harder and faster, and higher, until they moulded into one being. Showing him that she wasn't fragile and weak, and making hot, monkey sex was perfectly fine while she was pregnant, and horny.

After, when they got their heartbeats back to a normal rate, she explained that the baby was probably no bigger than a peanut. That made Gerry stop worrying that they could have caused harm to her unborn baby, but he honestly wasn't sure making love to Anna was a good idea now he knew she was pregnant with Edward's baby.

But Gerry was always a careful, but enthusiastic lover, and always put his sexual partner before his own needs. Anna appreciated that about him, especially after her sadistic, selfish husband forcing his sick, perverted sex on her, which made her feel dirty and ashamed, and even more so when he made her perform disgusting sex acts on him.

The pregnancy conversation had led to Gerry's next couple of questions that had been niggling him from the beginning. "What I don't completely understand is why you didn't inform the authorities of what was happening, because you had the evidence of his cruelty with the marks on your body? Secondly, you could have left him at any time in the past two years with Jayden. Why didn't you Anna? Why stay and take all that crap from him? It just doesn't stack up in my logical mind."

She stopped dressing to answer him, thinking she had already answered those pertinent questions. But wanted him to fully understand why she had come to him for help, because she couldn't have done it without his back-up and help. "No one in Atlanta would have believed me that my upstanding, loving husband and Jayden's father would ever abuse his beautiful wife. He also had the justice system and police in his filthy pocket. Nobody would have dared listen to me, or help me. His family are old Atlantan money, and everyone reveres them."

She finished dressing and sat back on their unmade bed, desperately trying not to cry, because Gerry hated

114

women's tears, and would stop listening to her. "I was desperate to leave him, and really tried a couple of times, but he found me, and gave me a terrible beating in front of Jayden, who tried to hide in a dark corner, because he was terrified of his father. That was why he stopped talking, and became a silent shadow of a child." That's when the tears did start falling down her pale face. "He-he threatened to take Jayden away from me, and that I would disappear permanently. I – I couldn't take that chance of it ever happening. That was when I started plotting my revenge. I knew he would kill me, if I didn't kill him first. I expect you wonder why his parents didn't realise what was going on under their stuck-up noses." That was when her face changed with hatred for her in-laws. "Of course they must have known, but he was their first born, who was going to be a judge, and rule the state. And one day even be President of America. He was loved by everyone, with a trophy, beautiful wife, and making a family to keep the Connors at the top of the pile of crap they called high society. A lineage of old money, that can buy anyone or anything to use for their own sick advantage, and even more money for their stinking bank balance."

Gerry didn't say a word, but shook his head and took her in his arms to console her with his love. Her problems were now *his* problems, and he didn't have a clue how he was going to help her. Hopefully Bazil would have an answer for them.

They hit the outskirts of Albuquerque at midnight. They had stopped twice for necessary food, and the ladies rest room for Anna. A humungous breakfast at I HOPS, where Gerry had watched Anna consume enough calories for both of them, so that they didn't have to stop for lunch to be able to keep on schedule for San Francisco. Then stopped early evening in a family run restaurant for a really satisfying home cooked meal, and again Anna ate more than Gerry. He was beginning to worry that at the rate of carbs she was wolfing down, she would be the size of a small apartment at the end of nine months.

Gerry was a rare steak and baked potato man, where Anna seemed to eat everything on the menu. But she was as skinny as a string bean, and so tall and slim she had told him that when she had carried Jayden, no one had realised she was pregnant until he appeared in public.

Gerry didn't argue with the pregnant lady, because he hated the way every man she came into contact with would love to get a piece of her, and he knew what piece. In truth, however big she got she would still be outstandingly beautiful, and there would be more of her to love, to cherish, and protect. Now she warmed his bed every night Gerry was a very happy man, and wouldn't want to upset that phenomenal piece of luck.

But luck that could eventually end his life, and hers. Was she *really* worth it? You bet!

While they ate in the family restaurant Gerry had rung through to a boutique hotel in Old Town, and reserved the best room for two nights, and they did laundry, which was a huge bonus as far as Gerry was concerned. He hated to have to wear anything that he had worn previously. All this travelling in a vehicle for days on end was not to Gerry's liking at all.

When they arrived at Hotel Albuquerque it was a quaint Mexican building, but immaculately clean and fresh looking. The complete opposite to last night's disgusting, seedy motel. Gerry had already decided that type of sleeping arrangement was not going to happen again. He knew once they got to their suite they would not be leaving to venture outside. So hopefully they were safe for the next two days and nights.

A bed that was kingsize, and looked and felt like a downy cloud, welcomed them as they both sank down onto it with huge sighs of relief, both laughing at the difference a long day of travelling had brought them to.

"You take the shower first sweetheart," Gerry had offered, even though it was big enough for both of them to shower together. He honestly didn't have a good fuck in him, and just wanted to go to bed and sleep for a week, at least.

When Anna came out of the bathroom, clean from head to toe, she found her usually ardent lover fast asleep on his stomach, with just his boxers on, spread-eagled over the duvet. "Poor baby," she crooned as she covered him with a soft, fluffy blanket. There was no way she was going to wake him up. She had known he was shattered from driving for the last twelve hours or so. He needed sleep more than he needed her tonight, and she was exhausted from her pregnancy, and sitting for too long in that uncomfortable truck.

When she looked at her side of the bed, she couldn't help but smile, and loved Gerry a whole lot more. Somehow along the way he had managed to purchase plain crackers, saltines, and bottles of ginger ale, for her in the morning. In passing she had told him that was the best sustenance for her when she woke up every morning. Of course Gerry had listened, and probably had asked in the family restaurant where they had eaten earlier.

Anna silently got into bed, and turned out the bedside lamp. Gently she snuggled up to Gerry, and put his out-flung arm over her upper body. Only then did she feel safe and secure with him so close. Immediately her eyes closed and she was fast asleep in seconds. Her dire circumstances alleviated for a few precious hours while New Mexico slept, as they did.

Early next morning Gerry fed Anna with crackers and ginger ale, and miraculously she didn't leave the bed to throw up. And, he most certainly made up for his lack of sexual activity, and for falling asleep on the job in hand. He made slow, thorough love to every part of her willing body with meticulous concentration, bringing her to an orgasm that seemed to go on and on, and had topped all the others before it.

Anna in turn decided to make him pay for what he had made her do, scream and bite until he had stopped playing her like a well tuned violin. She kissed and licked her way down to the part of his body that always gave her mind blowing pleasure. Her hands gently stroking his testicles, she took him into her mouth, and wouldn't stop, even though he tried to pull away from her, until she had emptied him of his hot essence. He vehemently cursed, and begged, but she was relentless, and on a mission to give him the ultimate pleasure that he always gave her.

Gerry couldn't believe that she had just done that, because he had never allowed anyone to do it before, not to that extreme. He felt unbelievable love for this woman, but he also felt emasculated, because he didn't have the energy, or power, to make love for quite a while, and that had never

119

happened to him before. Not Gerry Swane the exuberant and experienced lover of a great number of nubile women.

Totally absorbed with each other, they did not leave their locked suite for two days, and ordered mouth-watering meals from the kitchen. They were both using up a great deal of energy with their constant love making. Gerry was worried that Anna's pregnancy could be affected by the often too energetic and deeply intimate places their sexual fantasies were taking them. Sometimes dark and very erotic, as if binding their souls together, and becoming one with each other. But Anna kept telling him the baby wasn't big enough, or developed enough to be hurt in any way.

But even she wasn't really sure if that was true, but loving Gerry was now out of control, and she couldn't stop and think that what they were doing could harm Edward's baby. Of course she would be upset if she miscarried, but it could also be the best solution to an ongoing problem for her safety, and for Jayden's welfare. Edward's DNA in another child was not such a happy and comfortable thought.

Before they left New Mexico they drove to the nearest Walmart Supercentre to buy anything that needed replenishing. Particularly underwear, and medical essentials, and especially crackers and ginger ale for Anna. Gerry noticed that she was a very easy woman to get along with. Never pretentious, or particularly selfish, or needy, just a normal, everyday type of female, without any particular hang ups, or vices.

They entered California after eight hours of constant driving again, just stops for Anna to relieve herself, and stayed for one night in Bakersfield. Gerry chose once again a small innocuous motel out of the main drag, but he had learnt his lesson with the first one, this was a clean, well run establishment, and he had to use an alias, and credit card, which wasn't a problem for him. Anna stayed in the vehicle hidden away, and he drove around the back of the property, away from prying eyes.

The closer they got to San Francisco the more jumpy Gerry became, never nervous for himself, but for Anna he was seriously worried. He had been doing this cloak and dagger crap for years, but for the past five years had worked for Marcus, and his late brother Anton. Totally legal and often boring, but very substantially rewarding dollar-wise.

His nervous system had never let him down, even in the most dangerous episodes of his work. But the ice-cold fingers running up and down his spine were warning him to get out of Dodge, and not take any chances, even though he had a small armoury with him, which he would use if absolutely necessary.

Anna had noticed how quiet and withdrawn Gerry had become, which was not his usual persona. "Have I done something to upset you, Gerry? You haven't spoken to me for ages on the drive." When they closed the door behind them she put her arms around him to try and find out what was wrong between them, and to coax a smile on the serious looking expression on that handsome face.

He gave her a long lingering kiss on her full lush lips, trying to allay any worries she might have about going to San Francisco. He didn't want to spook her. "It's been another long drive, sweetheart. These four days have been exhausting for me. Let's go to bed, and try and get a good night's sleep for a change. Tomorrow is another five hours drive to San Francisco. I've been thinking about trying to find Bazil, and have been coming up short on the reason why we are really here. In my heart and head I would rather get on a plane and go back and pick up Jayden and just disappear for good." Quizzically, he looked straight into her pale multi-coloured eyes, and knew she wanted to go find her best friend, and he couldn't refuse her anything.

In answer he began to remove her outdoor coat, and boots, and then the knitted cloche that covered her gorgeous, curly black hair. She did the same to him, and then he gently went down on the bed with her, and the blending of two loving bodies began the mating ritual all over again.

Gerry completely forgetting what he had been worrying about, and why it was imperative they did *not* make their way to San Francisco.

Anna completely unaware that sickening danger awaited them tomorrow. But she put her heart and soul into that night of sweet loving, again unaware it would be the last time she would know Gerry's body intimately for a very long, torturous time.

CHAPTER ELEVEN

They left Bakersfield behind with a five hour drive in front of them. Anna by now really excited, and Gerry dreading what they were going to find, but didn't know why. Gerry decided to stay close to Pier 39, out in the open, as he felt that would be a safer option, instead of hiding in the shadows on the outskirts. His years of working undercover for the FBI were guiding him now, and pure instinct. More often than not, being out in the open was safer than hiding where you thought no one would find you, because more often than not, they usually did.

He also decided to treat Anna to a luxury suite at Fisherman's Wharf, having stayed there many moons ago, when a client was paying for his accommodation on a divorce evidence fiasco. They booked into the Hotel Zephyr, and took their finest suite for two nights. Gerry expected to be flying back to Los Angeles by then, after visiting Bazil, and finding out what he should do about Anna's huge problem.

From their balcony they could see the Golden Gate Bridge – Alcatraz – and Angel Islands, also the Marina and the famous colony of sea lions. Anna had to admit, this amazing area absolutely took her breath away, and she couldn't wait to go to Pier 39 for the delectable seafood, that was always talked about by vacationers when they returned home for San Francisco.

Gerry watched her get dressed for an early evening stroll on Pier 39. She was still so slim, probably too slim, but so utterly beautiful in her usual long flowing tunic, and matching long skirt, in shell pink silk. Her black, shiny curly hair held back in a matching silk scarf. His woman was an utterly stunning Mogadishu female, and he was proud to be holding her hand as they sauntered through so many tourist attractions on the Pier.

They rode the tram laughing at the antics of the silly Americans always trying to enjoy themselves. Sometimes too enthusiastically, and sometimes far too elderly to be able to cope with the rigours of walking too far, too long.

They fed each other from stalls and kiosks full of clam chowder – succulent crab – shrimp – and lobster claws. Gerry and Anna did not want to be confined by the interior of a cool restaurant, but wanted to be free to wander and take in the antics of jugglers, dancers, and madcap loonies, who were determined to entertain the tourists who had dollars to spend, and throw away.

But by ten o'clock Anna was showing pregnancy tiredness. So they took a cab back to their hotel, and crashed into bed after showering together, with the usual consequence of making love under the spray, and again before they fell into a deep sleep of a very tiring day, and a sweet, slow, but fulfilling love-making.

A beautiful, unforgettable day with the person you loved, and that love was growing out of control daily for both of them. And that situation was becoming extremely dangerous for them, because they were taking their eyes off an extremely dangerous adversary, Charles Connor.

Gerry woke up after a couple of hours, as he had set his watch on a silent vibration for that time. He hadn't told Anna that he was going to find Bazil on his own. He smelt danger in the air they breathed, and the cold at his back was getting colder.

Silently he dressed in the dark, and out of his travelling hold-all took his preferred hand gun, a 9mm Glock. Also a small, very sharp blade was secreted in his boot. The gun and knife were deterrents, but Gerry never actively looked for trouble, but unfortunately it often found him. Killing another human being was not in his mindset, but to save his own life he would without any doubt.

He had never known a day like yesterday, and he would cherish it until the day he ran out of luck and died. He had seen the other side of a life he had never known. Just being a tourist, and walking, talking, and eating with someone you loved and cherished, and enjoying the camaraderie of normal people just enjoying their moment of relaxing, and letting the world go by.

He now couldn't take the chance of allowing Anna to walk into a trap, and possibly lose her life and her unborn child's. He could look after himself much easier without her to worry about.

Gerry had studied Bazil's property on Google. He lived within a gay community in a ground level bungalow that was standing on its own amongst plenty of bushes and trees. It was a cinch to be able to get in and out of that property in the darkness of night without being seen. And Gerry intended to be in and out just long enough to have a very quick but informative chat with Bazil.

It was situated roughly five miles on the outskirts of San Francisco, a very quiet, seemingly wealthy area. Evidently adult escort services must have paid Bazil extremely lucratively, as he seemed to be living the high life. Gerry could only pray that he wasn't working tonight, as he didn't want to surprise any awkward situation.

He had left a note for Anna telling her she was to stay put, and under no circumstances leave their suite, and if all was OK at Bazil's he would come back for her as soon as possible. He had just signed it 'Gerry', as he wasn't a man to use flowery words of love, and didn't expect to change any time soon. Taking the door card, he locked the door on the outside, after kissing her gently, and covering her up with a soft blanket against the cold of the room. She just mumbled something he couldn't decipher, and turned to cuddle his pillow close to her. That made Gerry smile, and feel good about what he was doing, because she would be furious when she woke up. The last thing he did was to put the 'do not disturb' notice on the door before he left out of the back emergency stairs, and kept to the silent shadows of the corridors, praying security was fast asleep in their office.

He drove to the nearest Walmart, and purchased a pay as you go mobile phone, and paid cash with his Pier 39 cap pulled over as much of his face as possible. If anyone was looking for him, he wasn't going to make it any easier for them. He wanted a phone that no one could get into, and trace him. If everything got fucked up from now on, he wanted to get in touch with Marcus because they had a plan of evasion. Then that phone would be thrown in the ocean after one telephone call of distress, so that Marcus couldn't be held accountable, or traced at all.

Gerry had learnt over the years from working with the LAPD, and FBI, and the DEA, to never take anything at face value. The best laid plans could be fucked up by one tiny mistake, however much planning you put into it. Bazil was an unknown factor, and Gerry didn't know what he was walking into, and his life was as precious as the next mans.

He liked how his face was arranged. He was strong and pretty fit, except for a niggling cough, because he smoked those damn cheroots he couldn't give up, and Anna was starting to give him the evil eye every time he lit one up. So perhaps he would have to try harder next time. He was happy in his own skin, and didn't want a mean S.O.B. messing with any part of him. Yeah, he led a singular life, which seemed to be hitting the skids right now, and that scared the crap out of him.

Gerry stopped the truck a couple of streets before he came to Bazil's street. Cutting the engine, he just sat there studying the area. It was quiet and nothing out of the ordinary for the middle of the night, and there was a sliver of a new moon, which again was a bonus. He was dressed in black from head to toe, and began to move stealthily and slowly towards Bazil's bungalow.

His breathing was slightly erratic, but Gerry actually thrived on excitement. He wasn't a keep fit maniac like Marcus, who never missed a 5K run every morning, fucking numbskull, when he could be cuddled up to Mia in a warm comfortable bed. Gerry would rather have a cold beer in his hand watching a game of football in his super comfortable easy chair.

Lately his life had become boring and sedentary working for Marcus, until Anna had exploded into that comfortable existence. In truth he couldn't understand why he was so worried about Anna's friend. He was probably fast asleep in his warm comfortable bed, while Gerry was freezing his balls off in San Francisco's bloody cold weather. Los Angeles felt tropically warm against this temperature.

And, Gerry could only wish that he was in bed with Anna, fucking his brains out, which was a possibility as they couldn't leave each other alone for any amount of time. If they were in bed, they were constantly at it. If they were in the shower, they were constantly at it.

Constantly at it, was Gerry's new mantra!

He stopped walking and leant against a solid tree, and grinning, he chuckled and said to himself, "Please God, don't ever let this stop. 'Cos I've never been so fuckin' happy in my entire crappy life. And, I can't believe I am talking to God. A God I *absolutely* do not believe in. But, if I am putting my life on the line for a woman, I really must love her, but please don't tell her, God." Gerry then realised he would have to marry her when this was all over, because that would be the end game, and a fantastic result.

"Keep this between you and me, God, because I could change my mind at any given moment. Marriage to an outstandingly beautiful woman with two young children sounds way too much for me to cope with. Yeah! Ridiculously stupid to take on for the rest of my goddamn life. Why am I even considering it? There you go, God. I've already changed my mind. Sorry for taking up your extremely important time. But I had to get my head straight, and I knew you wouldn't try and talk me into such a ridiculous idea."

Gerry began to slowly and carefully make his way to Bazil's home. "Honestly, I really don't deserve a woman in my life like Anna. Because you and I know that there is no redemption for a dishonourable bastard like me."

Again he stopped at the back entrance to the over neat back yard. "You know God, that shit happens, and usually to me, even when I don't deserve it."

CHAPTER TWELVE

Like a shadow he had kept to the trees and bushes, and if someone was watching the bungalow, they couldn't possibly have seen him. Now he was at the back entrance he felt safer, and not such a target for a trigger happy over-zealous idiot.

But his euphoria was short lived, because the back door was slightly ajar, and he was sure Bazil wouldn't have been that stupid to keep it unlocked. Slipping on a pair of thin latex gloves, he retrieved his Glock from his shoulder holster. When he had his old friend 9 mm Glock in his hand he always felt safer, and invincible, which was really ridiculous because it couldn't stop a bullet coming his way. Just the fact that with luck on his side he could get the first shot in, ahead of his adversary.

But he stopped in his tracks, because the Godawful smell hit his lungs like a tsunami of overwhelming putrid depravity. "Shit! Fuck! Shit!" He said under his breath. He had smelt that human waste a few times previously, but would never get used to it, never, ever.

Glock in hand, he silently made his way through the kitchen, trying in vain to hold his breath, and in fact held a handkerchief over his nose and mouth. He found what was left of the human being called Bazil in the small lounge off the kitchen. The poor bastard had been literally hacked to death. Completely naked, tied to a kitchen chair, with a cover over his mouth, probably to silence his screams of agony.

Whoever had done the work was an experienced master of extreme, prolonged pain, and then death. Bazil had been sliced over his entire body, but that had only been the foreplay, and the pleasure for the masochist who had worked on him. His mouth covering had been lowered, presumably to be able to answer their questions. Then his testicles had been severed, again presumably because they found out he was a beautiful looking gay man, which must have upset their delicate sensitivity.

How Gerry managed to hold down his late dinner he would always marvel at. Bazil's eyes were closed, but his mouth was open in screaming agony, as his blood covered the floor under the chair. At least now he was beyond anymore brutality given out by a man who had no soul, no humanity for another living, breathing human, and was the devil incarnate.

As God was his witness Gerry prayed that Edward's brother, Charles, had not been the perpetrator of such evil, and barbaric work. If he was, then Gerry was petrified that he would somehow get his hands on Anna, or himself.

Without a doubt he now had Anna's new identity, and Jayden's. But, Bazil hadn't known about Gerry, or where he lived, or where Jayden was being hidden, with Marcus and Mia.

Gerry didn't touch anything in the bungalow. Hated to leave Bazil beyond anyone's help, but when he was far enough away from the scene, he used a local pay phone to call the cops and give them the address.

But now he had to tell Anna, and what not to tell her. Then worked out that he had to tell her almost the truth, because they had to move quickly, and get out of the area before the assassin caught up with them. Picking up Jayden was now out of the question for his safety, and hers. Convincing her was going to be a huge problem, but he had to be ahead of the game, and in control, even if he had to drug her to stop her from trying to get back to her baby. Also Marcus and Mia's family had to be out of the situation now, because it had become far too dangerous for them to be involved.

On the way back to the hotel Gerry stopped at the 24 hour Walmart, and bought another pay-as-you-go cell phone. There was one last call he had to make to Marcus that couldn't be traced. He could totally rely on Marcus to do as he asked. It would cost a couple of million dollars, but would be worth every dollar.

Marcus wouldn't argue about the cost after Gerry explained what those wicked, evil, deeply immoral bastards had put Anna's friend through. Marcus was a thoroughly decent, loving, giving human being, and would carry out Gerry's request without a second thought.

Marcus made his millions on the World Market gambling on futures. Pigs – sugar – grain - oil, and gas. He had an IQ off the scale, as his brother Anton had, but he had used that intelligence to outsmart the legal authority at every turn. While Marcus wanted to help the poor, and under-privileged of every colour and creed. So to help Gerry and Anna, he wouldn't balk at spending a couple of million as pay back for Bazil's demise.

And Gerry prayed that outcome would keep Anna and himself safe from that psychotic bastard Charles Connor.

Dawn was still a couple of hours away yet when Gerry quietly let himself back into their hotel suite. Hoping that Anna was still fast asleep, and he could get back into bed for a couple of hours shut-eye before they really had to leave. But that wish was dashed when he found her fully clothed, bag packed, and bristling with fury. He couldn't get a word in before she bit into him.

"How could you? How could you go to see my best friend without telling me, and leaving me behind?" His note telling her to stay in the suite was screwed up in her hand. "How dare you tell me to stay here, and that you would get back to me. You are a fucking, controlling bastard. Bazil is my friend, not yours. And – and, I don't want to be with you anymore. I – I am going to find Bazil, and ask if I can stay with him. I don't know what you have told him, but he – he loves me, and will want to look after me."

She was crying with anger, and he let her rant and rave at him, because what he had to tell her would almost finish her, emotionally and physically. Anna was already on the edge of giving up against a family who would want to destroy her, and take Jayden away from her, and possibly kill her. Bazil had been her anchor and a friend she could totally trust and love without a sexual agenda. After losing her parents and siblings in such awful, dire circumstances, he had probably saved her from insanity and suicide.

Firmly, but carefully, he took her in his arms, and then sat her down on the bed. Right at this moment he would give anything not to have to tell her what had happened to Bazil. But, it had to be the truth, because he had to frighten her enough to let her son stay with Marcus and Mia for his own well being and safety. From now on she couldn't even keep in touch with that family, because if Charles found out where Jayden was hiding, he would get to him whatever it took. People going missing seemed to be a sideline of Edward and Charles, without impunity or logic.

"Anna! Anna, please listen to me carefully." There was no way he could sugar coat this diabolical conversation. "Please Anna! I know you are angry with me, but I had to see for myself if it was safe to visit Bazil. I couldn't take the chance that you could get hurt, or picked up." He sat down next to her, and took her hand, even though she made it difficult for him. "Bazil is dead, sweetheart. I found him dead in his home, and I'm sorry but I had to leave him there. But, I did phone the police so they will find him, and take good care of him."

Suddenly she got up, wrenching her hand from his, and with all her strength slapped him round the face so hard his head jerked back with the impact. "You are lying! You lying son-of-a-bitch! No one in Atlanta knew that Bazil and I were friends. And, tell me mister know all, how could they have found out? That ridiculous story doesn't hold water."

Gerry's jaw hurt like hell, but he stayed calm. He realised this was too hard for her to take on board, because she had truly loved Bazil like one of her brothers she had lost. He managed to stand up and with resistance took her in his arms, because the truth of his announcement was getting through to her logical brain. "Sweetheart, I am not making this up. Bazil is dead! I have seen him with my own eyes, and have never lied to you, have I?"

Anna crumbled, and putting her hands over her eyes she began to sob heart-wrenching sounds. Then she dropped to the ground, and began to keen, an eerie wailing sound that didn't sound even human.

Gerry went down on his knees to hold her tight, and just let her get her torment out. He could only wish that someone could love him that much when *he* died.

After what seemed an eternity, Anna pulled herself together, and looked at Gerry with tears still flooding those beautiful eyes. "Please tell me the truth Gerry. Did they kill him mercifully? He was such a wonderful guy, and so exceptionally good to me. I can't bear the thought that he died because of our friendship, and in awful pain."

"Sweetheart, it was a clean shot to the head. He wouldn't have even felt it. But, I'm pretty sure they got out of him that you have changed your name, and Jayden's. So we have to move quickly, and can't go back to Marcus and Mia." He knew she would eventually realise that Bazil had been tortured to give them her new identity, and possibly himself helping her to evade capture. Hopefully that wasn't so, because he didn't know if Bazil actually knew about his existence, as Anna's old flame.

He pulled her up from the floor, and sat her back on the bed to explain their next move. "We really have to get going right now, Anna. It's best if we make for Los Angeles and my office. I don't really want my home to be involved. I have a very good friend in the LAPD, and hopefully he will know what to do. I now truly believe you are going to have to hand yourself in for your own safety. Those evil bastards are not going to stop until they have you in their clutches, and I am only one man trying to stop them." He gave her one last comforting hug, and a long heartfelt kiss. Gerry knew they were walking a tight-rope of danger, and could fall at any given time.

She leant into him, and returned the kiss with all the love in her heart and soul. She knew how dangerous this was for him, and all he had done was to try and help her. "Remember Gerry, if I get taken in, I have left something with Mia, that will explain why I did what I did to my husband. I couldn't take the chance of keeping it with me, or giving it to you. I could not lose it under any circumstances. It could be my get out of jail free, or nobody will believe it, and then I am toast. So, you must let me go if I am picked up, because I had to kill Edward, or be killed. I need to fight this fight from now on by myself. I love you too much for you to get hurt, or even killed like Bazil. When we get to Los Angeles, I will let your friend arrest me, as I am sure I can trust him. And, I am also sure that there is an All States Arrest alert out on me."

She kissed him again with tears flooding her eyes, knowing their adventure, and loving was coming to an end.

She just hoped she was strong enough, and determined enough to give up her beloved son to Marcus and Mia, who already loved him as family.

And, to give up her darling man, who she knew deep in his heart loved her, as much as she loved him. That type of love only came once in a lifetime, and to lose him was like cutting out her heart while it was still beating.

CHAPTER THIRTEEN

For the time it took to reach L.A., which was five hours, they travelled in silence. Each with their own chaotic thoughts of what to do next. The time for freedom and flight were long gone, and a serious path of where their road led in the future was staring them in the face.

Anna was huddled in her large wrap-around warm coat fast asleep, or pretending to be. To stop any further conversation about her decision to give herself up to the LAPD, which Gerry wasn't really happy about. But knew it was an inevitable circumstance.

Gerry was still dressed in his camouflage of all black. A roll-neck black silk jumper. Tight black jeans, which he thought showed off his manly package to its best advantage. And an ancient Harley black leather bomber jacket kept from his youth. With his blond hair and a forever tan, Gerry knew he looked good, and he wasn't wrong.

But, none of this was important now, because his mama hadn't whelped an idiot. The only outcome of their shared problem was about to hit the fan. Anna had to give herself up to Lieutenant McCreedy to be able to keep safe. Gerry had known this when she had walked back into his life just over a week ago. But this infuriated him, because he was usually a problem solver, and this was way beyond his capabilities. If anything untoward happened to Anna, he had asked Marcus to organise a huge favour for him. Gerry would wreak damage on Charles Connor *so* bad, he would pray to die quickly without mercy.

Halfway on their journey Anna had to stop at a rest area. Gerry couldn't understand how on earth women wanted to have kids. With morning sickness that often lasted all day, perpetual tiredness, and needing to pee every hour, it was so unbelievably restricting to a normal life. He was pretty certain nothing was worth all that sickness and inconvenience, especially to his sex life.

While he waited impatiently once again, he texted his friend, Lieutenant Daniel McCreedy, a cop in the LAPD. A self-made man who Gerry would trust with his life, and now Anna's. He asked him to meet them at Gerry's office roughly a couple of hours after they got back there. He did give a quick rundown on what was happening, and McCreedy agreed it would be safer for Anna to be taken voluntarily into custody. There was an All-States look out and detain regarding Leanne Zeema Connor. McCreedy gave his word that he would keep his meeting with Gerry and Anna under wraps until he actually took her to the station. That was all Gerry needed to know, that there wouldn't be a media circus, because Anna was too fragile for all that crap to surround her, and he would have to stand back and let her and McCreedy get on with it.

When she got back to the truck he helped her manoeuvre the high step up, and then tucked a blanket over her for comfort. Gerry knew she was fragile, and extremely worried and tetchy, that she didn't have a choice but to leave her gorgeous child with Marcus and Mia. He now understood just how much that must be costing her to let Jayden go until her life would somehow get back to some normality. She also knew that Gerry would always make sure that her small son was happy and safe.

He didn't mention that he had got in touch with McCreedy, because she needed another couple of hours rest without worrying about what was going to happen once they got to L.A.

Before he parked around the back, he let Anna out, and told her the entrance to the office would be open, because Ben, the young lawyer, would already be at work, as he always started early every day. Gerry decided to leave their sparse luggage in the truck, as who knew where they would be next.

Anna in lock up. Gerry probably with Marcus, trying to work out how to get her out of lock up, free and clear.

As he pushed open the glass front door, he called out to Anna to be a sweetheart, and make him and Ben a strong pot of coffee. And he would go out and pick up donuts, and whatever she wanted, as she must be as hungry as he was.

But it wasn't Anna who answered him, and his sharp reflexes came to the fore, and he immediately went for his Glock. "Leave your gun where it is Mr Swayne, otherwise we will have to hurt Leanne, and we really don't want to hurt a woman, do we?"

Oh shit! Now Gerry knew they were in big trouble, so he decided to play cool and innocent, to be able to help Anna get out of this psycho's clutches. And probably save his own skin as well.

He quickly scanned the office to see if he could easily get out of a dire situation. Ben was nowhere to be seen, and that worried Gerry, because he must be in the building somewhere, and hopefully unscathed. There were two very large, very ugly men standing menacingly in the background. A tall, very good looking, very well dressed younger man held a gun to Anna's head, and Gerry knew he was capable of using it, if provoked. Seeing Bazil so brutally murdered left Gerry in no doubt that Edward's brother was as evil, and psychotic as Edward.

"As you can see, we have found your sweetheart, Mr Swayne. And now I want to know where my sweet little nephew is hiding, *please*. As I know you saw what we did to poor Bazil, and he had to tell us what Leanne had done. Can you believe it? Anna Weist? So common, just like the low life black whore she is."

Anna managed to shake her head so very slightly, telling Gerry not to tell this maniac anything, because her boy would not be safe with his uncle.

"I'm sorry, but who are you? And, why are you in my office? And where is Ben, my lawyer? Mrs Weist is my client, and only my client. I always call women sweetheart, because I have a shocking memory, and I am a chauvinist pig without good manners."

The smile left Charles' face, and a third man had come up behind Gerry and put a gun in his back, taking his Glock from its holster, and making sure he didn't have another weapon. "Don't waste my time lying to me Swayne. I had you watched in San Francisco, and you were both extremely close, too close for my taste." He turned and backhanded Anna's face very hard, she almost came off the chair she was sitting on, but didn't make a sound, even though a trickle of blood was dripping from her chin.

Gerry went to spring to her defence, but again she shook her head, very carefully this time. She kept blinking her eyes, trying to stop crying from the pain in her cheek and jaw. Gerry realised she was used to suffering much more pain from Edward, and it would be so hard to break her. She would rather die than tell this sick S.O.B. where Jayden was. Especially now he was safe and loved by the Medina family.

Gerry took the path of least resistance, because whichever way he jumped, he knew he would either be dead, or hurt extremely badly. He had to think about Anna before his own comfort, because loving her had changed him beyond anything that had come into his life before her, and Jayden. He felt they were a family now, if he had to give his own life to save her, he would. That was not the old Gerry Swayne, who went through life, selfish, a lover of beautiful women, without a care in his own small world.

"First, you tell me where Ben is, and I will tell you exactly what I know." Gerry needed to know if Ben was OK. He was a young, black lawyer, who gave up his precious time for the poor black community, or immigrants, who couldn't afford legal help.

"Mr Swayne, you are testing my patience. Your black lawyer is safe. In his office next door, tied up, and gagged. I'm afraid my guys did get a tad rough with him, but he is still breathing, and in one piece. So be very thankful that we can be lenient *if* we want to be."

Gerry knew that they were not going to include him in that leniency. So he had to make his story as near to the truth as possible. He didn't know how long they had been following him and Anna. "A few days ago Anna turned up at this office

146

saying she had left her possessive, controlling husband, who she was terrified of, but did not have her child with her. She said she had driven for four days and nights from Atlanta. I immediately told her to contact the police and get help. But she said that as we had met five years ago, had a very short fling, and I had left her, I should help her now. I was extremely unhappy at what she was asking me to do. To find her best friend, Bazil de Frey, who had organised a whole new life for her. She never mentioned that she had a son, only that she didn't have any family to help her."

Gerry shook his blond head, and raised his hands at being so gullible. "Look, I'm a private investigator, she is a stunningly beautiful woman. Honestly, how could I turn her down, and my dick over-ruled my conscience. As a P.I. I have to often work under the police radar. And truthfully, I thought she was making the whole ridiculous episode up. I believed that she had run away from a possessive husband, and wanted me to find her lover."

Charles began to slowly clap his hands, and looked at the other three gorillas and smiled, and they smiled back. "Thank you so much for that fairy tale. Now, I am going to tell you exactly what happened, shall I?" Gerry held his breath fully expecting that Marcus and Mia would be involved.

"My black bitch of a sister-in-law murdered my wonderful, loving, hard-working brother. She came to you out of the blue, hoping you would remember her from five years ago, and so you did. You have been fucking my esteemed brother's wife. That must make you so proud, Mr Swayne. We managed to shadow you in San Francisco, when we found Bazil de Frey. Who I might add that my boys did a thorough job of emasculating the black gay whore."

Anna put a hand over her mouth to stifle the sobs that needed to be set free. She had known that Gerry had lied to her about how Bazil had died. She knew that her brother-in-law hated the blacks, and gays, with a vengeance. And poor, beautiful, passionate Bazil must have suffered beyond human tolerance before telling him about Gerry and where he lived. And, thank God, she had never told Bazil where Jayden was hiding. That was her only comfort. She had to speak up now to save Gerry. It would shatter her if she was the cause of his death.

"Please Charles, Mr Swayne is telling you the truth. He didn't want to help me, but I begged him to find Bazil in San Francisco, and then to leave me there. But when he found Bazil dead, he couldn't leave me. I came back with him to be able to disappear again. I will come with you now, and won't cause any more trouble, I promise."

Charles looked at her with hatred, and mockery. "Leanne sweetheart, you are going with me, right now. And, you will tell me where my nephew is, or else. And, you will not want to know what my capabilities are, extremely nasty and painful, waiting just for you." He smiled at her as he said his next vitriolic words. "Please don't worry about your so called lover here, because my boys really enjoy the work I pay them for." He turned to the two gorillas in the background. "Now guys, we don't want him dead, because the cops will be after us, but just enough to incapacitate him for a few weeks, so he can't follow this piece of black trash."

He took Anna's arm and pulled her out of the chair. She looked haggard and exhausted, but went docilely, knowing there wasn't any choice. There were four men against the two of them. As she went past Gerry, she looked straight at him, her eyes wet with tears, and mouthed silently, "I'm *so* sorry. I love you with all my heart", and then was dragged out of the door.

"George, get the car please, and hurry, I can't wait to get out of this fucking piece of shit, Los Angeles. Can't wait to get back to our private plane and Atlanta, and finding out where sweet little Jayden is."

As the door closed behind Anna and her captors, Gerry closed his eyes, and prayed to a God he still didn't believe in to be merciful, and let him die quickly, without too much pain. That was how desperate he was.

But when the first blow came it fucking hurt bad, and then after a relentless battering, God was merciful, because the lights went out for Gerry.

And the pain was a long distant memory he didn't want to come back from. He found he was hovering above his inert battered body. Then a very concerned voice was calling him back to a living hell of pain.

"Fucking hell, Gerry Swayne. Who the fuck did this to you? Stay with me, you stupid sod. No! Don't go back, take my hand and hold tight. I'm just calling an ambulance, they will be here ASAP."

Gerry tried to focus on his friend, Daniel McCreedy and whispered brokenly. "No! Phone Dr Perez at the Santi Clinic, he – he is the best." Then Gerry lapsed back into unconsciousness, and no pain.

"OK buddy, you've got it." He placed the call straightaway. "He is on his way Gerry, hang in there. He says he is only fifteen minutes away."

CHAPTER FOURTEEN

Lieutenant Daniel McCreedy would not leave Gerry, because he feared he would lose him. He had been systematically brutally beaten almost to death. Instead he summoned his two most senior detectives who he could trust without question. They arrived at the same time as Doctor Perez from the Santi Clinic.

McCreedy was still holding Gerry's hand tightly and hadn't let go, but Doctor Perez insisted he move back to give him more room to examine his seriously sick patient. Gerry had been at the clinic when Perez had saved Mia's life when she had been shot with her husband, Anton, who had died at the scene. Gerry had helped save Mia's life by getting her to the clinic so quickly.

Perez would work tirelessly to save Gerry.

Daniel left the doctor to help his friend, and quietly told the two detectives to go find the young black lawyer, Ben, next door. Gerry had somehow managed to tell Daniel that he could have been hurt badly, because of his colour, and work with the minorities. The psycho's who had beaten Gerry so badly, and possibly Ben, were white supremacists on a mission to kill any blacks who got in their way. Edward and Charles were high up in that sickening group of mentally unstable Nazi type psycho's.

Ben was found, tied up and gagged in a cupboard, and absolutely furious that he had left Gerry's door unlocked allowing the men to walk in and hurt Gerry so badly. Sure, he had been roughed up, but nothing like his boss, Gerry, and he managed to give an accurate picture of what the men looked like. But Daniel told his detectives to sit on what Ben was telling them, as he didn't know yet which way Gerry was going to jump regards Anna. Daniel had assumed this was a tricky situation, because it wasn't in the LAPD jurisdiction. Anna was probably back in Atlanta by now. And under the Agency that this Charles Connor worked for.

In their last phone call, Gerry had quickly explained to Daniel what had happened to Anna, and who she actually was. So Daniel was putting the lid on her being missing, and his friend, Gerry's involvement.

Then Daniel and his detectives were helping the good doctor move Gerry carefully into the private ambulance. Perez told McCreedy that Gerry needed to be in surgery immediately if he was going to repair all the damage to his battered body, and possibly save his life.

McCreedy got in the back with Gerry, as he was a paramedic and could keep an eye on his vitals, while Perez drove the small ambulance, slowly. The detectives, Lewis and Carter, were told that McCreedy was taking a few days off work that were owed to him, and he would square it with the

Commissioner. They were also told to keep their mouths shut at what had happened this morning, and he would also put that right when needed.

Lewis answered, "Whatever you say Boss, but this is going to cost you a double at the bar, when you get back. But good luck with Gerry, he is well liked in the force. Never known him to be caught out before, ever." And the doors closed on the private ambulance, leaving the detectives shaking their heads, and Ben with tears in his eyes, blaming himself for causing so much pain to his friend.

Lieutenant Daniel McCreedy was a stalwart, straight as a dye copper. Couldn't be bought. Couldn't be coerced into any illegal shenanigans. Six foot four of impeccably dressed, handsome, and muscled male, born in L.A. with parents from England. Mother Fay from Wales, and pregnant with Daniel when arriving in L.A. Father Jack from Glasgow, and on a work exchange permit from his police force to America. He had worked tirelessly to become a Captain in the L.A.P.D., and recently retired.

Daniel at twenty-one had graduated from The Police Academy. Had served his time as a rookie, and detective, and now Lieutenant. He had met Gerry when he had graduated at the same time, but Gerry was two years older. They had become firm friends, as rookies, and detectives, and Daniel trusted Gerry to watch his back, always. They had been partners in crime busting, and on patrol in stake-outs, bringing in many an L.A. criminal to justice. They had been the perfect team when the LAPD was not the pristine unit it was now.

But in the end Gerry couldn't take the restriction and regulations placed on serving policemen, and women. He turned his back on a rising career, and became a private investigator. Often helping Daniel with his career by working undercover for the police force, and finding out what the underbelly of the dark side of L.A. was up to. He also worked for the FBI as a non-contract free agent, again in deep undercover to help bring down the unsavoury drug and gun traffickers. Daniel and Gerry had both been instrumental in trying to bring down the Santi empire of Theo and Anton Santi.

Daniel knew that was how Gerry had met the lawyer brother of Anton Santi, who was as straight as a dye, while his father and brother were as illegal as get-go. Marcus and Gerry had become firm friends, and Daniel was the third wheel in that friendship.

Gerry and Daniel were like chalk and cheese, but had been best friends for almost twenty years. Gerry was blond, designer casual, and always got the beautiful women in his bed. Daniel was dark, total designer, and brooding. In the shower had a great deal to be proud of, whereas Gerry did not. But he never got the woman if Gerry was in the vicinity. He had a boyish charisma, and *the* chat, which always got a beautiful woman in his bed, while Daniel had the equipment, and often went home alone and frustrated. Gerry always commented that Daniel had a stick up his ass that needed to be removed surgically.

But early in their friendship Gerry realised that Daniel was shy around the female population. He rarely communicated with police-women, and got tongue-tied if he had to give them orders. With the men he was sharp and to the point. The younger guys looked up to him, because he always listened to their beefs, and was always fair. But with women, he was pretty hopeless. For all his shyness with women, Daniel was a tough cookie. He had played and enjoyed college football, until a knee injury had left him on the sidelines. As a defence player he had been battered and bruised, but was full of testosterone, and thoroughly enjoyed the bone crunching tackles to win.

Now he would stay with Gerry until he was out of danger, because his friend didn't have anyone else to care about him, locally. Daniel had loving parents, and a married younger sister with two kids, and he adored all of them.

He would keep Marcus advised on how Gerry was doing daily. Hopefully he was going to survive this savage and brutal beating. If Dr Perez was as good as Gerry had indicated, he might get his patient back on his feet. Only then could Gerry, Marcus, and Daniel decide what they were going to do about Anna, and her ongoing predicament.

Until then Daniel would stay by his friend's side. They had made a pact that they would look out for each other if in trouble.

And Gerry was in a shit load of trouble!

Twice on the journey to the clinic they had stopped the ambulance so that Dr Perez could work on Gerry, because his heart had stopped. Stefan Perez believed that he'd had a massive blow to his chest that was now affecting his heart to beat normally. But they had managed to make it to the clinic with Gerry clinging desperately to life.

Now he was undergoing scans, and tests to find out exactly what Perez was going to have to do to patch up his patient. As Gerry went through the swing doors of the theatre, Daniel asked the gowned and masked Perez how long was he expecting to operate on Gerry. "Honestly, I haven't a clue, but the Sister in charge will keep you posted. Sorry, I have to go, Gerry needs me to get on right now, and try to rectify the damage." He shook his head, as if he wasn't sure he really could do what was being asked of him. But also knew he was the very best trauma surgeon in L.A. and would do his very best.

Daniel hung around the theatre for a couple of hours, but realised he couldn't do anything to be helpful, so asked at the nurses' station which would be Gerry's room when the operation was over. The sister in charge said he would go straight to Critical Care, and then to his own room, number 10. There were only ten rooms in total, and that was the quietest one. The Santi Clinic was a private hospice with a small number of elite staff, paid for by Anton Santi, and Marcus Medina.

Daniel decided to check out the room, and make sure it was OK for his injured buddy, and was surprised at how pleasant and comfortable it would be for Gerry. It had a day bed for a visiting relative. A well appointed bathroom with a spacious shower and facilities. There was also a small table and a couple of armchairs in the main area. He decided to go home and pack a few clothes and toiletries so he could stay with Gerry until he was back on his feet. He could work from his computer and cell phone to keep in touch with his work, and could tackle the reports pending in his in tray. He rarely if ever took time out from his job, so he was owed a great deal of down time. And, nobody above his rank of Lieutenant could grouse that he was shirking his duty. There were others in command who could now step up to the plate for a change.

Away from his very tidy desk he could tackle the usually overwhelming back-log of paperwork, a big part of his job he really hated. But in his desperate need to be a Lieutenant, and slowly move up the ladder to the top job, he hadn't realised just how much fucking red tape and paperwork there was to catching the bad bastards in society and putting them away.

He went back to the nurses' station and spoke to Martha, who had told him she was going to be in charge of Mr Swane while he was in their combined care. "I've decided to go home and pick up a few necessities, so I can stay with Gerry Swane until he is on his way to recovery. Of course if that is OK with the rules for visitors?"

"If you are here as the police, it is OK to keep your gun in view, and your badge of course." Martha had noticed the big black gun in its holster under his arm, and guns were not allowed in the grounds of the Hospice. Daniel would agree with that rule normally, but his friend had been brutally attacked, because he hadn't had a chance to use his fire-arm. Daniel's fire-arm wasn't going anywhere without him, now or in the future.

"I am here as a law enforcement officer to keep Gerry Swane safe, and to make sure no one attempts to kill him again. I will at all times wear a jacket to conceal my weapon, and will be extra careful if I have to leave his room." He smiled shyly at the two women as he turned to leave. No way was he giving up his fire-arm, and when he met the bastards who had done this to Gerry, he would make sure his aim was straight at their balls.

Martha watched him saunter down the corridor to the garden exit, with his usual easy gait that was all athlete and extremely fit guy. She didn't breathe until he left the building. "Wow! Was he hot or what? He is Mr Gorgeous personified. There is no way I would ever throw that hunk outta my bed. No mama! Not for a couple of weeks anyway." She began to fan herself with a large folder.

"Martha honey, you never throw any man outta your revolving bed. P-lease, give me a break and let me have him for a change." They both gave out peals of laughter, as if their husbands would ever give them the chance.

Daniel was always totally unaware of how he affected all women, every day in every way.

Gerry was floating in a deep, dark, peaceful no-man's land, and he had decided he wanted to stay there forever. Outside this idyllic plateau, he could hear someone calling him, but he knew fangs of red hot fire and all encompassing pain were waiting on the edge for him. So he decided to stay exactly where he was, whoever was calling could fucking wait for someone else to take his place, and feel whatever was waiting for him out of this shield of darkness. If someone was kind enough to put a glass of rare scotch in his hand, and a cheroot in his lips, he would happily stay where he was forever, and enjoy every fucking moment.

And, if this was death, it wasn't such a bad place to be in, especially with a drink and a smoke available. And, for some goddamn reason sex didn't seem so important here, which came as a surprise to Gerry, as sex was at the top of his important list. The absolute top of his fucking list.

Well! Why wouldn't it be?

"Gerry, we really need you to come back to us, so that we can see if our patchwork is successful. I am sure you can hear me, so open those baby blues right now. I know you will be in pain, but I can give you strong pain meds to counteract that situation." Dr Perez was talking quietly to his patient, who was in Critical Care, and had been for quite a few hours. He needed to have a serious conversation with his friend, as he had been almost beaten to death, and Stefan's skill as a trauma surgeon had been truly pushed to the limit.

Halfway through the long complicated surgery Gerry had flat-lined again, and it had been touch and go if he would pull through. But earlier Stefan had called in an associate. A truly eminent heart surgeon who luckily was working with Stefan to repair a small tear in a blood vessel in Gerry's heart, which was now working perfectly. They had both presumed that their patient had had a violent and hard punch to the heart area, and many more blows that Stefan had worked hard to perform miracles on. Gerry would have to work exceptionally hard and take time to recover fully from this sadistic and prolonged beating.

And Stefan knew Gerry only too well. Patience and hard work were not in his DNA. But if he didn't try he would end up disabled, and half the man he was used to living with. A totally mean S.O.B.

Stefan had patiently continued to talk to his critical care patient, knowing he could hear him, but was not responding as he should be. "I know that you can hear me Gerry Swane, so I am not going to sugar-coat what is ahead for you. The next month is going to be extremely difficult for you, and extremely painful. Your lazy attitude is going to have to go out of the window, and pretty sharply."

Stefan waited, but still no response from his seemingly comatose patient, but Stefan knew better. So he listed the ravages caused by the savage beating.

"Your jaw is screwed and wired back to give it time to heal properly, so speech is going to be difficult. Your left knee again is screwed and wired to try and get it back to normality, and for you to be able to walk without a limp. Your right hand has had major surgery to put each finger into place, as it was smashed almost beyond repair. Your right shoulder has been completely replaced as it was shattered beyond use. Four ribs are taped and kept immobile until they heal and are out of pain. The tear in your chest has been clipped, and you are out of danger of your heart stopping and going out of sync, again. I'm afraid your damaged eye-socket is waiting for an eminent eye specialist to take a look at tomorrow, as he wasn't free today. So, taking everything into account, you are a very sick man, Gerry Swane. And, hopefully the amount of hours I worked on you with two other surgeons won't be wasted, as you decide you don't want to come back to us."

Stefan waited patiently again. "Luckily Lieutenant McCreedy is already here to get you through it. He is a fitness fanatic, and, bless him, he has taken unpaid leave of absence from the L.A.P.D. As soon as you are well enough, he is taking you home with him, to make sure you adhere to my demands, Gerry.

"You want to be a disabled, sad, son of a bitch, then be my guest. Because that is what you will be if you play dead, and disregard all our hard work on keeping you alive to live another goddamn day. You selfish bastard."

Gerry slowly opened his good eye, and whispered without moving his jaw. "Fuck you Perez! Why didn't you let me die? You fuckin' asshole!"

CHAPTER FIFTEEN

Anna could not get warm, in fact was beyond feeling cold, freezing cold. She was rolled tightly into a foetal ball, trying to survive another night in the hell that Charles had incarcerated her at least two weeks ago. She was lying on a thin old mattress, with just a flimsy blanket covering her, and wearing thin cotton surgical scrubs, which held no warmth to her shivering body.

She thought she was in the basement of premises that belonged to her brother-in-law, having been brought here with a black covering over her face. The three men who had been with Charles when she had been taken from Gerry in Los Angeles were taking it in turns to keep her imprisoned and making sure she behaved, and didn't try to escape. They didn't seem to understand that she didn't care anymore if she was dead or alive. Because the moment they arrived at their destination Charles had taken great delight in informing her that Gerry was dead and at the bottom of the ocean, feeding the occupants of the sea.

Anna hadn't cried. Hadn't screamed out her agony. Hadn't fallen to the concrete floor and prayed to follow him into the abyss of death. She would not allow Charles to intimidate her, and see the meltdown that was happening inside her. It actually did the opposite that he envisaged, because now she was really determined to overcome everything he could do to her, and make sure she survived to bring him to justice and his entire evil, despot family. She hated him with every cell in her body, and loathed him with every fibre of her being.

Evidently Charles wouldn't give up until she told him where Jayden was, and that was never going to happen. Anna would never allow her beloved child to live and be brought up by Edward's vile, corrupt family. So far nobody had guessed that she was pregnant with Edward's baby. Her baby!

But it was conceivable that she could miscarry at any moment with the diabolical treatment they were putting her through daily, and especially every night.

She didn't actually want to eat anything, but only did so to feed her unborn child. Breakfast was a weak cup of tea, and a piece of toast that was often burnt and stale. Lunch, a sandwich which she couldn't determine what the meagre filling was. Evening meal was another stale sandwich of the same ilk as lunch. Luckily drinking water was always on the menu, and Anna made sure she filled up her hunger with plenty of it. The big problem was that she had to use the toilet facilities in front of at least one of the gorilla's guarding her. There wasn't a shower, or any privacy for her in this prison, and Anna was a private and quiet person. So the situation she found herself in was brutal for her, and so very embarrassing.

But! None of that was the worst part of her incarceration. The light was never turned off in her concrete prison, so she rarely slept an hour or two in tandem, and was absolutely exhausted.

About two a.m. every night Charles came to her, after telling her guard to get lost for a time, as he wanted to grill her about his nephew, and didn't want a witness. Every night he lost his volcanic temper, and continually hit her when she would not tell him where his nephew was hidden.

But that was not the worst part, the pain of his blows she could withstand. She would never let him know where her child was living; loved and extremely happy. For Jayden she suffered cruel and painful rape every night. For Anna it was a repeat nightmare of Edward all over again, but that had taught her to cope mentally, and to rise above torture and rape.

If she wasn't pregnant with another precious child she would somehow have ended her Godawful life. She would have joined the love of her life in a heartbeat. Gerry had meant everything to her, and she still couldn't believe that he was gone out of her life permanently. He was too big – too charismatic – too gorgeous, to not be walking and talking anymore. She had lost all her beloved family in Mogadishu, and suffered at the evil hands of Edward Connor, her vile, psychotic husband.

Enough was enough!

Now she had even worse to cope with, his younger brother Charles, who was trying to diminish her self-esteem, and make her feel absolutely worthless. He was even more a psychotic madman, and trying to wear her down mentally and physically. But Anna was her father's daughter, stoic, complex and mentally strong, and not dependent on physical comforts. Never needing love and sustenance from people she didn't need or want in her personal orbit. He was wasting his effort in trying to get her pregnant, because he couldn't get his hands on Jayden.

Honestly, she prayed he wouldn't kill her in his effort of spawning another evil family member for their delectation, and perversions.

Internally she was shaking with fear, but he would never know. It was well past midnight, and she knew he would walk in any moment, because her guard had just left his post. Charles was meticulous that no one knew what he was doing to her, except of course the usual rough stuff of knocking her into silent submission. His men expected that of him, because he was a mean, sadistic bastard.

This was Anna's hell! She didn't believe her life was ever going to change. When was it all going to end? In her death? And, what had she ever done to deserve the hell she was going through right now?

"Leanne, please tell me where my sweet little nephew is, and then this tiresome meeting every night will stop. As much as I weary of fucking you, you black whore, I do have other much more pleasurable commitments in my diary. It seems that beautiful wholesome females yearn for my formidable penis to give them extreme pleasure. Beautiful, white, innocent females of course. Not black, filthy bitches like you, Leanne Zeema Connor. It's no wonder my beloved brother Edward had to beat you into submission to get you pregnant." He grinned like the psychotic madman that he was. "And, I am absolutely determined to make you pay for what you did to him. When I have finished with you, I will make sure you are sent to the worst prison imaginable to serve out the rest of your fucking black life being raped and sodomised by its inmates."

Anna was sitting on the side of the bed with her eyes closed waiting for the inevitable to happen, and as usual it did. He back-handed her so hard she fell onto the floor, but quickly got up because he would beat her until she did manage to scramble back onto the bed. Every night they went through the same painful procedure, as if he was winding himself up to be able to perform.

"Now take off those fucking disgusting garments and lay back with your legs wide open, ready for me." Over his hard breathing she heard him lower the zip of his immaculate trousers and grunt when he freed himself. As usual after hitting her he was ready for action. This was when her play acting came into the drama unfolding. To keep from being brutalised she had to pretend to have an orgasm, otherwise he wouldn't stop fucking her until she did. She had to pretend he had the best and biggest penis she had ever encountered, and enjoyed. But the opposite was true.

She closed her eyes, and clenched her teeth, and waited for the pain to start. He was rough and unfeeling, and first bit her nipples, as he thought that was foreplay. But her breasts were already sore and tender from her pregnancy, and she had to stop herself from crying out in agony. Then he thrust into her hard and fast, and her body was dry and fragile, again from her pregnancy. But of course no one but Gerry had known she was pregnant, and never would. That was their sacred secret.

"Open your eyes you black bitch, and know who is fucking you. And tell me that I am bigger and better than my stupid brother, who married you when his brain must have been addled with booze and drugs." He was screaming this with spittle covering his mouth, while he used her mercilessly, pounding into her with his full weight behind every painful lunge.

But, she didn't let him win, because in her mind and soul it was Gerry making love to her in his sweet, caring, beautifully gentle way. And she could only hear his words of love he whispered in her ear, as they came together in a wonderful completion.

So she told this sick madman what he wanted to hear. That he was bigger and so much better than his dead brother, as she pretended to come and enjoy his disgusting, and brutal rape. But if she ever got out of this hell of a prison she vowed to herself and God that she would avenge Gerry's death, and what she was going through every night to save her little boy's life.

Charles Connor would see the inside of a prison, and never see the light of another day again.

But first she had to survive, and hopefully not miscarry the baby she was carrying safe in her womb. But, with little food, freezing cold, and brutally used every night, it would be a miracle if this baby survived, with its mother.

CHAPTER SIXTEEN

It was three weeks since Gerry had sustained the beating that almost took his life. He had survived only because of the dedicated skill of Stefan Perez, and not because Gerry was the perfect patient at the small hospital. In fact he was the complete opposite, and Stefan was literally throwing him out before any of his exemplary staff walked out of their jobs, and left.

Gerry was a bad tempered, and thoroughly demanding patient, who wanted to go home and start searching for Anna. Nobody knew where she was, or if she was still alive. Gerry assumed she wasn't, because Charles Connor had taken her to God only knew where, and hurt her badly if his vile treatment of Bazil was the benchmark.

Daniel was being extremely careful in his enquiries, as he didn't want to ruffle the airwaves on who knew her whereabouts. He had friends in many police forces, and the FBI, and other agencies, but no one had heard a whisper so far. But Daniel knew the story had to leak before much longer, because only one person had to break their silence then he would hear something of interest.

But right now Daniel McCreedy had for his sins taken over Gerry's recovery, and he was merciless in his programme of getting Gerry back on his feet. He was the epitome of a Drill Sergeant, and Gerry hated his guts, and his punishing workouts. Daniel hadn't allowed Gerry to go back to his own apartment on the beach, but had taken him to his town house on Marina del Rey. His home was completely kitted out with a state of the art gym, and an exercise pool. Had an amazing view of the Marina with its upmarket restaurants and designer shops, which Gerry wasn't allowed to visit yet. He was still walking with crutches, because of his shattered but rebuilt knee, and a right hand that hadn't responded to treatment so far. Luckily he was left-handed so that wasn't too much of a problem. But eating and moving his damaged jaw was still painful, and his badly injured eye was on the mend, but he would now have to wear glasses, which seriously pissed him off.

To be truthful, in Gerry's mind his life was a living hell, because while he was in recovery he was still in a great deal of pain. Pain had never been on Gerry's agenda. So he was grumpy, difficult, and absolutely desperate to find out where Anna was, and if she was still alive. He missed her desperately, and couldn't believe she had become so important to him so quickly.

Charles Connor appeared to be worse than his older brother, which scared the life out of Gerry, and Daniel as well, but he never voiced his concern to his sick friend. He knew Gerry's recovery hinged on finding out what had happened to

171

Anna after she had been taken out of Gerry's office. Daniel hadn't told his friend that he was already making very quiet and slow enquiries, but to no avail. Nobody was leaking a whisper, because they were terrified of Charles Connor. The man was a manic psychopath, and was the head of a serious crime agency that allowed him the excuse to pull in people off the street, guilty or not, if he felt they needed interrogating violently. Hence the reason Anna was being held in a bare cell in the basement with no basic comfort.

Gerry was sprawled out on a comfortable recliner on Daniel's balcony overlooking the Marina. He was totalled after a punishing workout provided by his friend, and now enemy. Daniel had accomplished the same workout, but was not even out of breath, and was relaxing with a glass of rare bourbon, which Gerry was not allowed to sample yet. He was on too many painkillers, and strong antibiotics, so only soft drinks were allowed for at least another week. Gerry had vowed he was going to get so drunk in a week's time when Stefan Perez gave him the green light for alcohol.

Gerry decided he was going to get his own back on Daniel by asking him questions about his failed marriage, which Daniel never, ever referred to. "What was her name? Was it Beverley? Yeah, I think it was, wasn't it. What happened Daniel? One moment you were happy, and single. Then a year or two after you were a miserable son of a bitch,

172

and divorced. I am your best mate, and not one of us ever met her, or had even seen her, except in magazines, or on the local news media. What the fuck happened in those two years? You moved out of the apartments that I still live in, and moved into this luxurious town house, and still live here, and God knows how you can afford all this on a Lieutenant's salary." Gerry gestured at the view, and the ocean, and the pristine yachts bobbing up and down on the swell of the ocean. "And I know that you don't take back-handers, and are as straight and decent a cop that I have ever come across."

Daniel gave Gerry a loaded, filthy look. He never answered any questions about his marriage, or his ex-wife. It was a closed book on a time in his life that was a total embarrassment, and not up for discussion. Not even with Gerry, his best friend for twenty years.

But Gerry was not going to give up. Daniel was putting him through torture every day, so this was payback time. "Sorry Daniel, but I am not moving from this chair until you tell me the truth, and nothing but the truth, and it stops with me right here."

Daniel knew that his friend would not give up, so he took a deep breath, and set his mind nearly five years back, when he had been hopefully passing his exams to becoming a lieutenant. He was content and fairly happy with his life, but probably thinking about settling down with a wife and family, but ridiculously shy around women, so that was going to be a non-starter.

"Her – her name was Beverley Hart, and I met her when she had been burgled in this property. I offered to cover the complaint, as there wasn't anyone else available. Well! She was absolutely stunning. Tall for a woman, and slim as a read. Straight, brilliant, glittering blonde hair to her immaculate shoulders, and the biggest deep blue eyes imaginable, and as sexy as get-go. And Daniel McCreedy fell straight into lust. I can't believe I am saying this, but we ended up in bed that afternoon, and she was shit hot in the sheets. That was so against the police rules, enough to get me sent down immediately."

Gerry couldn't believe what he was hearing, because Daniel was a stickler for rules and regulations. For him to break any rule was so against his code. A code that had been drummed into him by his father, who himself was a top notch policeman, but was now retired as a captain.

Daniel gulped down a large portion of his drink to be able to carry on. "Two weeks later we travelled to Las Vegas and were married. I didn't tell anyone, just that I was going on holiday. I was just following my ecstatic dick, I had never had so much sex in my entire life. She was insatiable, not only never said no, but always instigated it at least five times a day. But, the warning signs were there, because she didn't

174

take my name, which upset me. Also, when we got back, I moved into her home, and I began to realise just how wealthy she was, and that I really didn't know her at all.

"Then she made it abundantly clear that she was using me to get pregnant and that was the reason for out of control sex. Believe me, it sounds great, but I began to feel like a piece of meat, a stud performing to produce a child. It got even worse, because she did become pregnant, but continually miscarried. Then we had floods of tears, recriminations, and it was evidently all my fault, as my DNA must be faulty, because she'd had tests previously to make sure she was healthy to carry a baby."

Daniel stopped for a moment to rub his eyes with the heels of his hands, obviously it still upset him that he had been mentally abused by a beautiful, cunning woman, and he had fallen for it all, hook line and sinker. Not a great feeling to cherish. In his view the whole sorry incident was best forgotten.

"The marriage was finished within six months, but we limped on for two years. By then I honestly couldn't get it up, and perform anymore. I was a shell of a man, I was pitiful, and I felt ashamed, beaten up, and feeling desperately sorry for myself. I came home one evening and she had left a note saying she had gone with her physio, and was pregnant by him. Was I relieved? You bet! And just felt sorry for her

175

physio, who was a really good guy, just not strong enough to stand up to Beverley Hart."

Gerry had to ask the obvious, because Daniel had fallen on his feet, and was set up for life, but at what cost? After listening to his friend he realised *he* couldn't have kept the marriage going for two painful years. Whatever Daniel had come out with, it hadn't been worth the pain, and misery, and mental instability.

"When I went to the divorce lawyer, which Bev paid for, I was totally unprepared for what she wanted me to have. And no amount of arguing would change her mind." He blew out a long breath of release, he needed to keep his composure, because he could still feel upset at a marriage that should never have happened. It had turned him off that sacred union for good. He had always wanted a couple of kids, and a comfortable marriage, like his parents had. But that was never going to happen now, so his work was the major factor in his life.

"I got this town house worth a tidy fortune. A very nice yacht in the Marina, which I love. A very expensive Porche, which I cherish. And to top all that, a million dollars put immediately into my personal bank account, which gives me the opportunity to live my life as I see fit. But, I love my work, and decided to stay in the police force, and strive to climb the ladder of achievement and honour."

"For fuck's sake Daniel, who was this Beverley Hart, that she could give you all that for two years of marriage?" And Gerry couldn't help adding, although he was only joking, "And has she got a beautiful, wealthy sister?"

"Fuck you, Gerry. She was a total nightmare for me." Daniel felt as if he would never get over what she had done to him in that two years. She had emasculated him. Used him like a piece of prime rib, and thrown him away when she had used him up, like a piece of trash.

"She was at the top of her game, as a millionaire realtor of absolute prime properties in New York. She had the world at her feet, but could not have the baby she craved for, and I'm pretty sure she never will. She told me that she was pregnant when she left, but I found out that she miscarried again, so that was not down to me – thank God."

Daniel had had enough of recounting his sorrowful past, and decided to change the subject. A subject that Gerry would want to talk about, and churn over. "I promise you that if you behave and do everything I say to help you with your rehabilitation, I will do everything in my power and knowledge to find Anna. I am certain she is still alive, because this Charles Connor will want her to suffer unspeakable torment and pain in prison. Something that I will not allow to happen. Believe me, my friend, we will find her with help from our friends in the FBI." He went over to his best friend and clasped his shoulder, but very carefully because of Gerry's painful injuries. "I promise you faithfully that we will find her, and get her to a safe environment that we can trust."

Gerry sniffed loudly, and wiped his eyes with his fingers. He trusted Daniel, and knew he would do his best for Anna, and that was all that Gerry could ask of anyone. "I am so desperately worried for her, especially as she is pregnant with Edward's child. That family will do everything to get their evil bloody hands on Anna's children." He sniffed again, and wiped his nose on a napkin. "I love her *so* much. She is a beautiful woman inside and out, and I can't believe she has left me. Anna doesn't deserve any of this. So far her life has been total crap, and I want to look out for her, and give her a much better life in the future. And I have to believe we have a future together." He gave Daniel a watery smile, which had never happened before in twenty years.

"You have my sacred word that we will find her, and get her away from that bastard who has taken her liberty away" Daniel promised.

"And I will work with you to get back to health as quickly as possible, so we can work together. No more moans, or arguing, or trying to get out of your awful regime, and totalian workouts. You can boss me around to your heart's content, and I won't say one word, or swear vile words at you. I will be the perfect patient."

Daniel looked askance at Gerry in total disbelief, because that was never going to happen, and both of them knew it. Gerry was lazy, laid back, and hated being told what to do by anyone, and especially Daniel, his best mate.

They both clinked their glasses in total agreement. One with orange juice, the other with Bourbon. "Can I have just a small wee Bourbon?" Gerry begged, as orange juice didn't help his desperate mood. "Shut up! Absolutely not!" Daniel answered. He knew that Gerry was never going to settle down to a strict healthy routine. But if he didn't, Daniel would get him back to hospital in a heartbeat, and wouldn't waver on that. Gerry's complete recovery was in Daniel's hands now, and he was not going to let him down.

Gerry back on his feet. Anna's recovery and back in Gerry's life, only then would Daniel relax and get back to the job he loved. Christ, he wasn't asking too much was he?

Or was he?

CHAPTER SEVENTEEN

Anna woke up before dawn, she only knew it was dawn because it was just turning light through the tiny window in her awful prison. Her guard was still snoring loudly because of the amount of liquor he had consumed when Charles had finished with her. It had been the worst night so far, he had raped her three times, because she had been too tired, and too traumatised to be able to fake an orgasm. He beat her between every rape, because she was apathetic, and would not praise him for his prowess, and having a penis bigger and more powerful than his brother. She had learnt not to put up a fight, because that was what he wanted, and became more violent, which he enjoyed far too much, and would rape her again, and again.

Immediately she realised that something was terribly wrong as her loose trousers were wet and sticky. Also she had an ache in her belly, which wasn't so unusual when her rapist was so rough with her every night. She reached out for the roll of toilet paper that was by her rickety iron bed, and stuffed a couple of small sheets inside her to try and stop the bleed from getting any worse.

At that moment her mind went down two pathways. Was she pleased to be losing Edward's baby? Or? Was she upset to be losing her beloved child, who would never breathe or cry on the outside of her womb in the real world?

She lay very, very still, and let her mind wander to her darling Gerry, and the wonderful time they had spent for just a few days in San Francisco. They had been so in love, and so compatible, and now he was dead and cold somewhere, and she would never be able to feel his warmth and vitality, and love ever again.

If she lost this baby she wouldn't have any reason to go on living, and that really scared the hell out of her. Even though her life had been truly awful since meeting and marrying Edward, and the death of her parents and brothers, Anna still had a spark in her to keep trying for a better life. If not for herself but for her children and their future.

She placed both hands on her still flat belly, trying to remember clearly the two miscarriages she'd had with Edward's babies. They had been excruciatingly painful, and she had cried through both procedures. This leak wasn't anything in comparison, and she began to think that it was just a show of blood that she had read about previously in a magazine.

Very carefully she levered herself out of bed, being extra careful not to wake her obnoxious, hateful guard. He always watched her avidly while she washed herself and used the disgusting toilet. She never took all her dirty garments off, so that he wouldn't see anything of interest in her ablutions.

In the past few days she had been given a bar of carbolic soap, a disgustingly thin towel, and a toilet roll. Three things of luxury after having nothing to help her to keep clean. Also another pair of thin cotton scrubs, so at least she could wash one pair and wear the other. But no underwear, or socks to keep her warm. Anna was constantly, and seriously cold, and beyond hungry. She ate every meagre morsel of food they gave her, because her baby needed nourishment. She didn't care about herself, because the love of her life was dead, and her heart had died with him.

There wasn't a mirror in her prison, but she didn't need to see that she had become rail thin, and her luscious hair a mass of knots and tangles. Gerry would not have given her a second glance if he had met her now. He had been gorgeous, and to die for in every way. Anna still could not believe all that charisma, love, and high energy personality was gone. They had loved, laughed, argued, been inseparable for such a short time. But that time had been gold dust in a desert of loneliness and pain that Anna had suffered at the hands of Edward Connor. And now his sick, perverted brother had got hold of her, and she couldn't see how she could end this, without her own death.

She went back to bed as she was doing every day now, because she didn't have the will or energy to do anything else. She was mortally cold, and began to plead with God for an escape from this purgatory she was enduring. Immediately a plan came into her head, she could use this slight blood loss as an excuse to stop Charles from raping her. He was the type of man who would not have intimate relations with a woman having a period. That would be too much for his finer sensibilities. She would be unclean and untouchable.

Yes, he would force a woman to have sex against her will, but a common malady like a show of blood would faze him, and disgust him.

"You are a filthy black whore. I need to teach you a severe lesson tonight, because I will not get my just reward for the death of my beloved brother."

Those were the usual disgusting triab of vile words screamed at Anna, who would not cower or beg for mercy, especially from this psycho maniac.

But deep inside she was desperately scared. Charles was capable of just about anything that was evil, excruciatingly painful, or even bad enough to cause death. But truthfully she was past even hoping for a tiny glimmer of reprieve from him. Death really was her only option now, and she prayed that God and Gerry were listening to her.

"Gary, go and get that equipment we use for difficult and dangerous prisoners." Charles nodded his head at the youngest guard, who looked with open sympathy at their prisoner. When Charles turned away Gary closed his eyes and shook his young head in sympathy.

Anna knew that if she was going to get help from anyone in this God forsaken hell-hole it would come from Gary. He always averted his eyes when she had to use the toilet, and when she washed every morning. She knew she was being watched on video every moment of every day, but Gary seemed to know when there was a gap in the surveillance, and very carefully gave her a coffee from his thermos, and a spare biscuit if he had one. Charles would have hit the roof if he found out, and Gary would be long gone, in every way. So Anna kept her mouth shut, mainly because that coffee and biscuit were akin to a five course meal when you were starving.

She truly tried to stay calm and composed, but it was impossible. Her insides were shaking, and her legs felt like jelly. Edward had been a walking nightmare, and depraved beyond repair, but his brother was in another league.

He was the devil incarnate. Psychotic, despotic, sadistic, and the worst was that he did not have one modicum of conscience. He was a wasteland of common decency, and Anna now feared for her life, and the life of her unborn baby.

She couldn't envisage what kind of torture she was going to be put through. But knew she would have to endure or die in the process, because Charles was completely mad, and beyond normal reasoning.

CHAPTER EIGHTEEN

"Wake up Gerry! Wake up you lazy son of a bitch." Daniel was trying to wake up his friend who should have been up at least an hour ago, but was still fast asleep. Daniel had already been on a 5K run on the beach, his usual start to the day.

Gerry stirred, grumbled, and went back to sleep. These days lying in bed against Daniel's fitness routine was absolutely the winner. "OK! You're not interested that we've had a breakthrough in Anna's whereabouts."

Daniel stripped off and made his way to his own shower in the next bedroom. Grinning, he waited for the explosion from Gerry's bedroom. It came roughly thirty seconds later.

"You fuckin' bastard! Why didn't you make sure I was awake properly before disappearing?" Daniel continued soaping and rinsing before he answered, knowing it would bring Gerry to a boiling point of desperation, and anger. He loved to wind him up.

He came out of the glass cubicle and began to dry himself with a large, soft bathroom towel. "Had a very interesting conversation from an Agent in Connor's Serious Crime Agency. He had heard my name mentioned regards the mysterious disappearance of Anna Weist, and hacked into the L.A. police computer, and managed to find my cell phone number. He rang me via a pay phone in a small town outside Atlanta's perimeter. This young man is terrified that his boss, Charles Connor, will find out what he has done. I had to give my word he would not be mentioned when the shit hits the fan." He looked straight at Gerry. "Right now this is between you and me, and I need your word as well. This guy believes he is a dead man walking if Connor finds out." He could see that Gerry was as white as a sheet, and his eyes were suspiciously wet, and he hadn't moved from the doorway as if he was struggling to cope with his overwhelming emotions. Daniel realised that Gerry had resigned himself that Anna was dead. This information, if true, was hard for his friend to take on board.

"Honestly, I believe this guy, because he gave me so much info, and detail. She *is* alive Gerry. But, let's not get too excited because she is in a very bad way, that is why he decided to get in touch with me."

Tears unashamedly ran down Gerry's face, something Daniel had never seen before. "Where is she? We have to get to her. I will kill that fuckin' piece of crap if he has hurt her real bad." Gerry wiped his eyes with the heels of his hands, still not quite believing he might see his Anna again, hold her, spoil her rotten, and love her for the rest of his life.

"You have to calm down, buddy. Anna *is* in a really bad way. This Charles Connor evidently has treated her really badly, and we have to be careful how we try to get her away from him." Daniel got dressed in a pure white T-shirt and immaculate jeans, trying to take time before he had to explain to his best friend that he wasn't going anywhere when Daniel and the FBI broke into Connor's Agency.

But, Gerry needed the complete facts on Anna's condition. However upsetting it was going to be, he had to know, because he had to make a decision on getting in touch with Marcus regards Connor's future.

"I'm not giving you anymore info until you shower and get your head together. I will get breakfast going, and a pot of coffee. Then we will sit down and discuss exactly what we are going to do safely to get to Anna, and make sure we keep her safe. If this Connor thinks we are on to him, he will swiftly move Anna to a secret location, and we could lose her for good."

Gerry just nodded his acquiescence, and like a robot went straight to the bathroom. There was no way he was going to hinder Anna's recovery. He knew what that psycho bastard was capable of, and in his head he was already plotting his downfall, a very painful and deadly downfall. Nobody, but nobody hurt a woman that he loved. Charles Connor would know and feel the worst scenario of his worst nightmare, and never recover from it. And that mantra kept Gerry sane at this truly awful time in his life.

Daniel put a loaded breakfast in front of Gerry, ham, eggs, tomatoes, and mushrooms. Also orange juice, and a strong black coffee. He had already loaded dishes in the washer, and the kitchen was immaculate. He was immaculate, and his home was immaculate. And all that put Gerry's teeth on edge. His friend was one fuckin' immaculate, ridiculous great guy. And Gerry couldn't fault that, but it drove him fuckin' crazy, because he was the exact opposite, and somehow beyond reasoning how their close friendship worked. Talk about opposites.

"Sorry Daniel, but I can't eat anything. I need to know everything about Anna's whereabouts, and what we are going to do about it. Like, right now."

"Gerry! Eat! We are not discussing anything until we eat. I am starving, and you need to get back to full health so that you can help Anna on her road to recovery." Daniel began to tuck into his plate of food. This time of day he was always hungry, as often in his job he didn't get the time for a leisurely meal.

He watched Gerry try to eat as quickly as possible, and actually felt sorry for him. If he was in his shoes he would be worried sick about the woman he loved. Even though he had never fallen in love yet, but there was always hope for the future. He wanted a solid marriage, and kids. A family he could come home to every night, keep them safe and comfortable within his very capable arms, and work hard so they never had to worry about money. Was that too much to ask? Daniel didn't think so! His parents had a rock solid marriage, and still loved each other, and his sister Louise was married with two great kids. Daniel loved his close family, and would do anything for them, as he would Gerry. Gerry didn't have any immediate family. That was why he had taken leave of absence from the job he loved, but knew he had to get back to work sooner rather than later. He just needed to make sure that Anna was out of the clutches of Charles Connor, and in hospital under surveillance. She had after all murdered her husband, and would have to stand trial, and take the consequences of her actions.

"I'm sorry Gerry, but you are not going anywhere. You would be an accident waiting to happen." Daniel put up his hand at Gerry's blistering answer, he was not going to be swayed from his official directive. "It's all been planned with the FBI. They have been trying to bring down all the Connors for years, but have never been able to get water-tight evidence. If Anna is being held prisoner in secret, and he has misused his power by abusing her in any way, this is concrete evidence. I am going in with two of my FBI contacts, who I can trust implicitly, and the detectives from my department, again, who I can trust without question. We cannot go in heavy handed, and it has to be at night when the Serious Crime Agency is quiet and almost empty." Daniel could see that Gerry was going to put up an argument, but wasn't having any of his crap, not this time. Gerry could talk his way out of any problem, and usually win the argument. But not this time, because Anna's life hung by a thread, and Daniel was not going to lose her under any circumstances. Charles Connor appeared to be a psychotic maniac, and they would have to tread very carefully if they were to get Anna out of her prison still alive.

"I have to go with you Daniel. I can't possibly stay behind and wait. I will be frantic with worry, and need to be there to make sure she is OK. If he has harmed her in any way, he is dead. I will make sure of that, and have the situation already in hand should the need arise." He didn't mention Marcus in that situation, because Daniel would not allow it to happen. He was a straight and dedicated copper, who wouldn't dream of using justice against anyone, however bad they were. For him a life sentence in prison was the only outcome, but Gerry begged to differ, sometimes a very prolonged and painful death was the only answer for pure unadulterated evil, and that was Edward and Charles Connor.

"Sorry my friend, but it ain't going to happen. I will lock you in the basement with no way out if you fight me on this. You are still not up to speed. Not fast enough, and not thinking straight. My team are going to have to be totally on the ball, fast on their feet, and totally without any agenda. Three things you aren't capable of. I need your word that you will leave it to me to expedite Anna's safety and release." He saw Gerry hesitate, and needed his friend's word, which he knew he *would* keep if given.

Gerry nodded, and gave his word. He knew that Daniel would give his all to get Anna out of that diabolical situation. It wasn't easy for him, but he realised he didn't have a choice. He just wanted Anna back, but dreaded what she had gone through at that maniac's hands. He cursed that bastard for leaving him so weak and sick, so he couldn't be there for his woman, who needed him so badly.

Gerry watched Daniel with envy as he eased into his shoulder holster and gun, slid his police badge onto his belt, and clipped his handcuffs onto the back of his belt. He had changed into his usual light weight dark Italian suit, and cotton dress shirt, the attire for work. Daniel was always absolutely neat and tidy when at work, and every time he left his home.

"I will keep you in the picture as much as I can. I will use my burner phone so nobody, however clever, can listen in." He gave Gerry a careful man hug, because he was desperately sorry for the poor besotted sod. If he was in his shoes he would be desperate to be there for the woman he loved.

He was deeply worried about what they were going to find in that basement, Anna could already be dead, or so badly hurt and abused she might never recover.

He was going to meet the other four men who were going to have an extremely dangerous and difficult time that night. They were flying out of a small private airfield in an FBI plane to Atlanta, hopefully to bring out Anna Weist alive, and to bring Charles Connor to justice. Also to close down the nefarious world of the old-money Connor family, and their disgusting evil fingers in the justice system, police force, and political world. Many in high office would hopefully tumble tonight if everything went to plan.

Daniel was going to make sure it did. He was sick to his stomach of people in high places taking backhanders to look the other way when miscreants weren't held to account for their lack of human good behaviour, and down-right illegal money-making schemes. But was he holding his breath? Absolutely not, because it was the way the world had become, and he was a man out of his time, honest, trustworthy, and caring.

This was why Gerry Swane and Daniel were such good buddies, because they were two of a kind, and had absolutely no thought or design about changing.

The world needed to change! But they both knew that was never going to happen – not in their lifetime!

Selfish, self-centred politicians had taken over good sense, good manners, truth and honesty. Men like Daniel and Gerry were just a few who battled daily trying to rebalance the status quo. But they feared they were slowly losing the battle against the many who constantly balked the legal system, and were making money hand over fist. Illegal millionaires.

CHAPTER NINETEEN

Silently, the five men entered the back entrance of the building, and were extremely thankful that there didn't seem to be any obvious security. There must be CCTV, but no one appeared to stop them from entering.

They were using hand signals that had been organised on their journey earlier. Agent Clancy was in charge of the night's proceedings. He had told the detectives, Lewis and Carter, to go through the building with their fire power on show, and to lock all the staff in a secure room. And, to make sure every piece of technology and their cell phones were locked down separately. It was imperative that the person in charge could not be warned ahead of them.

Daniel and the two FBI agents had their own weapons drawn ready for any eventuality, as they made their way down to the basement where their informer had explained Anna was being held. But were pleasantly surprised that there was only a skeleton staff working at the end of the day.

Everyone working in the Agency must feel safe and comfortable in their environment. They either didn't know what their boss was up to, or just didn't care, or were complicit in what he was up to on a daily basis.

Taking back handers – blackmail – torture – racial hatred – rape, and even murder. If it was illegal, and created wealth and power, then Charles Connor had been working it for years. How had he got away with it? His wealthy family had judges, police, and the FBI in their filthy pockets. That diabolical state of affairs had been going on through previous generations of the Connor dynasty.

No one had been strong enough, or fearless enough to try and change the status quo in Atlanta. If they had been, they were pulled in line with a pay-off, or generally disappeared permanently.

Agent Clancy stopped at the top of the stairs leading down to a locked door, which looked as though it was the only entrance to the basement. He whispered to Daniel, "It's fuckin' freezing down here, I sincerely hope Anna hasn't been kept here for a month. If she has, I think we have a diabolical situation on our hands."

Daniel shook his head in despair, he had been thinking exactly the same awful thought, and thanked God that Gerry wasn't there, because he would have become very dangerous to the outcome. Clear heads and steady hands were always essential in this type of search and rescue situation. Gerry would have been a time-bomb waiting to explode, and would kill anyone involved in Anna's capture and imprisonment.

Clancy, Stead, and Daniel had already taken into custody two cigar smoking heavies who were playing cards in front of the locked door. When they had looked down the barrel of three lethal looking firearms they immediately put their hands above their heads, and were relieved of their weaponry and phones. Now they were locked securely in an empty storage room with hands and feet in handcuffs and chains, going nowhere except a secure prison facility.

Agent Stead opened the door a fraction almost silently, and the three men were surprised when they were able to enter the room without anyone attempting to stop them. But, stopped in their tracks to cover their mouth and nose because of the Godawful stench. It smelt as if someone had died in there a week ago.

There was a large cage in the middle of the room, and as far as they could tell, a lifeless body laying amongst filthy bedding in just as filthy garments.

Daniel's heart almost stopped beating. This skeletal figure could not be Anna Weist. Please God, he prayed, let it be some other poor bastard, abused victim. He didn't even dare to move closer to check out who it was, because his gut was telling him it was Anna.

A young guy came out of the shadows with his hands above his head, and then laid his fire-arm on a small table in front of him. "I'm Gary, the guy who phoned Lieutenant

197

McCreedy. I am so relieved you are here, but I am sorry to say I think you are too late. She hasn't moved at all since this morning."

Agent Clancy barked out in reply, "Don't move, and keep your hands where we can see them. We need to know who is in that cage, and who put them there." He turned to Agent Stead, "John, you are a paramedic, check on that poor soul to find out if we are too late."

Immediately he moved to check the inert body, and he gave a deep sigh of relief. "Still with us Boss, but not looking good. It's a woman, very emaciated, extremely cold, and she has been bleeding from the vagina. Boss, we need to get her to a hospital facility ASAP." John shook his head in despair, he had never seen anyone this badly abused, or misused. The female was truly a pitiful sight.

Dreading what he was going to find, Daniel went to stand next to Agent Stead, and just about held down his last meal. Kneeling down next to the ridiculously rickety bed, he took her hand, and said softly, "Sweetheart, are you Anna Weist? Just move your hand if that is all you can manage. We are here to take you to safety, and put you into a hospital, and I will stay with you to keep you safe." Daniel couldn't believe that the vile monsters who had done this to Anna, if it was her, had actually shaved her head completely, as if she was a prisoner in the Second World War.

Agent Clancy shouted at the young guy who had been guarding his prisoner to find some warm blankets, and a hot drink for the woman in the cage. He had seen some sights in his long career, but nothing ever as bad as this God forsaken basement, and the lethal looking cage. It wasn't human, and someone was going to pay big time for this atrocity.

Anna drew on her waning strength and really tried to concentrate on what the man was saying to her. She just about managed to move her hand in his big warm one, and then opened her beautiful eyes to look straight at him and whisper brokenly, "My name is – is Anna Weist. Th - thank you for rescuing me, I thought I had died, but you are here at last. Thank you!"

Daniel wanted to cry with an overload of emotion at finding Anna at last, but she was in such a bad way, he wasn't sure that they had come too late.

"Gerry has been frantic to find you, nearly driven me to despair. We are all so relieved that you have survived, and we can now get you to a medical facility."

But Anna's last ounce of energy was depleted, as she closed her eyes again, she somehow managed to give a tiny smile. "Gerry is alive? They told me he was dead."

"Boss, we are going to lose her. Where is that fuckin' Elite Team of rescue and secure? They have a senior medic

199

and all the equipment on board. And, blankets, we need to get her warm, and she is still bleeding from the inside. We need to stop the bleed, now."

Daniel didn't let go of her cold, lifeless hand. "Come on Anna, stay with us. You are so close to getting the help you need." He turned to John to explain. "She is pregnant, but it looks like she is losing the baby. Someone please explain to me what kind of psychotic maniac treats a beautiful woman like this, and shaves her head." He wiped his eyes and face with a shaking hand, not quite believing this could happen in this day and this country.

Agent Clancy pushed past Daniel and covered Anna with a couple of warm blankets. He was talking into his scrambled A-class phone, and nodding his head. "Elite Team are here, just entering the building. They have been on red alert, and waiting on our information. I'm sorry McCreedy, I know you and Gerry Swane are close friends. The Team will do their very best to stabilise her. I need you to take a statement from that guy. It's urgent he tells us where this Charles Connor is, because we don't want to let him get away. Do we Lieutenant?"

Daniel had one eye on what was going on in that cage once the Elite Team powered into the basement, and took over from the two Agents. They were lethal looking power-houses of seriously armed uniformed combat figures.

He couldn't imagine anyone getting the better of that group of men. Scary wasn't a word to use about them, they were terrifying, even to Daniel, who always upheld the law, and never strayed across the legal line of demarcation.

Daniel couldn't stop young Gary from talking once he started. The only reason he worked for Connor was because he had threatened to annihilate his young wife and baby. They had been in diabolical debt, and Connor had paid it off, and by then Gary was committed. But in the last few weeks he had moved his family to Puerto Rico, where his wife had been raised, and he had made sure Connor hadn't found out. Gary was cutting his losses and going to make his way to Puerto Rico to be with his family. But had stayed to try and help Anna, because he had come to realise that his Boss was out to kill their prisoner slowly and painfully, and Gary couldn't allow that to happen. Hence the phone call to Daniel, which could have got him killed if the other guards had found out what he had done.

"We were never allowed to be here when Connor came in late at night, and he turned off all the cameras. I am pretty certain he brutalised her, and raped her every night. She was always in a bad way when he left, but we were never allowed to touch her, or help her." He looked over at Anna where two men were working on her frantically trying to stabilise her, and both FBI agents were talking worriedly on their phones, obviously getting information on what to do next.

Daniel could see that Gary was getting really upset about what had happened to Anna, and that he should have sought help earlier. They were all upset about Anna, even the seasoned Elite Team, who had worked in war torn countries. This had happened in America, under the watch of a Serious Crime Unit. Many people working here were going to have their lives torn apart by this horrendous event by going to prison for a very long time.

"Do you know where your boss is now? Because it is paramount we secure him ASAP. He is evidently a serious threat to everyone's life, and needs to be found." Daniel asked Gary, who was getting more and more upset, especially with the combat officers' appearance. He wanted them to know he wasn't there by choice, and had never hurt anyone.

"He came here earlier than usual, which was unusual, and didn't ask me to leave, again unusual. But as soon as he saw that Anna was bleeding he started to scream a blue streak at her. Saying she was a disgusting black bitch whore. And, how dare she have a period when she should be servicing him. What worried me was that she didn't respond, even when he kept slapping her around the face, really hard." Gary had tears in his eyes when he spoke again. "I'm *so* sorry

Lieutenant, but you cannot win against that sick bastard, he probably would have shot me if I had tried to intervene. I would have left after he had gone, but I was so worried about poor Anna, and had decided to try and help her, even though I would have been in a great deal of trouble myself."

"It's OK Gary. You have been truly helpful to us beyond anything we had expected." He gave him his notepad with Gary's statement written down. "Now check this carefully, sign it, and full name underneath to verify the signature." While Gary was carefully reading the statement, Daniel went over to confer with Agent Clancy about what was going down now. They spoke seriously for a few moments, and Daniel nodded and went back to the extremely worried Gary.

"Four of the Combat Team are going to the Connor family home to search and secure the household and property. Two are staying here to do exactly the same to this property, and open and empty the safe of its contents, and hopefully give us pertinent answers to what has been going on here. The two working on Anna are coming with our team of two detectives, two FBI, and myself back onto the aircraft we came to Atlanta on. And of course with Anna, who we cannot leave anywhere near this area. She is going to be put into a safe hospital environment with the two Elite Team guarding her, in a secret location in Los Angeles."

Gary had to butt in on Daniel's explanation of everyone's job and location, but the one person who was in serious danger, himself. "I can't stay here Lieutenant, I will go missing by tomorrow. You haven't a clue who they have working for them, and you never will. I am desperate to see my family again, and they need my income to be able to survive in Puerto Rico." He would go down on his knees and beg if he had to. Those military trained warriors didn't have a clue what they were up against. A group of millionaires who literally ran the state they presided in, and anyone who broke ranks, or went against them, disappeared overnight.

Daniel picked up Gary's weapon and put it in the waistband of his neat trousers. He never took chances, however cooperative another person he didn't know was. "We're not leaving you here, it's not a problem. You are going to a very secure safe house in our area. I'm afraid you cannot go back home, not even to pick up any personal items, it is far too dangerous. We can provide you with all the necessities you need, via our government expenditure. When this is all over and Charles Connor is in a secure prison facility, I will make sure you get to your family in Puerto Rico. You OK with all this? Because it isn't an option, this is a need to know operation, which means you won't know what is going on unless I tell you."

Gary completely understood and was just pleased to get away from this diabolical situation with his life spared, and in one piece. "I have everything I need in the boot of my old Jalopy at the back of the staff car park. As I didn't expect to ever go back to my home again."

Daniel nodded and shook Gary's hand. He was pleased that at least one person was coming out of this complex, dire situation intact. "One of my detectives will have to accompany you, and be as quick as you can."

He looked over at Anna and the paramedic, and could see he was packing up ready to move his patient, very carefully and very slowly. Daniel spoke into his phone, and immediately Detective Lewis came running through the open door, ready for action, with his partner hot on his heels.

"Lewis and Carter, we are packing up and leaving with Anna and two of the Elite Team, and I need you to go with this gentleman to his car and pick up his personal gear. Make sure you have your weapons ready for any intervention from an unknown source. I am pretty sure we are not out of the woods yet, so be extra alert. Two of the Elite Team are staying on the premises to tidy up and secure, and the other four have gone to the property belonging to the Connor family to search and secure, and to make numerous house arrests.

"Until we are all on the plane headed back to L.A., be careful. Be alert. We do not know who the exact enemy is

205

here, so keep your thoughts to yourself, and work quickly. Agents Clancy and Stead and myself will meet you in the car park at the vehicle we came in." Daniel looked across to Agent Clancy, who just nodded his greying head in agreement. Clancy wouldn't relax until they were all in the plane heading for home.

When they got there it was going to be a long, tiring night, making sure that Anna Weist was comfortable in a safe hospital environment. And Gary was placed in the FBI safe house, and no one was the wiser as to who or what he was. But he was not going to write up the facts of what or where they had been, until he knew who needed to read his statement and Gary's. Tomorrow was another day and soon enough. He needed to find out if the FBI Elite Team had accomplished their search, rescue, and secure situation. They always came up trumps, so he wasn't going to waste sleep on that outcome.

So when everything was nailed down and David Clancy managed to get home at last, he was going to have a hot bath, a very large scotch, and fuck his very patient, gorgeous, loving wife. In that very satisfying order!

Life was very good to Agent Clancy!

CHAPTER TWENTY

Daniel edged his large vehicle into his underground garage, turned off the engine, but didn't get out. Putting his arms on the steering wheel, he rested his pounding head on his arms. He was despondent, sick to his stomach, and beyond exhaustion. Did he still want to be associated with the police force anymore? That was up for serious debate. In all his time on the police force, he had never seen such depravity, cruelty, and mental sickness. The clothes he was wearing would all have to be permanently binned, because he would never get the stink of what he had seen and touched over the past twenty four hours out of his clothes, or out of his head.

Now he had to face Gerry, who, without a doubt, would be waiting for him to find out where Anna was. But, how much of what she had been put through could he tell him? If it had happened to someone Daniel loved, he would have gone ballistic, and Gerry was reasonably unstable right now. But, was it fair on his friend to try and sugar-coat what had happened? Surely he should know what the psychotic maniac was capable of.

But, mentally and physically Daniel was incapable of keeping his emotions strictly under control. He needed at least twenty-four hours of uninterrupted sleep, because he couldn't remember when he had last had a proper night's rest.

Gerry wasn't sleeping well, and kept Daniel up to all the hours given talking about Anna, and how they were going to find her.

Well! They had found her, and Daniel wished it hadn't been him that was given the honour. It had been a total nightmare of huge proportion. How the five of them had kept their last meal in their stomachs when they had opened the door of that basement was beyond Daniel's comprehension.

And, Gerry was not the hard-ass that he let people believe that he was. He always gave out a false perception of himself. Yes, he was laid back, but never lazy or boring. Often he had risked his life doing favours for the FBI, and the LAPD, and other Agencies. Many professional people owed him a lot of favours, and Daniel now feared he was about to call in those favours. His speciality was deep undercover, and had never blown his cover. That was why he had survived up until now.

Daniel was seriously worried what Gerry would do when he digested what Anna had gone through. He had always been a singular male, never loving another human being, and then Anna Weist had walked slowly into his life. And Gerry had fallen deeply in love, had fought it for five years, but now would give his life for her, which he almost had done.

Daniel could only wish that he had a love as strong as that. He adored his parents, sister, and her brood, but a loving partner seemed always out of his reach. Perhaps in the future it could happen, but he wasn't holding his breath.

Slowly, with utter fatigue, he got out of his vehicle, and began to make his way up the stairs to confront his friend. He knew he had to tell him the truth, it was the only thing he could do, because if he found out from someone else, Gerry would never forgive him. And Daniel treasured his friendship with Gerry beyond any other.

"How is she? Is she OK? Where is she? When can I see her? Please Daniel, I am going outta my mind here, and I am desperate for answers."

Daniel had purposely walked past his angry and highly agitated friend, and poured himself a very large fine Jack Daniels without saying a word. Only when he had emptied his glass in one hit, had he answered Gerry. "I am going to have the hottest shower I can stand, and am binning these clothes I am wearing, then I will answer all your questions. Then, I am going to sleep for at least twenty four hours straight. Then, I am going to my office to write up my statement with Detectives Lewis and Carter. Then, I am going to make my decision to stay in my fuckin' job, or not, because I do not know who I can trust anymore. I am a fuckin' law enforcement officer, and lately I am stymied every time I need to make a watertight case, or an arrest against someone." He blew out a deep exhausted breath, and walked out of the lounge and upstairs towards his bedroom trying to stay calm against all the odds.

Daniel came back into the intimate lounge dressed in boxers and a T-shirt ready for the long rest he craved. Gerry was pacing the balcony extremely agitated, but he knew if he pushed Daniel too far, he would clam up completely. His friend was always stoic, and patient, but when he did lose it, his temper was volatile to say the least. "I am warning you now Gerry, the last couple of days have been truly horrendous. I could sugar-coat what happened, but I can't do that to you, buddy. Anna is going to need your love, your understanding, and compassion, and utter patience. I cannot emphasise the importance of those four emotions. She has gone through the worst hell imaginable, and is desperately ill, and is going to take a very long time to recover from what has happened. Is this something you can cope with? If you can't accept what I am going to tell you, I will completely understand." He poured himself another strong drink, trying to give himself the courage to carry on. "In truth Gerry, I never in my entire life ever want to go through another day like yesterday. It was not what I signed up for, and neither did my detectives, the poor bastards. They had to go home to their wives and kids, and honestly I don't know how they did it."

There was a set of wrought iron table and chairs on the veranda, and both men sat opposite each other. Daniel sitting upright, as he was *so* tired he didn't think he could last much longer, and Gerry slumped in his chair, worried that he was going to be able to cope with what his friend was going to tell him.

Daniel didn't hold back a solitary moment of what had happened from entering through the back entrance of the building, and loading Anna onto the plane. Halfway through Gerry had his arms braced on his thighs and his head in his hands. By the time Daniel stopped his diabolical monologue, Gerry's shoulders were shaking, it was obvious he was actually sobbing quietly. The man was evidently in horrendous pain.

Daniel didn't move, didn't make a sound, didn't try to mollify his distraught friend. He realised that Gerry had to get it all out of his system, just as he had when they got off the plane.

Gerry sniffed loudly and wiped his eyes with the heels of his hands, and then spoke quietly but with extreme anger and disgust. "That piece of shit is a dead man. He is mentally deranged, and no one, and I mean no one, is going to treat my Anna, my beautiful Anna, who wouldn't hurt anyone, not

211

even with disrespect, as if she was worse than nothing, a piece of dog shit to be used like garbage." He put up his hand when Daniel tried to argue with him, because he was past allowing the law to put Charles Connor behind bars for the rest of his fucking goddamn life. It wasn't painful enough, or permanent enough.

"When I finish with him he will plead to die and to die quickly. He will see the fires of hell for all his sins, and I will laugh at his demise and funeral."

"Please Gerry! Let the law take its course. I can truly understand how you feel, but he isn't worth doing time for, no one is. And, we can't forget that Anna murdered her husband. She will have to be held accountable for that when she recovers, and is well enough to stand trial. You will only make her circumstances more difficult before a jury. Sorry Gerry, but you must listen to what I am saying to you as a friend, and a law enforcement officer." Daniel was extremely worried about what Gerry was going to do. If he went out for vengeance on his own, and something happened to Connor, Daniel wouldn't be able to help him, because he had his badge of office to stymie him. His hands would be tied, and his friend would face a murder charge, as well as Anna.

"Go to bed Daniel, and get some well earned rest, you look like shit. And, when you get up you can tell me where Anna is, because I have to see for myself that she is actually alive."

Daniel nodded, he did feel like shit, and couldn't keep his eyes open long enough to argue with his friend. He also felt bad, because when he had said goodbye to Anna, she had whispered to him, even though she was in a great deal of pain. "Don't tell Gerry where I am. I can't ever see him again. I am all used up, and that madman has made me feel unclean and disgusting. Please Daniel, I am begging you, let me go." Anna had then fallen into unconsciousness again, before Daniel could even promise her that he would keep her whereabouts from Gerry. After what Anna had been through, he could understand exactly how she felt about her future. And, he would abide with her regarding her love for Gerry. It was impossible for her to be with the love of her life, and resume what they'd had together. That bond had been shattered and could never be repaired.

Daniel stood up slowly and moved towards his bedroom as if he was an old man, but stopped before opening the door, and turned towards Gerry. "Give me your word that you won't leave this house before I wake up. We need to work together to decide what we are doing next. Our informant, Gary Gomez, has been put in a safe house. Anna is in an extremely safe environment FBI hospice. Charles Connor is under house arrest with two very able Elite Team guarding him, with two more in rotation. Everything has been taken care of until the FBI let me know what they are going to do in the future. The FBI have waited a long time to bring down Connor, and will not allow him to evade their might." Daniel waited for Gerry's answer.

"Go to bed Daniel, you are asleep on your feet. I'm going to have a rest as well. I am knackered with all this over the top emotion. See you buddy when you wake up."

Daniel was so exhausted he didn't notice that his friend hadn't given his word about not leaving the house. He shut the door behind him and fell onto his big, comfortable bed with a weary sigh, and was asleep in a nano-second.

Gerry checked that Daniel was fast asleep, as he knew he was by the low key snoring coming from the bedroom. Immediately he began to get ready to leave. After all, he hadn't given his word that he wouldn't. He had a great deal to organise and he couldn't do that in Daniel's home, or on his own cell phone. He needed to find a very large Walmart, and a bank of pay-as-you-go telephones. What he had to organise needed to be done today, and in complete secrecy.

That psycho piece of shit was breathing his last clean air on earth, because he didn't deserve to walk amongst decent, hardworking people. Gerry was certain that no one would weep at that man's funeral, except his parents of

214

course. And, he could join his brother at hell's furnace, stoking the fire through to eternity, and beyond.

CHAPTER TWENTY-ONE

Gerry felt bad, but needs must. He took Daniel's keys for his SUV Porsche, and intended to use the vehicle to get him quite a few miles to find a very large Walmart, and a phone that no one could track into.

He knew without a doubt that Daniel was still out like a light, and would be for quite some time yet. So Gerry had plenty of time to accomplish what needed to be organised ASAP. His shoulder had healed, and he was capable of driving competently and carefully. He did have to wear dark glasses in the sun, and glasses for reading, but otherwise his damaged eye was doing well. He was still walking with a cane, because his knee had been shattered. His right hand had been rebuilt with wiring, and nuts and bolts, and eventually would be almost back to normal.

Twenty miles later he drove into the car park of a super-store Walmart, and made sure he parked in a dense area of cars so no one in the future would be able to identify the Porsche as being there. He had dressed in black, nothing showy or designer. With the bill of his cap pulled over his face, he left the vehicle leaning heavily on his cane, as if he was elderly and disabled, and it was difficult for him to walk. As always, Gerry's camouflage was impeccable.

He always carried a phone card on him in case of emergencies, and this was an emergency, and luckily Marcus picked up on the fourth ring. "Can you talk Marcus? Without that sweetheart of a nosy wifc listening in?" Marcus's wife, Mia, always wanted to know what was going on in her husband's busy life, because she always wanted to join in the fun, or danger.

"It's OK Gerry, I am out in the stables, and Mia is shopping with my mother. So go ahead and put me in the picture. Daniel has kept me on board as much as he could, but evidently you are on the mend now, so what's going on? Obviously you have found Anna, and how bad is it? I can imagine pretty grim. And, how are *you* coping?"

Gerry outlined the whole situation, desperately trying to keep his emotions under control. But, anything to do with Anna's welfare and imprisonment almost had him on his knees, when pictures entered his head of what she had gone through, and he hadn't been there to help her, and keep her safe.

Marcus rarely used bad language, but he couldn't hold back when Gerry told him what Daniel had found in that stark, freezing basement, and Anna's fragile hold on life had been. "Jesus! What a fucking, psychotic maniac. How could anyone treat another human being so badly? Anna is very strong and very capable and in time will get through all of the

217

trauma. It is going to be difficult for you, as she will probably turn away from your love and help. It almost broke me when Mia refused to see me, but we survived because we loved each other so much. Stick with it Gerry, as the end result will be so worth it."

Both men went silent for a moment, their thoughts on the women they loved, and the danger they had been in, and survived.

"What do you want me to do, Gerry?" We did discuss it loosely when you realised how evil this Charles Connor was. And, you know that money isn't a problem on my side. But, The Executioner has retired. The guy we used when my Mia was left for dead, when those twins abused and raped her over hours of torture. But, I hear whispered that his nephew has taken over his specific work, and is just as excellent at carrying out anything needed against any atrocities. He goes under the pseudonym – The Judge."

Gerry made sure that he had his back to any cameras in the vicinity, because lip-readers were often used by the illegal rats in the community. Gerry never took any chances of being recognised, or listened to by the under-belly of society, or even rogue cops of which there were aplenty.

"That is why I am phoning you. I can't thank you enough Marcus. I won't settle down until that piece of shit is six feet under in the worst possible scenario. Slow and painful death is too good for him. Make sure you explain to this guy, The Judge, that nothing is too extreme. I know it is almost impossible to get in touch with him, but I do know that he lives In a remote part of the Nevada Desert, as did his uncle. But, if he knows that you are willing to pay him millions, I am pretty certain he will get in touch with you. You know I can never repay you, ever. But Anna means everything to me, and I am sure you have come to love her son, Jayden. But, when all this is over, we will come back to collect him. Anna is adamant about that, she loves that boy more than her own life."

"Mia and I, and our kids, all love Jayden, but have always known that one day he will leave us, and we pray for that day when Anna is free again. Mia and I will never forget how you helped save her life when my brother Anton was murdered. I can never, ever repay you for that. Before you go, where is this Charles Connor now, and how can our guy manage to get to him? He is extremely good, but he needs a starting point."

"Connor is under house arrest on his large estate. He is being guarded by four of the Elite Team, FBI, two on and two off. It isn't going to be easy, but that is why our guy is paid big bucks. I never heard that The Executioner failed, and his nephew seems to be even more lethal, and a perfectionist." Gerry was beginning to get a bit worried about how long he had been away from Daniel's pad. He didn't want Daniel waking up and finding that he had escaped. If The Judge managed to get that son of a bitch, and teach him a lesson he would never forget, Gerry had to be able to prove he was an innocent bystander.

Daniel was slick, and knowledgeable, and would want to find out who had orchestrated Connor's demise. Gerry and Marcus would be top of that hit list. Marcus hadn't got where he had in the world of finance, and mega-rich by being naive and stupid. He would cover his involvement with a rock-solid alibi, and Gerry had never left Marina del Rey, and had never used his cell phone since being beaten up. So, that should cover all the bases. Charles Connor must have a multitude of enemies that he had crossed in his under-world dealings in handouts to so many officials in high places.

Let some of them take the heat. The slimy assholes deserved everything that was coming their way once Connor was taken down, and his personal safe opened up and examined for evidence of his extreme life-style.

"Keep in touch, Gerry. Let me know how Anna is doing. In fact let Daniel get in touch with me. This conversation never happened. I am getting rid of the number you are using as we speak."

And the line went dead!

CHAPTER TWENTY-TWO

Daniel had been to his office and made his statement with his detectives, Lewis and Carter. He was still on leave, but knew he would have to return soon. He couldn't believe how well behaved Gerry was, by not asking to leave Daniel's home, unless it was in his fitness regime. This worried Daniel because it just wasn't Gerry, which made him suspect something else was going on. But, what could it be? It must be to do with Anna's imprisonment and trauma.

They had already discussed that to death and Gerry had to realise that they had to let the law take its course, which could be slow and lumbering. But, with Anna and Gary's evidence, there couldn't be any wriggle in Connor's defence.

Only that morning, before Daniel had left for the LAPD, Gerry had been arguing, then begging to be allowed to see Anna, which was not going to happen under any circumstances. She was far too sick for visitors, even the FBI agents were champing at the bit for information to bring down Charles Connor and his cohorts.

But, Daniel hadn't told Gerry that he knew where she was, and was going to take a chance later today to try and get to see her. After seeing her so sick in that basement prison, he couldn't get her frailty and almost demise out of his head.

He needed to see that she was on the mend and looking as if she was a human being again, and not a trapped animal that had been so badly abused, and almost starved to death.

Anna was being looked after in a small private sanatorium, which had a specialist suite that the FBI used when they needed to keep someone safe who was important to an ongoing serious incident. The FBI were totally aware that human intelligence, and feet on the ground, and ears, were far better than computers, or satellites. And Anna was serious human intelligence. She was the major factor in bringing down Charles Connor, and the tentacles of illegal crime that radiated from his family and wealth.

But as luck would have it, Anna had asked to see Daniel, and the FBI had got in touch with him at his office. So he didn't have to worry about just turning up at the Hospice, and cajoling her guards for a quick visit. He was really doing this for Gerry, who was frantic to see the woman he loved, and to make sure she was having the very best treatment, and was responding to that care. Unfortunately, Gerry would not be allowed to see Anna for some time, as the case against Connor was being built, and Anna's testimony was crucial to that end.

Daniel was not happy to have to give his friend the run around, but Anna's whereabouts were on a need to know basis. Gerry Swane was not on the list of need to know, so Daniel had to keep to that process of acute safety for Anna's life.

Daniel was totally taken aback when he finally was given permission to enter Anna's medical suite. She was of course still painfully thin, and her once beautiful face was gaunt with the trade mark of dehydration, and malnutrition. Even with the plethora of tubes entering and exiting her weak, fragile body, she was smiling a warm welcome to him. The last time he had seen her Daniel thought they were going to bring her back in a body bag. Her demeanour now was nothing short of a miracle. This woman holding out her hand to him to come closer must have the strongest mindset of any person he'd ever known. She had been beaten, abused, and raped continually, but had never given in. To Daniel, she was a power house of strength, but also of humility, and he could understand why Gerry absolutely adored her.

Her voice was weak and scratchy, and he could see that it was still an effort for her to use her vocal cords, where Connor had tried to strangle her for sexual gratification. Daniel was seriously worried that she would ever allow any male to get close to her again, which didn't bode well for Gerry. And, Gerry was a hands on sexual animal, who was used to sex whenever he felt inclined, which had been daily before his encounter with Connor's hoodlums.

"Lieutenant McCreedy, I can never repay you for finding me." She smiled a very watery smile, and squeezed his large hand. Hers seemed so much smaller, and feminine, and wasn't very powerful yet. "I honestly believed that I couldn't hold out for another day, and was praying to God to take me away from that disgusting, diabolical cage I was being kept in. I do not remember you charging in to save me, or being brought here to this wonderful facility." She rapidly blinked her eyes to stop the tears from falling, because she had cried far too much since waking up from the nightmare of Charles Connor.

Daniel always tried to be truthful in every situation he encountered, so he stood by the creed when he answered her. "If I am being honest, my heart sank when we got to you, because I thought we were too late. But, luckily one of the FBI was a paramedic, and started work on you, and told us that you were very weak, but still breathing, just about. I can't tell you how relieved I was, not only for myself, but for Gerry as well. Telling him you hadn't made it would have been my worst nightmare. In truth, I don't think I could have done it."

He bent down and kissed her softly on her cheek. Daniel McCreedy was always gentle with females, and wanted to put his arms around them in protection. He was always calm and low key with women, but was tough and hard with any bad boys that came into his vicinity, especially at the LAPD. "He is desperate to see that you are OK, and making good progress. Really that is one of the reasons I have come to see you today to ask that you give your permission for him to visit. You have an embargo on visitors right now, but can ask for permission to see him. And, please call me by my given name, Daniel. I'm sure Gerry must have told you we have been the best of friends for at least twenty years."

Anna actually laughed, even though it was still too painful for her to do so. "Yes Daniel, he told me all about your dangerous escapades, but I'm pretty sure he was the actual trouble-maker between the pair of you. He also said that you had the perpetual stick up your butt that needed removing surgically."

Daniel grinned and shook his head, he hated it when Gerry said that about him, because it was too close to the truth. Gerry was danger personified, while Daniel thought carefully through everything he did, which drove Gerry almost into a frenetic meltdown every time they had to make a quick decision, which didn't happen with Daniel on board.

"Will you let him visit please Anna? I haven't told him I am here today, because he is wearing my flooring out pacing up and down. I don't know just how much longer I can keep him housebound. He is swearing and losing his temper at everything I say to him. All he talks about is you, and how much he loves you. I'm sure you realise that Gerry does not find it easy to talk about loving anybody, because it has never happened to him previously. He has been a loner by choice, and perfectly happy in that singular situation, without committing to anyone or anything." He grinned playfully at her. "Then you came along, and he went down like a ton of bricks. In my bachelor opinion it couldn't have happened to a more difficult bastard."

But Daniel would always love Gerry for the amazing friend that he was. If Gerry was watching your back you were always safe, and Daniel couldn't say that about anyone else. But Anna's next words almost brought him to his knees, he had never expected to hear her say those words about Gerry.

"I am *so* sorry Daniel, but I can never see Gerry again." Tears started to swamp her beautiful eyes that were a myriad of colour. "I am all used up Daniel. I've been abused, sodomised, in truth fucked and used up almost to death. All the showers and soap in the world cannot make me feel clean again. Charles Connor has made me feel unclean, unworthy, and beyond disgusting. Gerry possibly still thinks he loves me, but every time now that we make love, in his mind he will remember what that maniac did to me. Then he will begin to hate me, and then hate himself. I know this to be true, because I already hate and despise myself for not trying harder to stop that madman from killing me right at the start of that torment and pain."

She looked straight at Daniel with the hurt and disgust written all over her face, and begged him to try and understand. "Believe me Daniel, I tried to live for my precious son, Jayden. I could not let that evil family get hold of my beautiful child. Sheer determination kept me alive when every time he put his filthy hands on me, I truly wanted to die. Believe me when I tell you that I never thought at the end that I was going to survive, that young guard Gary was my life-saver, because he showed me small favours that kept me going, and I am sure if Connor had found out, he would have killed him without a second thought. I probably owe my life to that guard."

Daniel tried to argue with her, but she put up her hand to stop him, because she was almost out of energy, and exhaustion was creeping up on her. She took his hand and put it on her concave stomach. "The sister has told me that I haven't lost my baby after all that trauma. I am *so* very relieved, and impossibly happy. This has to be one strong and resilient baby to have gone through all that stress and deeply disturbing trauma, and survived intact."

Anna kept hold of Daniel's hand on her belly, as if needing his strength and understanding as to what her future held. "When I leave here, and hopefully the FBI will help me get past my husband's death, and I can try and lead a normal life, my children will be that life. I do not want or need anyone else to interfere with that life, or be part of it. I love Gerry with all my heart, but it just isn't to be. Please, please, I beg you, help him, and explain exactly as I have explained to you why we cannot be together, and never will be."

She pulled him closer and whispered into his ear something she did not want anyone else to hear. Walls had ears, and Anna had learned the hard way not to trust another soul, except Daniel or Gerry.

Before Daniel could plead Gerry's case, or confirm what she had asked him to promise to do, they were interrupted. "Sorry Lieutenant, visiting time is over." She tsk tsk'ed loudly. "Our patient is still very poorly, and needs her rest. You have been here for too long Lieutenant, off we go now, and no more visitors today, thank you." She began to check all the ingoing and outgoing tubes, and then was taking Anna's temperature and blood pressure with perfect professionalism.

Daniel quickly kissed Anna's hand, and mouthed "I won't let you down, you can trust me. And, please reconsider about Gerry, he will be heartbroken."

Anna solemnly shook her head, and silently said, "Sorry Daniel. No!" Then laid back, her eyes drifting shut while the senior sister took charge of her ailing patient, and gave her an injection of a strong painkiller that would knock her out for a couple of hours, but wouldn't adversely affect her baby.

With heavy heart, and even heavier steps, Daniel left Anna behind. Now he had to go home and tell Gerry what she had decreed, and knew he would go ape-shit. In fact there was no telling what he would do. Gerry could be extremely volatile when he couldn't have his own way. He had always been adverse to rules and regulations; that was why he had left the Marines, and the police force. Anna's revelation was going to be a huge pill to swallow, if he did that is? With Gerry every day was a question, not always an answer.

The Elite Teamster spoke to Daniel as he came out of Anna's room. "How is she, Lieutenant? Slowly getting better I hope? Never thought she was going to make it, and she seems such a lovely person. Goes to show it doesn't always happen to the bad people. Shit happens to good and bad, doesn't it?"

Daniel was choked up with what Anna had gone through, and thoroughly pissed off with what he had to go home and tell his friend. "Do you know buddy, I am so fucked off with the world at the moment I want to just drop off, and never be found again."

The guard slapped him on the back, grinning. "Don't worry Lieutenant, everything always sorts itself out. It's another day tomorrow, and today will be in our past. And, there isn't a problem we can't sort out. Well! That's what my dear old mama always told me when she was alive. Gee! I just wish she was still here to tell me off. I really miss those clips around my ears, even though they did hurt like the blazes."

Daniel couldn't help but smile at the image of the guard's mama slapping him. He must be at least six foot four. A man mountain, full of packed muscle, and a mean-machine.

Daniel walked out of the medical facility, and made his way to his vehicle, and decided to take the longer route home. He knew he was only delaying the inevitable, but he needed to be calm and hold his tongue when Gerry found out he wasn't going to be able to visit Anna. He would hit the roof and some, but Daniel was not going to tell Gerry where Anna was being looked after. The facility was off the record, wasn't on any website, etc. So Gerry would wrack his brain trying to find out but wouldn't get anywhere.

Daniel hoped and prayed that she would change her mind eventually, but wasn't betting the farm on it. The good news was that she hadn't lost the baby, and he knew that both Gerry and Anna were looking forward to the birth, and extending their family, or not?

And, now Daniel knew where Jayden was hidden, he could visit and accumulate the evidence to keep Anna out of prison for murdering her husband, hopefully.

CHAPTER TWENTY-THREE

Alan Davis was demure, innocuous, and completely unnoticeable in a crowd. He was of medium height, medium weight, and wore clothes that were purchased at any mediocre super-store. His passport, driving licence, and social security number gave credence to that name, but try to find him on a computer and you would come up with a big fat zilch. Alan Davis did not exist.

The unknown male leaving Hartsfield Jackson Atlanta Airport in a rented non-descriptive family saloon was almost invincible. He had a greying goatee beard, and a moustache, with eye colour changing contact lenses, and an Atlanta Falcon Football Team cap, which he had purchased in the airport. He never stowed luggage onto the aeroplane, but always toted a small black backpack on his shoulder. When he arrived at his destination, he knew he would find everything he needed to carry out his objective safely and without any harm to himself.

As always, he was totally on the ball as the assassin who was being paid ten million dollars to rid the world of that evil bastard Charles Connor. The Judge was a techno genius, and had hacked into the complete set up of Connor's world. He had studied the bastard's secret life, his untold wealth, his goods on all the people he blackmailed, and the complete

232

map of his extremely large, and wealthy property. Connor did not stand a hope in hell of surviving past that night. Would be dead long before dawn.

The Judge never, ever, took on a job unless he was one hundred per cent prepared, and ready to accomplish the end-game. There was never room for any mistakes, because *he* could end up dead, and he loved what he was extremely good at. Permanently getting rid of the assholes in his country. He never worked outside America, except very occasionally in Mexico, because many mobsters, drug barons, and gun runners, slipped across the border to evade law enforcement.

For a very high price his expertise was needed to eliminate the truly bad guys in this world.

The Judge drove around the back of a twenty-four hour small convenience store, roughly two miles from his destination. It was already dark, but he had to wait a couple of hours until midnight. At midnight the Elite FBI Team would change their guards, that would be the usual procedure, and that would be the safest time for him to get into the Connor estate. Then he would leave it another couple of hours to allow the guards to relax their positions. Around two a.m., anybody in the house would also be fast asleep. He knew where Connor slept, and his parents. There were live-in servants, but they lived over the stables, and The Judge preferred that they weren't hurt in the melee. But if they were, then that was collateral damage, and couldn't be helped. He never killed or hurt anyone unnecessarily, but in every war there were casualties.

He changed into a hoodie, sweats and trainers to be less conspicuous as he jogged to the Connor estate. He always kept himself super fit, working out rigorously every free moment he had. Keeping fit was a necessity in his line of work, he always had to be faster and more alert than his chosen victim. A great deal of money was a prerequisite for his services, so keeping super fit was another prerequisite for him.

He checked the contents of his backpack for the last time. He carried enough accelerant to obtain his objective, and four vials of very toxic barbiturates, which he had mixed himself, and could knock out an elephant. In case any enthusiastic border and custom controller had asked to see the contents of his backpack, the four injections had been labelled as diabetic medication. He was so underwhelming in his looks and attitude, no one ever stopped him. The lighter and lighter fluid were also in his backpack, and he was sure they wouldn't have been considered as suspicious had he been asked why they were there.

On the way to his destination he had pulled into an out of the way garage and purchased a small can of

Kerosene. The young girl at the cash register hadn't taken her eyes from the romantic novel she was avidly reading, and had just taken the ten dollars without even looking at him, which was a bonus. There were a few decrepit cameras around the property, so he made sure his face was not in view, and could be recognised.

As the supreme caution he had sprayed his finger tips with a clear coating gel, which gave them a smooth finish, and only cold water would remove it. He was always extremely careful to never leave his finger prints anywhere on a job. He was in fact a living ghost. No one had ever recognised him, managed to get a photo, found a finger print, or anything that could be used against him in a court of law. Everything he did was always absolutely exact, and on time to the second.

He took great pride in his profession, because in his mind and conscience he was ridding the world of evil, psychotic maniacs. They were driven by power, greed, and a monstrous ego, and they punished the weaker, softer side of the world.

The Judge was an enigma. No one knew where he lived. No one knew what he looked like. No one had ever heard his real voice, as he always used a voice enhancer, he rarely had to speak when working anyway. He preferred silence, but today was an exception, because the customer, who had already paid his exorbitant fee, had asked to give Connor a specific message.

When he had heard what Connor had done to receive his death sentence, he immediately added a bonus to the request, and would finish the job with a spectacular end. It would be an absolute pleasure to complete the project to his own satisfaction. As usual, he would be at his professional best, until this was done, and he was on his way home to his pretty young wife, and baby, who were innocent bystanders.

The Judge walked silently and slowly through the wooded area surrounding the Connor estate. It was exactly two a.m. Two minutes ago he had disabled the guard on the front gate of the long drive to the house. He checked his state of the art phone, it was a part of him, he had built it himself. It could start or end a war. Could bankrupt a small country, or make it extremely wealthy. But, right now it was going to allow him entry to the Connor property unseen, and unknown. He was dead on time, because he was a man of principle, he did everything to a perfect time scale.

Without moving his entire body, he watched one of the FBI Elite Team relax and light a cigarette, and stupidly he laid his extremely expensive light-weight assault rifle on the ground next to him. Silently, like a wraith, The Judge came up behind him and pierced his neck with an injection that had enough barbiturates to fell an elephant. The guard slumped to the ground without a murmur of surprise or retribution. Immediately The Judge picked up the weapon, and gave it a quick once over with a satisfactory nod. It was light, not the latest model, but extremely accurate and deadly.

Swiftly he made his way around to the back entrance where the other guard was sitting on a large stone seat, evidently not expecting any intruders that night, or any arising problems. Again he silently approached the very stupid guard, and jabbed him straight into the back of his neck, and he went down immediately like a stone statue.

The three guards had only one area that was left vulnerable - their neck. Every part of their body was armoured up to the hilt, but for roughly an inch between body armour and head gear. The Judge knew exactly where they were vulnerable, and he had hit the spot without a problem. They wouldn't come back to the land of the living for hours, and probably, but definitely should be put back down the ranks of the lesser hierarchy in the FBI.

This was where his phone came into its own. It disabled every form of alarm in the house. It opened the main doors, and every other door that was locked. It did not alert any complicated system that was embedded inside or outside the main house. Any computers that were monitoring the cameras inside or outside the house would be showing the very last pictures before everything had been disabled. At two a.m. anyone supposed to be watching the screens would be asleep, or very relaxed, and not bothering to be that alert, because nothing apparently was happening. Especially as there were three FBI Elite Team guarding the perimeter, so all should be safe and secure. Nothing to worry about then, was there?

Swiftly and silently he made his way up the curved intricate gold staircase to the level where the bedrooms were all located. Every time he passed heavy velvet drapes he soaked the hems with Kerosene. When he came to the suite that Connor's parents occupied, he carefully locked the doors so they couldn't seek help. Unfortunately, they were collateral damage, but they had spawned their two evil sons, and had encouraged them on their path of destruction, and depravity. The Judge didn't feel an ounce of guilt in causing their deaths. He had done his homework on that disgusting dynasty, and it stank to high heaven, or hell. Many a poor, honest soul had lost all their hard earned money or their lives, because of this family's destruction, and mayhem.

He also knew that the FBI had stripped the family of every form of communication, so no one would come to their aid when he completed his night's work. All the staff lived over the garages and would have time to evacuate the premises

238

when it literally went up in flames, and it would be too late to save the Connor home.

Slipping into Charles Connor's bedroom he laid his backpack beside the bed, and took out the items he needed, very carefully. Connor was snoring, and hadn't heard him enter the room. Nobody ever heard the Judge move around, he would be a perfect cat burglar. Unfortunately that wouldn't have earned him enough money to retire early, which he intended to do before his luck ran out, which wasn't a possibility really, but you never knew, it could happen.

He nudged the sleeping man with the nozzle of the assault rifle, and waited for him to realise what had happened. It took only seconds as his target sat up wide awake, angry, and very belligerent. "What the fuck? Who *are* you? And, what the fucking hell are you doing in my home?" He shook his head to get rid of any sleep mode left. "And, where are the fucking guards, who are supposed to be keeping my family safe?" Again he gave the Judge a look of disdain, and utter hatred at daring to assume he could frighten him with just an assault rifle. "Well! Who are you? And what do you want from me, you stupid bastard?"

The Judge wasn't going to waste his breath on this piece of shit. "I am your judge, jury, and executioner. Now, get out of bed before I do you a favour and blow your brains out."

CHAPTER TWENTY-FOUR

He nudged Connor out of bed with the assault rifle, and was surprised when Connor put his hands on the back of his head compliantly. Obviously he wasn't taking any chances on his life being in danger. Little did he know, the Judge thought, smiling inwardly.

Of course Connor was naked, and he couldn't help but make comment. "Not much to boast about there."

"It does its work perfectly well when asked to perform." Connor snidely remarked.

"Yeah, I'm sure. But I'm informed that you prefer to use it for rape, sodomy, and brutality, with a violent beating as a backup."

Connor just shook his head dismissively, as if he couldn't care less how so many women had suffered at his cruel hands. Cruelty was part of his nature that he thoroughly enjoyed and encouraged.

With the barrel of the gun the Judge pushed him into the chair he had already put in the middle of the room with restraints ready for wrists and ankles. Quickly and efficiently he locked Connor's body in the restraints before he realised what was happening. Now, the Judge could relax a tad, because his prisoner wasn't going anywhere any time soon.

"Well! You idiot fucker, what are you going to do now? Beat the shit out of me? But, I hope you realise that I get an erection with any form of torture, and pain."

"I can assure you Charles fuckin' Connor, that you will not have the pleasure of any form of erection with what I am going to do to you." He put the barrel of the state of the art assault weapon into Connor's mouth, and looked into those depraved, maniac eyes. "I am your worst nightmare. I am your judge, jury, and executioner." He couldn't believe it when Connor winked at him, because he still did not believe that this calm, innocuous looking individual, with a ghostly quiet voice, could dare touch the great man, Charles Connor.

Slowly and carefully The Judge removed the small can of accelerant and poured it over his prisoner. That was when Connor realised exactly what he was going to do.

"You piece of shit! Whoever is paying you to do this to me, I will double it. In fact you can name your price. I have money in the Caribbean, Columbia, Aruba, and Switzerland. Anything you ask for you can have, I give my word." Coldly he smiled, thinking he had done a deal. Of course, he had no intention of paying out a single dollar to this ridiculous cretin. He wasn't worthy of a second coherent thought in Charles Connor's magnificent, corrupt, evil life. Anyway, the cameras sited all around the house were recording every moment of this ridiculous debacle.

241

The Judge smiled back without a modicum of humour, because he always took his profession very seriously. "I have been told by the bountiful benefactor who paid ten million for your truly horrendous death, that this is for Gerry Swane, and the love of his life, Anna Weist."

The Judge took a bandana and tied it around Connor's mouth, stopping him from anymore profanity. "May you rot in hell with the rest of your family, Charles Connor. My conscience is clear, knowing I have rid the world of a small part of corruption and dark evil work that has been performed in this house, and the Agency that you were the head of."

Calmly and carefully The Judge gathered everything that he had used whilst in the property. Only then did he flick open his lighter. "Oh, and thank you for telling me where your stinking money is, I will enjoy spending it all for you. Luckily I am a genius of technology."

He lit a paper napkin he had picked up on the way to Connor's bedroom, and threw it on his genitalia. That was the part of his body that needed to go up in flames first, because it had caused so much damage and pain to so many women.

Connor tried desperately to release the restraints, but it only served to tighten them. His face was contorted with fury, excruciating pain, and absolute fear, as he realised this inconsequential small professional hit-man knew exactly what he was doing, and enjoyed every single moment.

The Judge heard the whoosh of the angry flames as they consumed Charles Connor. He left the house as quickly as possible, because with the amount of kerosene he had poured on the drapes, etc, the property would be an inferno within minutes. He checked the guards. He had pulled them far away enough to be safe, and they were all still fast asleep, and now probably would be unemployed.

He left the way he came, jogging through the woods surrounding the late magnificent house. In the distance he could hear three different services descending on the Connor residence. The Fire Rescue trucks – Police department, and Ambulance service. The Connors were held in high regard in that part of Atlanta, especially to those who received generous back-handers to keep their mouths shut for services rendered.

Alan Davis smiled as he jogged to pick up his rental car, because a hell of a lot of bent people were now going to be a lot less well off, and out of work. And he most certainly could live with that.

CHAPTER TWENTY-FIVE

Daniel threw his car keys onto the side table in the lounge, he was incandescent with rage. It had been his first day back at work, and had been a really shitty day. The in-tray on his desk had been full to overflowing, and his out-tray empty. There were folders piling up that God only knew when he would get to tackle them. He had been away for a month because of Gerry, and there hadn't been anyone spare to take on his overload of work, which was always on overload.

Then around ten a.m. Agent Clancy had begun a video connection with him that went on most of the day. The two agents, Clancy and Stead, were back in Atlanta via a cargo plane before dawn, trying to make sense of what had happened at the Connor estate. The FBI were in a state of extreme agitation, because three of the Elite Team had been hospitalised and were all in a coma, so couldn't help with the enquiries of how and why Charles Connor, and his parents, had been cremated in an inferno.

The property was completely demolished, because it was over a hundred years old, and a great deal of wood had been used in its structure. The only way they knew that the three people had been asleep in the property, was because a guard, just before his shift had ended, made sure they were all in their respective bedrooms, as was the protocol of house arrest.

Daniel looked askance at Gerry who was comfortable in Daniel's favourite lounge chair watching a football game with a can of beer in his hand. That was when Daniel lost his usually held back and in control temper. They had had a nasty flare up between them a few days earlier, when Gerry had learnt that Anna would not let him visit. It wasn't Daniel's fault, but he was the messenger of doom, so got all the crap thrown at him, but enough was enough.

But now he was spitting mad, and needed the absolute truth, and nothing else would do. Something Gerry was a master at avoiding. Making up stories, and a fragile truth was everything that came naturally to Gerry Swane.

"I want the absolute truth, Gerry. No if's or but's. I have had the day from hell with a video call from the Agents Clancy and Stead, questioning me on the deaths of Charles Connor and his parents at their property early this morning. Three Elite Team have been hospitalised, and hopefully will survive. The property burnt to a crisp, with not a shred of evidence of finger prints, foot prints, or any evidence of who committed this heinous crime. They don't know how many people were involved, but was certainly out of the realm or capability of a singular person." Daniel's whole body was shaking with anger, because he did believe that somehow

Gerry was involved with this diabolical crime. "Did you have anything to do with this, Gerry? Anything at all? Because if you have, friend or not, I will take you in myself." And, Daniel meant every word. No one was above the law, and he knew that his friend often skirted around it, and often walked a fine line of danger.

Gerry had never seen Daniel so angry, but he could truthfully say that he hadn't known what The Judge was going to do for ten million bucks. He shook his blond head in almost complete innocence. "No! I do not know what you are talking about. But, it couldn't have happened to a nicer person. I can only pray he suffered excruciating pain, and I would like to shake the hand of whoever did it. And, I would like to remind you that Connor must have had a crowd of enemies waiting to help him to get to hell, and beyond, with his brother Edward."

Daniel glared at Gerry trying to weigh up if he was actually telling the truth, or not. "If I find out that you are involved in any way, we will part company for good, and I really mean it this time, Gerry. I cannot be involved in a crime like this, and keep my place in law enforcement, it wouldn't be right, or moral."

Gerry couldn't believe he had got out of that predicament so easily, and Daniel still had that stick up his ass, which must be so painful. "Honestly Daniel, where on earth would I get the money to arrange such a professional job? It did sound as if it was a top notch professional piece of work. Must have cost millions to organise. And, I haven't left here for a few weeks, and haven't got a vehicle, or a mobile yet." He raised his eyebrows, and his hands in supplication to his friend, as if, how could he doubt him?

Daniel could see Gerry's point of view, and apologised, because he knew that Gerry was without funds, until Marcus gave him money that he was due. Only then did the light come on. Now, Marcus was extremely wealthy, would he have bank rolled Gerry? Would he? Marcus was wealthy, extremely bright, adored his wife Mia, and she had been badly abused, as had Anna. Daniel wasn't going to pursue that thought any further. Marcus Medina would sue the ass off of any agency who tried to connect him with last night, and he would win. He was a top ranking lawyer.

Just when Daniel was going to get a beer out of the fridge, and sit down to watch the end of the game with Gerry, his cell phone rang. He looked at the caller number, and said 'fuck' under his breath. "Agent Clancy, what can I do for you?" He listened for a couple of minutes. "You are kidding me! Who on earth can do that, and be off the record? This has to be one fucking genius with computers, even more so than your forensic experts, and crime laboratory top people. Thanks for the heads up. Keep me informed, but I'm out of it now, way beyond my expertise."

Daniel put his phone next to his keys, and went straight to his aged Jack Daniels bottle. Poured a hefty amount into a glass, and drank it straight down. Then he poured one for Gerry, and another for himself. He needed to get roaring drunk after the day from hell he had suffered.

He gave Gerry his drink, and then sat down in the other armchair. He was beyond exhaustion. "All the heavies in the technology departments in the FBI have just managed to work out Connor's personal computer where all his money was hidden. It ran into billions, and they couldn't believe their luck, because it had been in a maze of different accounts in a multitude of countries." He leant back in his comfortable leather man-chair, and closed his eyes, a wicked grin on his lips. "While they were patting themselves on the back, one by one every account was emptied, and they scrambled to find out what had happened, but they were blocked completely on every channel, and couldn't get back to any account they had seen before." Then Daniel couldn't help but laugh. "When they did manage to get a connection on every site, a thank you came up from all the rescue agencies in the Western World. Save the Children – Unicef – Red Cross, etc., and starving in Africa, and Ukraine, were all recipients of Charles Connor's fortune. This guy was a genius at technology. The FBI technicians were scrabbling around the globe, while he was re-routing, criss-crossing every upside and downside on a computer, confusing everyone. Then they drew a complete blank on who it was, or where he was. The FBI was left with a thumbs up, and thank you."

Gerry couldn't belicvc what Daniel was saying, but then The Judge had been well paid for his work. "Wow! I bet that must be pissing off Connor, wherever he is. All that dirty money doing some good in the world, who would have thought it? Connor made all those billions out of corruption, murder, rape, and evil brutality. Now, hopefully it will help those in desperate need. Of course it doesn't help those people who have suffered at that psychotic mad man's hands, and his cohorts in evil pursuits. And, my Anna, it won't help heal her pain. But given time she can forgive herself, and me, for not keeping her safe. And, I can hopefully wait for that day to come."

Daniel raised his glass in salute to Gerry. But feared that day would be a long time in coming, if ever?

"Do you want me to leave, Daniel? I've been here over a month now, you must be absolutely cheesed off with me being so untidy, and eating your food, and not paying my way. I need to get back to working for Marcus, it's been long enough now, and I am almost back to normal." Whatever normal was, thought Gerry, without the one person you love with you. She was still in hospital, and refusing to see him, would only see Daniel, which totally pissed off Gerry. He wasn't jealous, because Daniel wouldn't try to get too close to Anna, he wasn't that type of predatory male. He was and always had been one of the straightest, and honest guys that Gerry had ever met, and admired.

"You are still not up to speed, Gerry. You are a pain in the ass, but what's new? You can stay as long as you like, in truth I don't much like living in this bloody palace on my own." It was Sunday morning, and so far Daniel hadn't been called into work as an emergency. They were still under-funded, and under-whelmed, without enough bodies at LAPD. "We'll go out for breakfast, and then go pick up your own truck and some extra clothes. You know I always go to my parents for Sunday lunch if I am not called into work. So, you can meet me there in your own vehicle. My family love it when anyone turns up on a Sunday. Nobody cooks a roast like my Mom, and Dad makes the gravy."

Gerry's stomach rumbled at the thought of Daniel's family roast, his Mom was a fantastic cook. He didn't realise just how lucky he was with parents who thought the world of him, and sister Louise with two lovely kids. Gerry had never had family or siblings who loved him regardless of what he did. That was why Marcus and Mia Medina, and their four kinds were so special to him, because they represented a loving family he could love without any questions asked. They were a family who loved big, and bold, with hugs and kisses given freely, without any prerequisites, or returns.

While they were at I. Hops eating a huge breakfast, Gerry decided to go for broke, as he really didn't have anything to lose regards Anna. He just couldn't go any longer without seeing for himself how bad she was, and if she was at last getting better, and might be leaving hospital. It was so unfair that Daniel was allowed to visit her, and he wasn't. As far as he was concerned, he was the innocent person in all this. He truly had done his very best to keep her and Jayden safe, but he knew it hadn't been good enough. Charles Connor had been far too devious and clever, and definitely had many more resources at hand to be able to find them so easily. For that mistake, Anna had suffered *so* much more than Gerry had.

"Daniel, I am not going to beg anymore, but I am warning you that I will somehow find Anna. I know she is in a safe environment, and it will be almost impossible to find her, but I *will* do it, because you know I have the contacts. Also, now the threat of Connor has disappeared, she will be allowed to leave hospital as soon as she is well enough to go."

Daniel pushed his almost empty plate away from him with a huge sigh of 'here we go again'. Gerry was like a starving dog with a bone he would not surrender to anyone,

251

and would fight to the death to keep it. "Look, it hasn't been my fault that you haven't been allowed to see her. I told you before that she won't see anyone, and especially you." Daniel hated to put that so plainly, but Gerry needed to understand the situation as it was. Anna was adamant that she would not see Gerry under any circumstances. But the beaten look on Gerry's animated face was Daniel's undoing.

"OK! Look, Anna is put to sleep every night, because she has such violent nightmares, which is understandable. I will take you in to see her once she is out for the night. No touching, or trying to speak to her, That is a total no – no. You can then see that she is responding to treatment, and is getting back to a fairly normal routine." He gave Gerry a fulminating hard glare that meant he wasn't going to take any shit from him. His friend had to promise to behave himself, do as he was told, or else this meeting wasn't going to happen. Daniel had to respect Anna's wishes. She had come out the other side of a horrendous episode in her life, and deserved to feel safe in the future. And that didn't include Gerry Swane right now, and probably might never again.

So very gently he touched the stubble on her head, remembering the glorious mane of almost black hair she once had. Sadness threatened to engulf him, because his Anna was still a beautiful woman, who had suffered such sadism, hardship, and evil intent. Of all the people he had admired and loved, Anna *so* didn't deserve what those two psycho maniacs had put her through.

At his touch she murmured in her deep sleep, and became restless, as if she knew who was touching her, and she was desperate to respond, but couldn't pull herself out of the chemical sleep aid that had her firmly in its grip.

Gerry turned to Daniel who was hovering at the entrance to Anna's room, trying to give Gerry some privacy, but also having to keep his eyes on him. He still didn't quite trust him where Anna was involved. Gerry sniffed, and wiped his fingers under both eyes. "She is going to be OK, isn't she? And please don't give me assurances that aren't true. I'm not stupid Daniel, my Anna isn't looking great, she has lost so much weight, and she is still very pale and gaunt. And, are you sure she is still pregnant, 'cos she certainly doesn't look it? She must be around four months gone by now, if my reckoning is correct." He bent down and softly kissed her on the lips, and she responded again, with a soulful sigh. As if she knew who was kissing her, and wanted more. "I love you *so* much, my darling. Please come back to me when you are well enough. So that I can spoil you rotten, love you, and try to help you forget the two men who almost managed to end your life, with their demands of warped sexual gratification, and hideous cruelty."

Daniel stepped forward and put his comforting hand on Gerry's shoulder. He was worried if Gerry carried on, he would at last wake Anna, which would infuriate the night sister in charge. That type of in charge female scared Daniel spitless. So he always kept on their good side, if they had one, but Sister Hadley needed a charisma bypass, and Daniel wasn't stupid, he kept away from the Hospice when she was walking the corridors.

"Sorry Gerry, but we have to leave. The Doctor and the Sister will be coming in about now, and I didn't get permission for you to visit Anna." He gave Gerry's shoulder a hard squeeze, when he didn't respond, and was still lightly touching Anna's arm. "Now Gerry! Or, I will have to manhandle you. I don't want to lose my visiting rights. You gave me your word that we would only visit for five minutes, and it's been fifteen at least."

Gerry wiped his eyes again, and bent down to kiss Anna on the forehead. He didn't speak until they walked outside the Hospice. "Fucking shaved her head." He sounded as if he was choking up with tears in his voice. "Like she was a victim of the fuckin' Nazis in the Second World War. Who does that crap anymore? And you have the audacity to question me if I knew who had murdered that psychotic madman. It's a fuckin' shame he is dead, because I would have enjoyed killing him myself, very, very slowly, and very, very painfully."

Daniel opened the door of his SUV Porsche to let Gerry climb in, they had both come in the same vehicle. "Don't lose any sleep on that account, Gerry. I am sure Connor died an excruciatingly painful death. Whoever did it knew exactly what they were doing. I can promise you that Connor must have known what was happening, and wasn't in a position to stop the assassin from carrying out his mission, and target. And, we still have to find out who that meticulously professional hit man, or men, were."

Gerry grinned to himself. Good luck with that Lieutenant, 'cos it ain't never going to happen, not in a million fuckin' years. But, he stayed silent, and let Daniel talk about nothing in particular, because his thoughts were on the love of his life. When he would be able to see her again, touch her again, and make fantastic love to her again, because they were so compatible.

He had to believe that! Otherwise his life wasn't worth shit. He wasn't on his own anymore. He had a family to take care of now. Anna, Jayden, and the unborn baby that she carried. Gerry was determined to step up to the plate, and be responsible for all of them. To be truthful, he was really looking forward to that life. He'd only ever been responsible for himself, and it was time he grew up, and grew a pair of balls.

But, now he had to convince Anna that he was the man for the job. After all that she had suffered he realised it was going to be a slow, very careful, and very patient time in his life. But for now Daniel was still twittering on about nothing in particular, so Gerry closed his eyes and took a well earned nap. He still wasn't back up to his normal, restless energy, but would never admit it to anyone, and especially Daniel. Because he would make Gerry eat healthily, smoke less, booze less, and exercise more. Four things he truly hated.

Gerry had also given up daily sex relief since losing Anna, and he didn't now want anyone else, which was unheard of in Gerry's sex life. Taking everything into consideration his life was poles apart from what he had enjoyed previously, when Leanne Zeema had opened his office door and declared she had murdered her husband, and changed her name.

So, you never knew what was waiting around the corner. Something Gerry Swane had never worried about. Some time in your life, shit hit the fan, and this was Gerry's time, and he wasn't griping about it. He had got away with being a single, very lucky guy, with *so* many one night stands to fill a stadium.

Now his life was about to change. So bring it on! He was as ready as get-go! He *would* have his love to warm his bed, and a ready-made family to keep him out of mischief, and extremely busy.

But would he? Life was a manoeuvre of twists and turns, as Gerry was about to find out. Thinking you had it cornered didn't always make it so. Fate had a habit of altering your well laid plans, and some.

CHAPTER TWENTY-SIX

He woke up with the full blown erection from hell. He had been dreaming about having explicit sex with Anna. Not a good thing when there was absolutely no chance of any relief in the foreseeable future. So, he made his way slowly to his en-suite bathroom. Slowly, because he still wasn't up to speed yet, and a full blown hard-on hampered his walking. He would have to relieve himself in the shower, but was intently pleased with himself, because this was the first time he'd had the energy to produce an erection of any sort. It had been a constant worry that his manhood had been compromised by his attackers.

No sex for the rest of his life, had had him worrying if he wanted to continue living, or not. So, question answered, he was going to make more effort in getting back to full health. Was, going to get in touch with Marcus today and try and get back to full-time work. Was, going to try and see Anna properly today, and find out what the true position was between them. Was *not* going to take anything negative in their relationship. They were a couple! A commitment he had never thought would happen to him, and it scared the shit out of him that she now didn't feel the same way about them.

Daniel called out from the kitchen as Gerry left his bedroom. "Breakfast is on the table. Coffee has brewed. Get a shift on you lazy bastard, because we are due at FBI headquarters in an hour. And I mean in an hour. Agent Clancy has just requested our presence for a meeting, and no, I don't know why. So get a move on as your breakfast is getting cold. We can't be late, and the traffic will be grim trying to get to 1100 Wiltshire Boulevard at this time in the morning."

As usual Daniel was dressed immaculately in a light weight navy blue silk suit, and pristine white cotton shirt. While Gerry had put on jeans and a tired T shirt, his usual attire if staying at home. "Lieutenant McCreedy, you will make a boring beautiful blonde a wonderful wife one day. There are no boundaries to your domestic excellence, and tireless good humour. So shut the fuck up and pour me a coffee, so I can start *my* day in a better mood than usual." Gerry wasn't a morning person, because he did his best work at night, or he used to previous to his injuries.

"That is so not funny, buddy. I suffered two years as a prisoner with no reprieve, or freedom. Learnt a lesson the hard way, and ain't doing that again. I realised that marriage is definitely not for me. And, she *was* blonde, beautiful, and exceedingly hot and needy." It made Daniel shudder just thinking about those two lost years, married to a raving nymphomaniac, and using him as a stud to reproduce.

Gerry drank his first cup of strong black coffee in one hit, and then Daniel poured him another, which he drank

259

much slower, enjoying the taste and smell this time. "Not much good in asking you what the meeting is about then, if you don't know?" Gerry squinted his blue eyes at Daniel. "*Or*, do you actually know, and are keeping it to yourself?"

Daniel kept a straight face, and really hated not telling the truth, because he had instigated this meeting, with a request from Anna. "It could be about something to do with Anna, and her husband's death. But you know the FBI, they keep their own knowledge close to their chests. So we will have to wait until we get to their headquarters to find out, won't we?"

Daniel knew exactly what was happening this morning, but didn't want Gerry working himself into health issues again, as he was doing so much better now. Anna was definitely not going to be at the meeting, as it wasn't necessary for her to be there. Daniel knew it was going to be truly gruelling, traumatic, and downright horrendous for everyone involved. He really wished he didn't have to be there, but Agents Clancy and Stead had told him to attend, or they would pick him up from home themselves.

Daniel McCreedy was not stupid, no one bucked the FBI. Also, he was totally involved with Anna and Gerry, and wanted to make sure their side of this ongoing investigation was taken into account, and used fair and square.

Daniel was a man of integrity and fair play, where his friend Gerry was often the opposite. So, if Gerry got out of hand if he was extremely upset, and he would be extremely upset at the meeting, Daniel would have to play Devil's Advocate, and shut him down hard. Otherwise Agent Clancy would close down the meeting completely, and Daniel wouldn't blame him.

Anna needed to know what was going to happen once she left hospital, and that was entirely up to the FBI, because they held all the information. What they did with it would be discussed this morning, and Daniel wanted to be a small part in that decision, amongst others who were involved, Gerry included of course. He had after all almost died for her, so that should be held into account in any major decisions about Anna's welfare, and future.

CHAPTER TWENTY-SEVEN

The six men in the conference room at FBI headquarters sat silent, white faced, extremely grim, and sick to their stomachs at what they had watched on the screen. It was just one of the small tapes that Marcus Medina had brought into the FBI yesterday.

The D.O. of the FBI had watched it early that morning with two of the senior lawyers in his office at the FBI. Immediately the Director of Operations had instructed his lawyers to inform the people involved in the Connor's arrest and death, his own wishes. Subsequently Agents Clancy and Stead – Daniel McCreedy – Gerry Swane, and now Marcus Medina, who had acquired the tapes from Anna Weist.

Halfway through the first tape Gerry had left the room and gone to the men's room, and been violently sick, and still hadn't returned to watch the explicit sex and violence that his beautiful Anna had managed to tape of her sick maniac of a husband.

And, with the statement of the young guard at The Serious Crime Investigation Unit, which had now been shut down completely, the D.O.'s decision was a no-brainer.

They had all watched in horror the violent abuse and explicit racist screaming spewing forth from Edward Connor's vile mouth. Anna had been beaten, spat on and used sexually in such a horrendous manner, the six men watching the drama unfold had a hard time watching the tape, and keeping their last meal down. Unfortunately Gerry hadn't been so fortunate, and had to exit quickly before he embarrassed himself completely.

The pitiful crying of Anna's little boy would stay with them for a long, long time. Her son pleading in his weak, broken voice, not understanding why his sweet mama was crying, and his papa was hurting her for no reason. "Mama? Mama?" Was all he could say, as his cruel, stern papa picked him up and literally threw him into his own bedroom, and locked the door. It was obvious he wanted to stay with his mama, who was the centre and love of his tiny life. They could hear him screaming behind the locked door. It made the hot blood in their veins turn to ice.

Edward Connor's ranting against his poor wife never let up. It was pretty obvious he was very drunk, but that could never excuse what he did. "You filthy black bitch whore, shut that fucking retard up, or I will shut the bastard up permanently." Then he had got hold of her long hair and swung her around to hit her against the bedroom wall. The worst part of that horrendous scene was that Anna never pleaded for mercy, never cried out at all. The six men all realised that Connor, from a previous scene, would inflict

263

more pain on her if she made any sound at all, especially pleading for mercy.

Then Connor watched her take all her clothes off, and lay on the bed with her legs open wide, waiting for him to rape her repeatedly all night. While he slapped her around the face, bit her breasts, and took her every which way he could think of in his sick mind, and as painful as possible.

They had watched the first and then only the last tape when Marcus stood up and turned off the screen showing the tapes. "I'm sorry gentlemen, but I cannot watch anymore of this sick, perverted, mad man's treatment of his poor wife. If he wasn't dead already, I would gladly go to prison for his permanent removal." Marcus sat down and put his head between his knees, and took quite a few long deep breaths. All he wanted to do was go home, and gather his loving family around him to kiss and hug them all.

Daniel spoke up, even though he looked and felt as bad as Marcus. He had seen some awful stuff in his work as a detective, but Edward Connor was the worst psychotic evil bastard he had ever had the misfortune to come across. "Can someone tell me why Anna never left this diabolical situation as soon as it started to get to this level of sadism, and sheer animalistic torture?"

Marcus lifted his head, his expression was full of hatred for Edward Connor. And guilt at being a male after

264

watching what a male could put a beautiful, sweet female through, because he was stronger than her. "She told my wife Mia, and myself, that she couldn't leave, because Connor told her he would find her wherever she went. He would kill her, and because of his standing in the community, he could get away with it, and would use his son for his own sexual gratification, and no one could stop him." Marcus turned his cold gaze on everyone in the room. "What could Anna do? She had to stay, and plot her maniac, unstable husband's death. That was the only way she could survive, and keep her baby safe.

"Would I have done the same? You bet I would. This beaten up, regularly raped, tortured, and abused woman needs our sympathy, and understanding. Under my guidance as her lawyer, she will never spend another minute in custody, or in a courtroom being vilified, torn apart, scrutinised by the prosecution, until somehow she will believe it was her fault. She will end up in prison, because she will believe she deserves it, and feels guilty." He looked straight at the two lawyers who were listening avidly to his words. "Anna has just escaped from a cage in a basement after being raped and starved almost to death for a month by Charles Connor. Her husband's brother unfortunately had the same sick, perverted mindset as his dead brother. Anna Weist will go to court over my dead body, and believe me, I am not joking. I am as serious as a heart attack regarding my client's welfare and future. Enough is more than enough, gentlemen."

Marcus sat down, and Daniel squeezed his arm in agreement with everything that Marcus had explicitly set out. At that moment a white faced Gerry came back into the room, and sat the other side of Marcus. He had heard the last few moments of his boss and friend's statement. Marcus was the very best of the best at his chosen profession, and Gerry couldn't ask for anymore for his Anna.

The lawyers were sitting opposite Marcus, Gerry, and Daniel, and the older one wanted answers to pertinent questions that were worrying him. Immediately Gerry went to get up in her defence, but Marcus pulled him back down, and whispered to his friend. "Leave this to me, Gerry, please. Anna's future and freedom are relying on keeping calm and civil to these eminent lawyers, and I understand where they are coming from. Please!"

Gerry sat down, but was glaring at the men opposite, as if he wanted to do them bodily harm.

Marcus realised what the lawyers wanted to know. Mia and Marcus had quizzed Anna on all these pertinent questions before she had left Jayden with them. "When Anna met Edward, he was charming, caring, and a thoroughly Southern gentleman towards her. She had just lost the love of her life through no fault of her own." He gave Gerry a belligerent look, as he was that procrastinator who had let Anna down, because he couldn't make a commitment to any woman, even though he had loved her. "Edward Connor was a player, and wanted to get into politics big time. He knew he needed a token wife, and two children as a game changer. This piece of shit preferred men as sexual partners, but used Anna to cover up any doubts on his masculinity. When she didn't get pregnant quickly enough, he began to change tactics. He separated her from any contacts she had, her close family had all been killed in Somalia, and that suited his agenda. She wasn't overly black, just of mixed race, her mother had been a white American, her father born Somalian. The Connors were all far right supremacists, who hated blacks, ethnic minorities, and migrants. Anna was a kind, sweet, loving woman, who didn't stand a chance against this truly racist family."

Marcus drank down half a glass of water. He hadn't given such a long speech since marrying his darling Mia, because he never got a word in when she was on a rant, and that was often in their manic household, with two teenage boys, and five year old twins. Marcus wouldn't change anything in his world, it was pure gold.

"And gentlemen, when she did at last get pregnant, he threatened that if she ever left him, he would keep the baby, and put a contract out on her. I think you can work out that my client's only get out of this hideous marriage was to somehow eliminate her sadistic, dangerous husband. She knew she would end up dead, and her baby sexually abused by its evil father. Anna did not have a choice, she had to put her baby son first, and plot for two years to murder her husband."

Marcus closed the notes that he had written earlier, there wasn't anything more to say. "You will ask why didn't she go to the police, or seek out an agency for rescuing abused women? She couldn't, because he kept threatening to take away the boy, if she opened her mouth about what was going on in that family home. Edward Connor had a multitude of high level people in his extremely wealthy pocket. Anna knew this was a fact, and who was going to listen to her, if she blew the whistle on him? Who could she trust? Not one living soul, because all of her close family were dead. She didn't dare tell her best friend, Bazil, in New York from her modelling days, because he was black, and gay. When Charles Connor found out about him, he was brutally tortured and murdered, until Charles found out where his brother's wife was, and with whom." Marcus looked at Gerry and nodded his head, because his friend had almost lost his life while trying to keep Anna safe, and her son, Jayden.

The elder lawyer for the FBI raised his hand in recognition of Marcus's excellent speech and answers on behalf of Anna Weist. "Thank you Mr Medina, you have explained everything clearly, and concisely. This of course has been recorded and my colleague and I have been taking notes of the main facts. I can now tell you that in conference with John Williams, the Director of the FBI, our boss, we came to a combined decision early this morning. We are shutting down any case against Anna Weist. There will be no more investigation regards Edward or Charles Connor, not now, or in the future. With all the evidence against this vile family, no court would convict Anna Weist, it would be a total waste of government money, and our precious time."

He gathered all his papers together, and leant over and shook Marcus's hand, then Daniel's, and lastly Gerry's. "This morning has been mine and my colleagues' worst morning ever. We have seen and prosecuted quite a few horrendous crimes, but what we have seen this morning has just about been the worst ever. Anna Weist is free to leave hospital, and be with her child, and hopefully will someday lead a loving, normal life, with someone who will show her that a good marriage, and a loving relationship is waiting for her in the future." He looked at Gerry and nodded. "Can you be that person Mr Swane?"

Gerry smiled with tears in his eyes. He was so relieved that his Anna was coming home at last. "Yes sir! I *am* that person, and always will be there for Anna, and Jayden.

269

These last few months have been truly awful for Anna and her son, and I am going to make it up to her, and even more so for the years she was married to that psycho bastard. May he rot in hell, and his maniac brother."

The lawyers turned to Marcus just before they both left for their own offices. "I'm sure you will understand that this meeting never happened, and anything pertaining to it will be destroyed, on our side, and yours. Edward Connor's death was engineered by an unknown assailant, and Charles Connor and family were killed in a house fire, which was an accident from the kitchen area, we believe."

They both smiled, but without humour. "We have been trying to bring down everyone in the Connor household for years. We knew what was going on, but everyone who was in their pay off, were too frightened to say anything. Quite prominent people in Atlanta have been disappearing for years, but we couldn't prove a damn thing. Now the brothers have been taken out, so many people are talking, and believe me, we are listening. Thanks to the courage, and strength of Anna, we are beginning to see the light. When you see her, give her our profuse thanks and regards."

Everyone shook hands and then the government employees left without a backward glance, because that was how they always worked. They always had far too much work to cope with.

Then the lead lawyer popped his neat grey head around the door. "Marcus, when you come back to L.A., please call into my office, because we have a lot of legalities to batten down, and completely negate." And, again he was gone on the run to the next emergency. Always ready to, listen – debate – negotiate, because they didn't take sides, or do favours. There would always be right and wrong in their world, and they had to decide what was right or wrong, and work with it.

CHAPTER TWENTY-EIGHT

The three friends stood talking beside Marcus's old pick-up truck, it was the ancient vehicle he kept at the private airfield he used when visiting L.A. He had flown in last night with two doctors who were his friends in Fort Worth, where he lived. James and Sally Collins were his local G.P.'s, and Sally also worked with newborn babies and mothers in the community, she was a qualified obstetrician.

Gerry was itching to get to the hospital and tell Anna the great news about her freedom from the law, and any recriminations in the future. He was literally pacing around Marcus and Daniel, swearing under his breath, because his friends weren't in a hurry to get him there, and he was furious at himself for not having his own vehicle. Daniel never rushed to get anywhere, and always discussed every move he made, the opposite to Gerry, and Marcus was similar to Daniel. He always worked out his strategy before committing himself. He was a typical lawyer.

Gerry hadn't been following the conversation, he was too impatient to get on the move, they could have been discussing the weather for all he cared. "Guys! Can we leave for the hospital, NOW?!"

Daniel shook Marcus's hand, and clasped his shoulder in friendship, he had come to admire and like

272

Marcus Medina. He was one of the good guys, extremely wealthy, but didn't flaunt his wealth at all, just used that wealth to help others who were in need, and desperate. Marcus was the ultimate philanthropist.

He financed an abused mother and child rescue unit, and the small hospice that had looked after Gerry. It was a modern facility for anyone who couldn't afford medical insurance. Mainly people who were unemployed and had fallen on hard times, and were chronically sick. Marcus would always be trying to pay back the world for his estranged father's life of drugs, guns, and violence. His younger brother, Anton, had been groomed by his father to take over his illegal, evil business of making money from the cesspool of humanity. Marcus had hated his father, but never Anton.

But for now it was time for Daniel to butt out of Anna Weist's life and problems. He had only been involved because he had helped rescue Anna from that disgusting cage. Then she had asked him to get in touch with Marcus and Mia, because she had left them with evidence of her husband's cruelty and abuse towards her for years. Daniel felt it was time he took a back seat on Anna's future, as she had made it obvious that she was leaving Los Angeles, and Gerry behind in a concentrated effort to get her life back on track with her beloved son, on her own.

Daniel told Gerry and Marcus he was going to wait in his Porsche while Marcus explained to Gerry what was happening with Anna. This was a particularly explicit conversation Daniel did not want to be part of. He felt sorry for both of his friends, because Gerry was going to go ballistic when Marcus explained the simple, but truthful mindset of Anna, and what *she* wanted now, and possibly in her future.

As soon as Daniel left, Gerry pounced on Marcus, his entire demeanour was uptight, and menacing. "What the fuck is going on here? Why are you both trying to stop me going to see my Anna? She is free after five years of being jerked around, abused, and God only knows what else, by that sick, psycho, her so called husband. And then his brother joins in the sadistic, evil party. For God's sake Marcus, I am begging you, please let me talk to Anna. I need to see with my own eyes that she is well enough to leave the hospital with me."

Marcus closed his eyes for a second, and took a deep calming breath. He rarely if ever lost his temper, or his cool in any emergency, but this could be that very rare occasion, because Gerry in full throttle was a mean, and vengeful bastard. "I am truly sorry Gerry, but I cannot let you go to the hospital to see Anna. She has told everyone who is looking after her that she will not see you, or speak to you. Whatever the outcome of today's meeting at the FBI headquarters, she would have gone down fighting if they had decided to prosecute. You must be wondering how Daniel became involved. Anna asked him to get in touch with me, as Mia had Anna's evidence against her husband. She asked me to give it to the FBI, that's why I flew in yesterday to present them with it, and also let them know that I would be representing her in the foreseeable future."

Gerry almost blew a gasket at being left in the dark while everyone else was rallying around the woman he loved. "I am *so* fucking angry I could spit blood right now. I am staying with Daniel twenty-four seven, but not a fucking word leaves his mouth about all this, and it's obvious he has been visiting Anna, and again, not a word to me." He shoved his hands through his over long blond hair in exasperation, because his so called friends had left him on the sidelines of *his* Anna's health, and future, and well being. "And, where does all this fuckin' crap leave me? Absolutely nowhere, Marcus Medina."

"Look Gerry, I can understand your anger, and your hurt at what is happening. Anna has been in crisis talks with a top mental health consultant for a week now, which has helped her come to terms with her critical mental and physical health, and well being."

Gerry shook his head, and mumbled very ripe explicit swear words. "You're still not telling me, where does all this shit leave me now?"

275

Marcus knew he had to give it to Gerry in straight and truthful, plain words. "Anna is coming home with me today to be reunited with her boy, Jayden. She is going to recuperate with my family, and doesn't want you, or anyone else interfering in her life. We have employed a qualified psychologist to come in every day to help her work through why all these horrific circumstances happened to her. Unbelievably, she believes that somehow she has been at fault. To be truthful, five years ago, when she met you, that was the beginning of her misery. She had already lost her parents and brothers in Somalia, and then out of the blue she met you, and fell in love."

Gerry put his hand over his mouth, and nodded his head in acquiescence. He had fallen in love with her, but because he was so scared of committing himself to any woman, he had left her without any explanation, or regret. He realised now, it must have been very traumatic for her, because she was such a sweet, loving woman, and also extremely beautiful, and still was. The then Leanne Zeema had been far too good for the likes of Gerry Swane. He was a solitary being, selfish and self-centred. He had truly believed he had done her a big favour by leaving her in that hotel suite after two nights of intense and magical sex. They were two halves that made a whole, and fitted like the end of a puzzle.

And that scared the crap out of the singular Gerry Swane, because he had always been alone, and self-sufficient.

Marcus did feel enormous sympathy for Gerry, because he had almost died trying to keep her safe from Charles Connor, but that bastard had still managed to get hold of her, and inflict vile pain on her. "Please Gerry! Please, give her time to convalesce with Jayden, Mia, and our family. I give you my word that the moment Anna asks to see you, I will get in touch. My heart grieves for you my friend, because I had to stand by and watch my love marry my brother Anton. I lived in a fog of misery, and heartache, until she came to me free to love me, as I loved her. So, do not think that I do not understand what you are going through. Right now the pain is unbearable, but you now have to get back to work, and carry on with your life as you did before Anna came into it. You cannot come to Fort Worth to be with my family, unfortunately that doesn't work for me, or Anna."

That was going to be very difficult for Gerry, but he understood that Marcus was being extremely fair to everyone. If anyone was going to look after Anna in the future, Marcus and Mia would have been his very first choice. Their family were unique in that love and hugs, and laughter were an everyday requisite in their comfortable, but rowdy and undisciplined home.

The two men gave each other a manly friendly hug, because for everything that Marcus had stipulated, Gerry had totally understood that it was all for Anna's welfare. "I am sure she will want to get in touch Gerry, but at the moment she is exhausted, feels dirty, and is embarrassed that she allowed Charles to abuse her in every way for over a month. Lastly, she doesn't feel that she is worthy of your love, and wants you to move on, and find someone that *is* worthy."

"Give her my love, Marcus. And tell her that I am waiting to hear from her, night or day. And, make sure she understands I do *not* want any other woman for my wife, only Anna Weist."

Only then did the two friends part company. Marcus to make arrangements for Anna to come home with him. Gerry to go home with Daniel, and try to come to terms with the fact that it could be a long, tiring, waiting game, until he would be with the love of his life. In his bed, and with his ring on her finger. Something in his worst nightmare he had ever envisaged happening to Gerry Swane. The proverbial one-night stand Lothario, with a string of beautiful women always in his revolving bed.

The old adage of when they fall, they fall harder, and faster, had certainly happened to him. In consequence Gerry couldn't wait, because he had fallen hard and fast, but hadn't realised until it was too late, and his love had been taken away from him. What an idiot he was!

Lesson learnt!!

Daniel drove in complete silence, words failed him at man's inhumanity, and vile sickness. He had been severely traumatised this morning, and hadn't realised what poor Anna had been subjected to by those psychotic brothers. Since talking to her, he had come to admire and respect her. She was sweet, loving, and never complained. Gerry was extremely lucky to have met her, and for her to love him, as she most definitely did.

Gerry was also silent, and ruminating about his past life. He had been a womaniser, loved women, and bedded many a beautiful woman, the notches on his bed post were phenomenal. But, Leanne Zeema had quietly and sweetly entered his hedonistic life, and he became toast. He fell deeply in love, and that would last a lifetime. Now he knew he had to behave impeccably, and win back that amazing love to be able to go forward into the future, with his Anna.

He was seething with anger and hurt against Daniel, who had kept him in the dark about what was happening with Anna, and he couldn't forgive him, right now. As soon as they got back to Daniel's home, he was going to pack up his few personal belongings and leave.

No fuss. No arguing. He had to return to his own apartment, and return one hundred per cent to work for Marcus. Had to get his shit in order to make a good life for Anna and Jayden, and the baby she was carrying. Because that baby *would* bear his name!

He couldn't envisage his life without Anna sharing it with him. So, he would wait patiently, not his usual trait, for Marcus to get in touch. They always had a monthly meeting regards Marcus's business affairs, only then would he be greedy and nail down his boss, with all his pertinent questions on Anna, and everything she was doing, health-wise, and mentally.

Did she miss him? Did she still love him? Could Gerry see her, and talk to her? PLEASE!! He would be slowly dying for any information he could get on anything about the love of his life.

But, there would be a time when he wouldn't wait a moment longer, and just turn up at the Medina ranch.

That was a threat, and a promise!!

CHAPTER TWENTY-NINE

A small body hurtled through the front entrance of the ranch house to throw itself at the frail, thin woman that Marcus was helping out of his vehicle.

Anna went down on her knees to hold on to the over exuberant child who almost knocked her onto her backside. "Mama! Mama! I can swim now, Mama. I am a big boy now, Mama, and can swim the whole swimming pool, 'cos Auntie Mia taught me how to, Mama, because I could have drowned if I didn't learn."

Anna covered his sweet, so loved, perfect little face with kisses, not believing she was holding her beloved child's small body at last. "You *are* such a big boy now, and have grown so much since I have been away. I cannot believe you are the baby I left behind such a short time ago." She looked over the top of her little boy's head with tears in her eyes at Mia, who was standing at the top of the steps, also crying for the sheer joy of their reunion. "Thank you Mia, my heart is full of love for you and Marcus for taking care of, and loving my son, and making sure he didn't miss me too much. And, I can never thank Marcus enough for getting my release from the authorities, and my case being dropped for good. I am overwhelmed with love for you both."

281

Marcus picked up Jayden, and put his arm around Anna to help her climb the steps. She was still very frail, and far too thin. "Believe me, Anna, helping you get your freedom was the best thing I have ever managed to do. From now on you are going to rest up, and get your strength and stamina back. And, you are not going to leave here, if ever, until you are one hundred per cent fit."

"But Marcus, I am without funds, and won't be able to work for a while. I cannot take advantage of your family's hospitality. I have to be able to repay you somehow?"

Mia and Marcus helped the walking wounded up the stairs to the suite they had allocated for Anna's stay, be it long or short. It looked out on the vast acreage that was Harmony Ranch, with its green pastures, blossoming trees and bushes, and paddocks filled with all manner of rare breeds, which the ranch specialised in promoting. It cost huge amounts of money to do this.

But Marcus was extremely wealthy, and his idea of always helping others, and spending his wealth on worthwhile projects, was the heart and soul of the Harmony Ranch, giving Marcus a great deal of pleasure, and happiness.

His father and brother, Anton, had made millions by selling drugs and fire-power to the highest bidder, causing so much misery and despair in the USA, and beyond. So everything that Marcus did was a payback in an extremely good way, for the diabolical sins of his father and brother. Anton had had a good, loving heart, but had been groomed by their father as his successor. Luckily Theo had left his older son, Marcus, with Sophia his wife, and she had raised him to be an exceptional father to his two boys, and now the husband to Mia, and her twin daughters, Anton's children.

Marcus and Mia hadn't managed to have any children together. His first wife, Bianca, had died the day she had given birth to their youngest son, Milo. And Mia had a difficult birth with Anton's twins, and now couldn't have any more children. They would have liked to have at least two children together, but were content with the four they already had.

Mia settled Anna into her kingsize bed while Marcus ran down to retrieve her luggage. When Anna had been taken from Gerry's office by her brother-in-law, Charles Connor, she had left all her personal items in Gerry's vehicle. The vehicle had been safe behind Gerry's office, and Gerry too ill to move it, so Marcus had retrieved Anna's cases before he picked her up at the Hospice early this morning. Everything she now owned was in two small cases, which was pretty pathetic in Marcus's opinion. But knowing his excitable wife, Mia, she would be helping Anna to spend his money, as soon as Anna was back on her feet. Mia loved to shop until she was worn out, which never happened, unfortunately.

Mia was akin to a keg of dynamite; if you lit her fuse, she went off like a fire cracker, waking up the dead, enthusing everyone with her love and energy. She was after all the biological daughter of America's iconic movie star, Madeline Maxwell. Too beautiful, over enthusiastic about life in general, beyond charismatic, full of laughter, and sexually greedy, any time of the day or night.

No wonder Marcus Medina was an extremely happy and contented husband. Would live his entire life trying to keep hold of his good luck, and never looking at another woman, because he knew his Mia would vandalise his dick if he ever did.

Jayden climbed onto his mama's bed, and put his small arms around her neck. "Can I sleep in your bed tonight, mama?" Of course he had to explain why he was asking. Jayden had found his confidence and his voice, so didn't stop to take breath now.

Anna snuggled closer to her beautiful, chubby son. "Of course you can, my darling. Mama is not going to stop you doing everything you want to do, from now on." Meaning that his cruel, violent father was not going to hurt them, ever again. Edward had stopped his baby son from doing anything that made him happy. Often locking him in his bedroom if he got in the way, especially when he was raping and beating his mother.

Marcus knocked on Anna's door, and walked in carrying a tray that Ria the housekeeper had prepared for her. "It's only a sandwich, cookies, and milk, because we didn't think you would be up to a large meal, yet. Mia is making sure that the kids are all behaving at the supper table." He shook his head, and rolled his eyes upward, because only Maddie, the most dominant twin, would play up, Like Mia, she had a fearsome temper, but was also the most loving and giving of their four children.

His two boys were older, but were completely under her arrogant little thumb. Mel, the other twin, was the complete opposite, gentle, studious, always trying to keep the peace in the boisterous, energetic family. She was God-sent, with Mia, who often sent the family into a tail-spin with her volcanic temper. Marcus always thanked God for his own wonderful, patient mother, and his amazing boys, who took after his mother, and not their Italian grandfather, Theo. Marcus truly loved all of them far too much for his own sanity.

"I also wanted to have a quick word, without my darling wife talking over me." Marcus smiled again, which lit up his gorgeous face, making Anna realise what a beautiful looking man he really was. "We all need you to understand that we want you to be a family member, not for a time, but for good." Anna wanted to say something, but Marcus didn't give her the chance to interfere. "Our home has so much room, and the ranch is endless with space. We have all come to love Jayden, as if he was our own family, and now you, who has been *so* brave, and you now need a comfortable, and loving home to bring up Jayden in safety, surrounded by people who love him."

Tears were slowly dripping down Anna's face at Marcus and Mia's generosity towards her and Jayden. But then a small voice piped up. "Please mama, can we stay, 'cos I love it here. I have two sisters, and two big bruvvers, and Auntie Mia, and Unka Marcus. Gramma Sophie is teaching me to write my name, and I am reading my own book about a doggie called Rex." Jayden didn't stop to take a breath, as he clung to his beloved mama. "And, we all have to clean the stables when we aren't at school, 'cos the kittens and puppies, and goats, and geese, all poo a lot, and I am big enough now to help."

Anna couldn't help laughing through her tears. "Well! It looks like my very grown up baby boy has made up my mind for me. It's wonderful the difference in him since I've been away for two months. Honestly Marcus, your generosity overwhelms me, but I can't bring anything to the table. I am still frail! I haven't any money! I haven't got any particular

286

skills to help on the ranch!" She had never felt so ridiculously useless as she did at this particular moment.

Again Marcus shook his head and smiled. "Don't worry, we have a job already waiting for you. My mother Sophia isn't getting any younger, and Mia is never going to be able to control four, or five kids. Mom has been coming in every day to home school the twins and Jayden, she was a teacher at the local school. The boys travel to Fort Worth every day for school. She wants to continue home schooling every morning, but would like to go home to her fairly new husband, Ward, after lunch. I get up at four a.m., and after a 5K run, work in my office until lunch time, but would then like to be out on the ranch helping the hands until late. You would help me enormously by just being there for the kids whenever needed."

Marcus blew out a long held breath, it was a long speech for him, especially when Mia was around. He had known he had to make a strong case to Anna, who was fiercely independent, and would hate being a problem for anyone, and couldn't pay her way.

Anna looked closely at Marcus, who seemed to really need her help. Then she looked at her darling boy who loved living with this family after the horrendous time with his vile father. Then she looked within herself, and made up her mind without hesitation.

287

"Thank you *so* much, Marcus. I would love to live here, as long as you need me. To be a part of your wonderful family, and I will be here for your children, and won't let you down, I promise."

Anna couldn't believe what was happening to her. She had lost all her own beloved family. Her wonderful parents, and four boisterous brothers in Somalia. Now, she had a new start with Jayden, and a baby on the way, in a few months time.

She patted her now rounded belly. "You haven't forgotten I'm producing in around three months? Is that going to be a problem? If it is, I will understand completely."

Marcus plucked Jayden from his mama's arms. "You are kidding me? We are so excited to have a baby in the family. Mia can't have any more children, so we are truly thrilled." He kissed Jayden's forehead, whilst giving him a loving hug. "Come on baby boy, your mama needs to eat, and then rest. And you need to eat your supper, and then straight to bed for boys of your age."

But Jayden always had the last word. "I'm sleeping in mama's bed tonight, 'cos she is very sick, and needs me to look after her, Unka Marcus."

"I know, my darling boy. Your mama needs your help, and if you want to sleep with her, that's fine with me, and Auntie Mia." He gave Jayden another squeeze. "Sometimes young man, you are far too grown up to be only three years old."

Marcus closed the door quietly behind him, and hurried down the stairs, because all the family were already in the dining room eating supper. By now Mia would be bursting, wondering how his conversation with Anna had gone. If Anna had declined his invitation to stay, he would have received an ear-bashing from his very verbal, very volatile, but gorgeous wife, who he absolutely adored, and always would.

But, what Anna had been through was undeniably traumatic, and criminal. No one would blame her if she wanted to stay single, and bring up her two children on her own, and not trust another living soul.

But, Gerry was Marcus's wing man in the Corporate World, and he had been dying to ask Anna what she was going to do about Gerry, and his love for her.

He was proud of himself, because he hadn't mentioned his friend's name, not once. Gerry was desperate to see Anna, and just talk to her, and tell her just how much he loved her, and Jayden, and the baby yet to be born. But Anna wasn't ready yet to have any man in her life. Perhaps she never would be, and who on earth would blame her?

CHAPTER THIRTY

Gerry and Daniel raised their glasses of aged Scotch whisky and said 'cheers'. For the past few Saturday nights they had met at the bar and lounge of The Excelsior Hotel. Around midnight at the weekends, a very talented young musician played the grand piano to an electric crowd, playing soul and jazz, and everything in between.

Daniel couldn't believe what he had seen at this location in L.A., and was thoroughly enjoying the experience. The lounge bar was a meet and greet, and sex, for the many celebs locally. There was an abundance of gorgeous unattached, or not, females, and extremely good looking males.

Since sitting at Gerry's reserved small table in the corner of the large lounge, it was evident that he was well loved, and respected. Harry, the excellent bar manager, who had worked forever at The Excelsior, certainly looked after Gerry, as if he was one of the celebs, and his best friend.

The whole time Gerry and Daniel were talking over their preferred drinks, so many of the gorgeous females, and they *really* were gorgeous, came over and kissed and hugged Gerry with enthusiasm. Daniel had never been so envious, and so invisible, in his entire adult life. It was pretty evident that Gerry had indeed bedded all these women. He had often boasted to Daniel of his expertise with the female population, but Daniel hadn't really believed him.

But now he most certainly did. Avidly, Daniel watched Gerry, trying to understand exactly what he had that attracted women to him. Sure, he was pretty boy material, with his blond, straight, floppy hair. He always had a glorious tan, and wore casual designer clothes that fitted perfectly his slim, tall figure. Taking that package into account, it was no wonder beautiful women were attracted to him. Also he loved women, and it showed in everything he did in their company.

Five years ago this had been a familiar haunt of Gerry's. Mia, an extremely talented piano player, had worked there then. This was where she had met Anton Santi, who owned the hotel, and they were married soon after. Anton had been taken out a week after the marriage, and she had been seriously injured, but somehow had managed to survive.

Gerry told Daniel that every male fell in love with Mia, because she was so beautiful, and captivating. Gerry admitted that he had fallen in love, or lust, with her, but knew he wouldn't stand a chance against Anton Santi. When Santi wanted something he got it, bought it, or used his strong-arm persuasion against his enemies to acquire it. In Gerry's view Anton Santi was the most beautifully perfect male he had ever seen. And laughed when he admitted to Daniel, even as the

291

straightest of heterosexuals, could have fancied Anton himself.

Mia had loved both brothers, but Marcus had his mother Sophia, and his two growing sons to consider. So he stood back and allowed Anton to sweep her off her tiny feet. But Gerry knew that Marcus was almost destroyed when Mia married Anton. When Anton was murdered a week later, Marcus waited patiently until Mia came out of hospital, but she was still very frail, and grieving. So he took her home to take care of her, and she most certainly wasn't the easiest patient to look after. But Marcus was a patient, and loving man.

But in the end Mia came to her senses, and realised that Marcus could be trusted, and had been there when she needed someone to comfort and love her. Now, they were the most devoted couple, and totally in love with each other, that Gerry had ever come across.

"I sold my 1970 TR6 Roadster." Gerry waited for Daniel's cryptic remark. Anyone who knew Gerry Swane would understand that simple acknowledgement.

Daniel choked on the whisky before he could swallow his mouthful. "Fucking hell! You are kidding me, right? That bloody piece of ancient history meant more to you than anything, or anyone." Gerry clapped Daniel on his back to stop him coughing.

"I've got to admit, when the guy who bought it drove away, I actually shed a few fucking tears." Gerry had ruminated for days before getting the courage to get in touch with a dealer who was desperate to own that particular Roadster.

"What on earth possessed you to sell your pride and joy? You actually bankrupted yourself to buy that piece of vintage shit, years ago." Daniel shook his head in disbelief, he never, ever, expected Gerry to sell that car. "Why? Why Gerry? There must be a reason for this sudden madness?"

"Anna! She is the reason! I am packing up here, Daniel. I am renting out my apartment to Ben, my lawyer from the office. He is young, single, and I know he will take care of it, if I have to return, which I am not planning to do. I'm sorry Daniel, but I have to go to Fort Worth, and visit Anna. It's no good shaking your head, because I won't change my mind." He glared malevolently at his friend. "If you whisper a word of my plans to Marcus, or Mia, I will never speak to you again, that's a promise, and not a threat."

Daniel wouldn't dream of telling anyone what Gerry was planning, but thought it was a fool's dream. "You know me better than that, my friend. But, I think you are making a big mistake with Anna, and her ongoing recovery. I've heard that she is doing well, and Jayden is loving having his mother back, and that they are living permanently with the Medina's."

293

Gerry raised his hands in frustration at Daniel's knowledge about Anna's welfare. It made him fucking angry that Daniel always knew more than he did. It was *so* unfair, because no one had got in touch with him, and kept him updated on how the woman he loved was coping out of hospital. But at least she was safe and secure living with Marcus and Mia, and their kids. That was a huge relief and comfort to Gerry, but didn't stop him worrying about her. He intended to marry Anna, and be a good father to Jayden, and the new baby when it arrived.

"I need money, if I'm going to marry Anna, and find us somewhere to live. That's why I sold my prize possession, that piece of crap was a gold mine, and I've sold everything possible. I've kept my vintage Harley, because I'm using it to get to Fort Worth. I don't think you understand how serious I am, Daniel. I can't live without Anna, I am a changed man. I haven't been out with anyone since being with her. She is the love of my life, and I have to go and persuade her that I can provide for her and her children." He gave Daniel an emotional smile. "And, I am leaving tomorrow." He looked at his watch, "which is now today. My Anna is seven months pregnant, and I intend to be at that baby's arrival, because I *am* going to be its father."

Daniel and Gerry said a brief goodbye in The Excelsior car park, because as far as Gerry was concerned, he could be back in L.A. within a few days. He wouldn't have a choice if Anna refused to speak to him, and Marcus was angry that he had turned up without being invited. But that didn't stop Gerry from giving it his best shot, because not trying wasn't going to happen.

Daniel had to put in his dollar's worth. "She loves you, buddy. Really loves you, wants you, needs you. You ain't coming back, not a chance. And, I'm going to miss you, even though you are a pain in the ass. A lazy bastard, who doesn't know the words 'keep fit, and 'eating healthily'. Hopefully Anna will change that ridiculous mindset, and let you live longer, and much healthier."

Both men then got into their individual vehicles and drove off. Gerry wasn't going to bother going to bed, because he wanted to leave before dawn and drive for at least twelve hours. In that way he could eat up the miles to Fort Worth in two days.

Gerry had changed his mind about the Harley, realising that twenty hours on the road would be too much on his ass and balls. He wasn't a teenager anymore, and cherished his manhood more than his Harley. So he had put his beloved Harley in storage, and if all went well with Anna, he could have it shipped out. Also, he could fill the cab of his flatbed Chrysler with his personal items, which could be safer when he had to stay at a motel. The rest of his gear was packed in two boxes, and left in his office. If he stayed in Fort Worth, Ben would ship the boxes out to him.

He wasn't stupid, he had to drive steady, and carefully. There were a multitude of assholes driving on the roads. He would stop at least twice to sleep in cheap motels, because expensive hotels would be a waste of money; those halcyon days were long gone. Money wasn't a problem, but wasting it wasn't on his agenda anymore. If he was going to marry Anna, and be a good father to her kids, that would take a great deal of change.

Over the next three days and two nights, he drove through Phoenix, which looked to be cultured, a great place to live, with plenty of open spaces, and all round good weather.

Then he drove quickly through Ciudad Juarez, not bothering to stop, because he didn't feel as safe as he should.

Arizona was sub-tropical, and humid hot, even in April it was reaching the nineties.

It always amazed Gerry that when you drove through America, it was so diverse, so different, in every state.

He reached Fort Worth late in the evening, and was tired, felt very dishevelled, and badly needed a hot shower, a close shave, and a large substantial meal. Fort Worth was cattle country, and well known for its amazing steaks. A very large one, still mooing, had his name on it. All in that order.

So decided to bed down for the night, and turn up at the ranch early tomorrow.

He was nervous! Excited! But really apprehensive!

Not knowing how Anna was going to respond to him just turning up out of the blue, was something he didn't want to get his head around. But he had burnt his bridges, and was here now.

If love was enough then he had that in spades, and more. And, if Anna still loved him, he was home and dry, and wouldn't be living in L.A. ever again.

CHAPTER THIRTY-ONE

Gerry parked his truck right in front of the granite steps leading to the entrance of the Medina home. Immediately, as he got out of the vehicle, a scream filled the air, and Mia came flying down the steps and threw herself bodily at Gerry.

"Gerry! Gerry Swane you bastard! You never let us know you were coming." Avidly she kissed him all over his face, as she clung to his body. "I've missed you *so* much. You know how much I love you, and not a word on how you were doing." Laughing, she came out of his loving embrace, and stood all five foot of her looking him over with a frown marring her beautiful face. "You are still one good looking bastard, but there are a lot of extra lines on that beaten up, gorgeous face."

Gerry gave her a smacking kiss on her pouty lips. "Thank you, I think?" He couldn't help but grin at her exuberant welcome. Mia didn't know how to hold back on her emotions, or words, good or bad. She loved or hated, there was no grey line with Mia, and she couldn't keep anything to herself. She was a typical Gemini, and couldn't be trusted with a secret, because it wouldn't remain a secret if you told her, well, not for long anyway.

Gerry looked up at the entrance to the house, and there she stood, more beautiful than even he remembered.

298

Tall, elegant, and now definitely pregnant. She was wearing her usual long, slim tunic, with cotton loose trousers to match in a beautiful shade of creamy pink. Her glossy dark curly hair now growing longer, and framing that sweet, perfect face, and he couldn't have loved her more in a million years.

Mia whispered to Gerry, so Anna wouldn't hear her. "She's been waiting for you, Gerry. Hoping that this day would come sooner rather than later. Anna loves you Gerry, but try to be patient with her, and take things slowly. She really is doing great, but you know what she has been through, and it happened to me as well. It takes time, sometimes never, to get over what happened. But Anna is strong, and is doing better than expected." Gerry bent down so that Mia could whisper in his ear, he was over a foot taller than her, but he still kept his eyes trained on the woman he loved, and dreamt about.

"The younger kids are schooling with Gramma Sophia, and Marcus can't be disturbed until much later. So, go with Anna up to her rooms, and get seriously reacquainted, Gerry Swane." She looked at his crotch, and winked. "You have my whole-hearted permission, and we do not want to see either of you until supper time."

Gerry slowly walked up the steps to Anna, who held her arms out to him. He walked into her loving embrace, and knew without a doubt that he had come home at last.

299

*   *   *   *

Anna locked the bedroom door, and then went to Jayden's room, and did the same. There was no way she could allow anyone or anything to disrupt the next few hours. These hours were entirely special between Gerry and herself. Could she make love with him, or would it be a total disaster? Only time would tell. She was as nervous as get-go, and terrified that her body would let her down. But, also knew she had to try to overcome the mental and physical trauma the two brothers had put her through.

She couldn't lose Gerry. Couldn't lose his love. Couldn't lose his friendship, and kindness. Even though he was brash, laid back, charismatic to numerous other women he had previously met, Anna knew that he did love her, and wanted to take care of her and Jayden, and the new baby. She would try her hardest to be a loving, sexual partner, even if she had to fake it.

"Anna, sweetheart. Honestly, we really don't have to do this today. I love you, and only want what is best for you. If I'm being truly honest, after two months of being without sex, sure it would be a relief to make love to you. I promise faithfully that I haven't been with anyone else since meeting up with you again." Gerry laughed without mirth. "And, you know me, that's about as serious as a heart attack, for me to go without for so long." He put his hand on her rounded belly,

300

"plus the fact that I have never made love to a pregnant woman before. Yeah, I know you were pregnant when we were together before, but it wasn't showing so much then."

His facial expression was one of amazement. "Wow! That baby has a kick to it, seems to me it's going to be another boy. Have you had a scan to determine if it's a boy or girl? I don't mind either way, I will love it."

Anna smiled at Gerry's simple reckoning, he did not have a clue about babies, birth, kids, which was a slight worry for her. An abused woman, with two children to take care of, was a huge undertaking for Gerry the outstanding, long term bachelor. Right now he was totally enthusiastic about their long-term relationship, but would that wear too thin when reality set in, and everyday boredom was the norm'?

"Stop over-thinking our future life together." He kissed her gently but enthusiastically. "I have left L.A. permanently. Have given up a life that I enjoyed, but I need and want to be wherever you are, and your kids. I'm not going anywhere without you. We are going to get married ASAP. We are going to find a home near here, as we won't find any better friends than Marcus, and Mia." He kissed her again, holding her as close as possible, but trying not to frighten her with an erection that wasn't going to abate. Slow, patience, and easy, hadn't got down to his dick, unfortunately.

"I promise I will stop immediately if you become frightened, or worried, that you can't cope with what is going to happen today. I completely understand that what you have gone through could put you off any man coming near you. But, I can't love you anymore than I do, so it's entirely up to you now, as to what happens next."

Anna took him by the hand and led him over to the king-size bed to answer him. She trusted Gerry and knew he would keep his word if she wanted to stop. But, she also loved him way beyond she had ever loved before, so was determined to let him completely erase the Connor brothers out of their existence.

This was Gerry's and her future, and she was going to relax, and enjoy every stimulating moment. Her Gerry was a fantastic lover, and she was so lucky to have found him again, and to be able to prove that she did love him, and want him as her partner for life. This was a new beginning for them both, and Gerry had to understand that.

Those deep blue eyes looked straight at Anna, with worry and sadness written in them. "Can I undress you, or would you rather do it?"

"I am Anna Weist, who loves you, and trusts you. This is the beginning of our life together, and I know that sex means a great deal to you. So I'm leaving it up to you to carry on as normal, because, my darling, you have had a great deal of practice, for which I am very grateful to be the harbinger of such practice, and expertise."

All the while Anna, who was obviously nervous by talking too much, Gerry was slowly undressing her. When he gently kissed her rounded belly, she pulled him onto the bed with tears welling up in her eyes. God, she loved this beautiful man, and knew he was going to be an amazing husband, and father to her kids.

Swiftly Gerry shucked off his clothes, and taking Anna in his arms, began a slow and careful seduction. He knew that this first time wasn't going to be comfortable for Anna. He was nervous, and she was more so. He was desperate to fuck her, and keep fucking her until he was completely empty, and his balls soft and pliable again. But, that wasn't going to happen this time, and probably not even the next time.

In fact couldn't stop kissing her, because he had begun to believe that he would never get to kiss her again. Never make love to her. Never have a future together. Not quite believing they were in bed together, naked, again.

Slowly he began to move down her beautiful, café au lait body, kissing his way down to where he wanted to be. He didn't hold her hands, but left her free to touch him, because she had been imprisoned, and shackled previously. He was desperate to get to the place where he could taste her essence, and make sure she was ready and willing to take him into her body.

Her breasts were now much bigger, and the nipples darker and more prominent, which was a complete turn on for Gerry. He definitely was a large breast man. So he paid a great deal of attention to both mounds of pleasure, suckling on both in turn until Anna began to move with his mouth, sighing his name. But when he went to move lower, she stopped him immediately with both hands on his head. "Please Gerry, don't. I can't deal with oral sex right now." Anna didn't have to explain what had happened to her previously, because Gerry understood completely.

He came back up to that generous mouth, and made love to it, without questioning her motive for stopping him. He had promised to stop, so he had. But, he realised that Anna had become upset that she had rebuffed him, because a lone, solitary tear fell down her cheek. And, that one tear made him feel even worse. At the same time he was willing his over enthusiastic dick to calm down, and behave. But, it was telling him to get a move on, and go – go – go.

"Sweetheart, it's OK. Please don't cry, or I might never get another hard-on. It's OK, we really don't need to do this right now. Truly, it's enough that I am with you, holding you, and just loving you. That's more than I've had for the last two months."

Anna smiled through her tears, and pulled Gerry even closer, so that he could feel the baby kicking him in the stomach. He was fascinated that women went through pregnancy with so much good humour, and love for their unborn child. While men just had the best part of helping to form the baby's DNA, and enjoying themselves at the same time.

"I'm fine, honestly I am. Can we just try again, but slowly and gently. I want you Gerry. I have to get past this first time, so we can have a normal sex life, enjoying making love together." She didn't add that she was frightened that he would leave her behind if he couldn't have sex with her when he wanted it. Gerry was caring, and loving, but sex was a large part of his make-up, and she wouldn't expect him to go without, however much he loved her. Anna knew that he did love her a great deal, but that could soon erode, if they weren't compatible in bed.

Gerry made a decision to go for bust, or lose her forever. He encased her darling face in both hands, gave her a long breath-taking kiss on the lips, and pushed his extremely hard, throbbing length into her warm, wet vagina, but didn't go any further, waiting for her reaction, good or bad.

Anna hitched a long breath, then blew out that breath, as pain hit her hard. She'd had multiple stitches inside to put everything back into normality. The stretching of those unused muscles screamed out their pain, but she breathed through that pain, and put her knees up and out, so that Gerry could go into her deeper, and she would be more open for his enjoyment, and hopefully hers.

Gerry watched her expression as he began to make love to her. He knew it was going to be difficult for her, but his woman would not give in, however painful or uncomfortable for her. So for just a moment he stopped, waiting for her to adjust, but when her legs opened up around him, he lost the will to stay calm and be too careful. With one final push he was in her up to his whole length, and groaning with anticipation.

No one could describe that exact moment when you filled the woman you loved with your hard length that was already pumping, and ready to explode with your essence that created a new life. But still he moved carefully, and gently, so he didn't hurt her unnecessarily. He had no intention of ruining this first time.

Anna realised what Gerry was trying to do, he was holding back, desperate not to hurt her, but that wasn't what she wanted. Every time he moved in and out, she began to move with him, bringing him even deeper inside her, and she felt the magic start to happen. She could feel her orgasm building and building, and with both hands she clasped his tight buttocks, pulling him even higher, and she went silently over the top, and tumbled into the first natural climax she'd had in two months. Whenever Gerry touched her, she never faked an orgasm, because she didn't have to, they fitted like a comfortable pair of old gloves, made for each other.

Gerry followed her into an overwhelming amazing climax. He had waited until she had gone over into a boneless heap, and then allowed himself the pleasure of doing the exact same of just letting go. He took them both onto their sides, as he didn't want to crowd her with his weight. But one thing he wanted to know was, the last time they had made love, she had been very vocal. Why this time absolutely silent? Making him think that she hadn't enjoyed it this time.

They were contentedly spooning and cuddling in the big bed, and he kissed her salubrious sweet neck, and asked that particular question. But wasn't happy with her truthful answer, because he knew that his Anna would never lie to him.

"Both Edward and Charles forbade me to speak or make any noise when they raped me. If I screamed or cried they hurt me even more. So I learnt to keep absolutely silent and still until they were finished with me." She now went absolutely quiet, as if not wanting to admit what she had gone through, and worried that Gerry would be angry with her.

"Oh sweetheart, I am so, so sorry. So sorry for mentioning it. I'm just truly happy that you managed to get through it with me, and overwhelmed that I gave you an orgasm, and that you loved me enough to go through that with me." He turned her head and kissed her on those luscious lips. "We're good, aren't we?" Gerry was worried that he had hurt her, and she would be put off from doing it again.

"My darling Gerry, it was *that* good, can we do it again, and again?" She laughed at his wry look of concern.

"Absolutely! But I ain't a teenager anymore, can you give me at least a few moments to gather up my strength and energy to make it as good again. Believe me, it's my absolute pleasure to make love to you until neither of us has the strength to leave this bed, and walk down for supper."

Anna put her hand behind her, and felt and stroked his slowly rising erection, and smiled. "Seems good to go to me, Gerry Swane. You're just making silly excuses to get out of fucking me. Didn't know I was going to marry a quitter!"

Gerry growled his reply, because it looked like she was going to be a whole lot of trouble. He turned her over, and went straight for his target to prove his point, or his dick. Sliding into her wet warmth, he did his very best to prove that he could still perform like a teenager.

His over-zealous dick was exceptionally happy!

Gerry would always try to prove he was up for it!

Anna was going to be the happiest, most contented wife in Fort Worth!

EPILOGUE

<u>2 Months Later</u>

Serena Joy Swane slipped into her capable daddy's hands with a sigh and a squeak. Her eyes wide open and already inquisitive for a world she would dominate and work hard in politics for almost sixty years.

Gerry, with tears in his eyes, looked with wonder at the miracle of birth and the beautiful child he would call daughter for the rest of his life, however long or short. He turned his gaze to look at the amazing woman he loved with all his heart, and grinned. Tired but exultant at managing the birth of her daughter, without screaming, or a temper tantrum. Anna knew she was extremely fortunate with child birth, because both of her children had appeared on time, and without any fanfare. And in under an hour of little pain, and effort, they had both ejected themselves, as if it was an everyday occurrence.

"Give her to me, Gerry. I need to see just how perfect she is, with ten toes, and ten fingers, and who she looks like, hopefully not her bastard father." She quickly changed that last comment, because she knew how Gerry felt about her two children, because they would always be his, with a Swane surname.

Gerry hesitated for a second. "Erm, she is much darker than you, my darling. Serena is a female of colour, not like Jayden." This wasn't a problem for Gerry, as long as she was healthy, and full of good heart, he didn't care if she was green – blue – yellow, or purple.

Anna indicated that she wanted to hold her new born baby right now, and when besotted Gerry laid her gently in her arms, she laughed out loud. "Oh my God! She is pure Somalian. She looks like my papa, and my brothers, who were all gorgeous looking. Out of all my parent's children, I was the only one who looked like our mama, American, and almost white, but not quite."

Anna looked at her husband of two months, to see if he really was OK to be the father of a coloured female. After being persecuted and brutalised by the Connor brothers, because of her café au lait skin, she couldn't be with Gerry if he had a problem with Serena's colour. As a dedicated mother, who loved her children beyond sanity, she couldn't stay with anyone who had even a tiny modicum of black hatred in him. She loved Gerry with all her heart, but would always have to put her children first, that was a mother's prerogative.

Gerry bent down and kissed Anna, and then his perfect daughter, Serena. "You know, my darling, that I would give my life for you, and our two gorgeous kids. Colour has never been a problem for me, and it never will. And, any jerk who makes it a problem is going to see the other side of my good nature, and my fist."

Sally, their obstetrician neighbour and friend came back into the room. She had delivered the baby in their bedroom, because Anna knew she wasn't going to have a difficult birth, and did not want to go to the hospital. "OK papa, we don't need you for a while, and I need to weigh the baby, and clean up Anna." She shooed Gerry out of the room, in her stern doctor manner. "You can go let the Medina household know, and pick up Jayden, who must be driving them insane with curiosity by now." As soon as Gerry left, she went over and picked up the baby from Anna's arms, who was looking tired, and frazzled, by now.

"Come to me, little sweetheart, I'm your Auntie Sally, and you are as beautiful a baby I have ever had the pleasure of bringing into the world. I think you weigh about eight pounds, as soon as we have cleaned up your precious mother you can have your first taste of her delicious milk." Serena gazed up at the woman who had brought her into the world, as if she knew exactly what she was saying, and understood. Serena would always look at people in that way, solemnly, and weighing up if they were telling the whole truth, and not a load of shit. In politics, standing up for black women especially, that ability would put her in good standing with her peers. She was made in her Grandfather's image, and would be respected the world over.

Gerry left their comfortable home on the run, because he couldn't wait to get back to Anna and the baby. This was all new territory to him, and now he understood how Marcus loved his four kids so passionately.

The Medina's had been overwhelmingly good to Anna and himself. A week after Gerry had arrived unannounced at the Ranch, they had allowed Gerry and Anna to be married in their garden with only the family as guests. After the wonderful, but simple ceremony, Jayden had held Gerry's hand, and asked if he could call him papa now. Gerry had almost broken down when the bright little boy had added. "I didn't like my other papa, he frightened me. But I like you, and really hope you like me, so you can be my bestest papa." Anna did cry, which nearly set off Gerry. He covered it up by picking up Jayden, and whispered that he loved him, and really, really wanted to be his bestest papa.

On that fantastic wedding day, Anna and Gerry couldn't believe it when Marcus gave a set of keys to Gerry, giving him the house and grounds that Anton had bought, but never got the time to live in. They both tried to refuse such generosity, but Marcus and Mia would not let them. Marcus explained it was five years since Anton's death, and it was high time a family were living there. Anton would have agreed

312

that Gerry and Anna were the right family to make it a comfortable and loving home. Gerry couldn't believe the generosity of the Medina's, and took their generosity as their way of showing their love to other family members, and helping others when in need.

When Gerry asked why they hadn't sold the property after Anton died, Marcus replied with a wry smile, "We just couldn't do it. Mia and I discussed it to death. But, Anton was desperate to change his way of life, and wanted to keep Mia safe from his enemies, and lead a much quieter life in the country, and live closer to his mother, Sophia, and my family."

That was when Gerry finally, with Anna's blessing, decided to accept the house and grounds. They both loved living there, and looked forward to bringing their family up, and loving each other, in the future.

It was a win-win situation all round. For the Medina family, having the Swane's a mile away, and Gerry able to work alongside Marcus in his office. And Anna helping with the children, now all six of them. The circle was complete, and was loving, and truly wholesome for everyone concerned.

It was a great dynasty that would be repeated for generations to come.

Printed in Great Britain
by Amazon